ST. MARTIN'S

MINOTAUR

MYSTERIES

PRAISE FOR THE MYSTERIES OF SUSAN HOLTZER

THE SILLY SEASON
"[A] witty and humorous tale."
—Harriet Klausner, *Painted Rock Reviews*

"Lighthearted and smoothly told."
—*Library Journal*

BLACK DIAMOND
"This relaxed, evenly paced mystery deftly entwines a century-old tale with a modern murder, and firmly unites three disparate sleuths in a common goal . . . Excellent . . . This satisfying story includes a surprising yet plausible finale."
—*Publishers Weekly*

"[This] promising series features appealing characters and skillful plotting."
—*Booklist*

"Enjoy the adroit intermingling of intrigue present and past as Holtzer bridges a hundred years to bring two generations of strong Swann women vividly to life."
—*Kirkus Reviews*

BLEEDING MAIZE AND BLUE
"Holtzer knows the territory. From the chaotic offices of the *Michigan Daily* to Zingerman's Deli and the Michigan League, the story sparkles with authenticity and suspense."
—*Detroit Free Press*

CURLY SMOKE
"Inviting prose, refreshing characters, and crisp plotting."
—*Library Journal*

"Anneke is the kind of friend with whom one gets comfortable, sinking into the sofa and sipping brandy, quietly conversing until midnight."
—*Alfred Hitchcock Mystery Magazine*

SOMETHING TO KILL FOR
Winner of the St. Martin's Malice Domestic Contest

"Engaging . . . Anneke is an appealing sleuth, her policeman a perfect foil and their case enjoyable."
—*San Francisco Chronicle*

"A marvelously plotted story . . . A satisfying conclusion."
—*Mostly Murder*

THE SILLY SEASON

SEASON

AN ENTR'ACTE

SUSAN HOLTZER

St. Martin's Paperbacks

This is a work of fiction. While Ann Arbor and the University of Michigan are of course real places, all the characters in this book are the products of the author's imagination. Any resemblance to actual persons, living or dead, is entirely coincidental.

THE SILLY SEASON, AN ENTRA'ACTE

Copyright © 1999 by Susan Holtzer.

Library of Congress Catalog Card Number: 98-45220

ISBN: 0-312-97039-0

Printed in the United States of America

St. Martins Press hardcover edition / February 1999
St. Martins Paperbacks edition / April 2000

10 9 8 7 6 5 4 3 2 1

For Mason and Loren,
who constantly remind me of the Why

AUTHOR'S PREFACE

● ● ● ● ● ●

Yes, there will be a wedding, but that's for the next book. After the serious and emotional content of *Black Diamond*, I felt that Anneke and Karl and Zoe—and their creator—deserved a break. Hence the *Entr'acte* in the title—and hence, the subject matter. This one, folks, was written strictly for fun.

One other note: The famous Ann Arbor Sightings of 1966 occurred pretty much as Zoe describes them in her stories, and caused much hilarity at the time. Also, the broad outlines of the Alien Conspiracy—the Greys, Majestic 12, and the like—are a more or less accurate representation of the New Mythology, give or take a flying saucer or two. Like most myth systems, it shifts and changes somewhat depending on who's telling the tales.

ONE

• • • • • •

"And it's not like he's really a dumb jock, you know." Jenna Lenski turned the topless '57 Thunderbird onto South U and proceeded slowly toward State Street and the promise of ice cream. "I mean, underneath all that silliness, he's got a first-class mind. He just won't—hey, what the hell is that?" She slowed the powerful car even further and pointed over the top of the windshield.

"What's what?" Zoe Kaplan peered upward into the blackness of the night sky. Overhead, stars blinked and glimmered, impossibly near.

"There." Jenna pointed again, toward the southwest. "Those lights."

"You mean those? Probably a plane."

"Uh-uh." Jenna, as always, spoke positively. "Can't be. They're not moving. See?"

"I guess. Must be stars, then." Zoe slumped, dropped her head back against the leather seat, somnolent with summer heat. One of those hot late-June nights, the air thick and still, sticky with humidity. She was more than ready for sleep, but East Quad was an oven after three straight days of ninety-degree temperatures. The stars seemed to shimmer in the saturated air.

No, they couldn't be stars. The lights—three of them?—suddenly swooped and whirled, then rose again to their previous position. At least, that's what it looked like. Zoe blinked and blinked again, finding it hard to focus. The night sky offered no point of reference, no perspective.

"That's weird." Zoe blinked once more, sitting up straighter. "They're out by the stadium, I think. Planes? Why would planes be doing maneuvers over the stadium in the middle of the night?"

"Beats me." Jenna shook her head. "Want to go see?"

"Yeah, I do." Zoe shook herself alert, feeling journalistic juices begin to flow. So far, summer school had been even more boring than she'd expected, especially with the *Michigan Daily* publishing only once a week.

"Okay." Jenna turned left on State, braking as the light at Hill turned yellow. Zoe's hands itched for the steering wheel; Jenna was the sort of careful, law-abiding driver who made her twitch. Why have a great car like this if you drove it like a Volvo?

"Are they still there?" Jenna kept her eyes on the road.

"Yeah. Just hanging there. No, there they go again. Sort of zipping toward the ground and then zipping back up again."

"Weird." Jenna accelerated fractionally.

"I don't suppose it's heat lightning? Uh-uh." Zoe answered her own question. "Balloons maybe?" She was getting really interested now. "Definitely somewhere over near the stadium. Can we go any faster? I'm afraid they'll be gone by the time we get there."

"Sure." To Zoe's surprise, Jenna took a firm grip on the wheel and picked up speed; the huge V-8 engine purred softly.

"Rebuilt engine?" Zoe asked.

"Partly. I had to replace the carburetor entirely."

"You did it yourself?"

"Yeah. I figure if you want a car like this you ought to be able to do the work yourself, y'know?"

"Right." Zoe, who loved cars but couldn't tell a carburetor from a carbuncle (and wondered what on earth a carbuncle was, exactly), was impressed. But then, Jenna was impressive all the way around. At least, when she wasn't talking about Ben Holmes. The trouble was, lately every conversation with Jenna ended up being about Ben Holmes, Michigan's great tight end.

Zoe had heard Jenna's litany half a dozen times since they'd met in East Quad at the beginning of summer school: Ben was irresponsible; Ben only wanted to have fun—"no matter what's going on in the world"—Ben never read anything more complex than the Michigan football playbook. Zoe forebore to point out that the Michigan playbook was probably as complex as a Derrida treatise—and a lot more useful besides.

She'd known Ben longer than she'd known Jenna, ever since she'd joined the *Daily* sports staff. She liked them both, but she thought that they were about the oddest couple imaginable. Jenna took everything seriously; Ben

Holmes took nothing seriously. Zoe wondered why the smartest people seemed to make the dumbest relationship choices.

"There they are—over that way." As they neared the Stadium Boulevard overpass, Zoe pointed to the right, where the lights still hovered overhead.

"I see them." Jenna steered around to the Stadium intersection and accelerated to the top of the overpass, where she slowed to take in the panorama of the athletic campus below. The huge bowl of Michigan Stadium filled the corner at Stadium and Main; Crisler Arena crouched next to it; beyond that, a tangle of buildings, playing fields, and parking lots sprawled north and east across several acres of precious Ann Arbor real estate. On the other side of Main Street, lighted windows glimmered along residential streets.

The lights they were following were still there. Three of them, in a vaguely triangular formation. Not blinking but steady. Funny, Zoe thought, they don't look any closer now than they did from South U. Maybe they were higher?

"They're over by Crisler." Zoe pointed again.

"Maybe it's a flying saucer that thinks it's found a friend." Jenna giggled, and Zoe joined in. The low, round dome of Crisler looked like a set from *Close Encounters*.

"Well, it's some sort of flying object, and right now it's definitely unidentified." As she spoke the words, Zoe felt the beginning of a small bubble of excitement. "Hey, you think we're really in on a sighting?"

"Of what? Little green men?" Jenna snorted with laughter.

"No, of course not." Zoe wasn't sure what she meant,

exactly. Except, a Sighting would be a Story, capital S on both words, and so far this summer she hadn't found anything at all worth writing about.

"Go on in through the parking lot," she told Jenna. "Around behind Crisler."

"Okay." Jenna steered past a big blue University bus and came to a stop. The dome of Crisler Arena was to their left; the dark wall of the stadium loomed up in front of them. "Now what?"

"Damn. The parking lot's too bright." Zoe threw open the car door and scrambled out. She continued to watch the lights—had they moved?—while at the same time registering the presence of four or five other people. They must have just gotten off the commuter bus, she deduced with one corner of her mind. But the lights captured most of her attention.

One thing—here, they were even brighter. Too bright to even consider that they might be stars, unless a whole cluster was going supernova all at once. So bright, in fact, that they almost blurred together. The closer she got, the harder it seemed to focus on them.

"Damn," she repeated. "I wish I had a camera."

"I have one," Jenna said unexpectedly.

"Yeah? Where? Can I use it?"

"It's in the glove compartment; I was taking some pictures in the cemetery yesterday. Hang on." Jenna turned back to the car and returned with a small 35-millimeter camera. "Self-focusing, with a coupled strobe. You just look through the viewfinder and push that button."

"Great. Thanks." Zoe took the camera and aimed it upward until she had the triangle of lights in the viewfinder. She clicked off a couple of shots.

The lights moved suddenly. One moment they seemed to be floating over a corner of the stadium; then, abruptly, they were directly overhead. Zoe heard a babble of voices, and turned to see a small knot of people staring upward.

"Must be something military," a young guy in torn blue jeans was saying.

"Not necessarily," a balding man in a heat-rumpled business suit contradicted. "There's plenty of aerospace research going on in Ann Arbor." Zoe recognized him as Gerald Cochrane, an assistant dean in the lit school.

"Big difference," the young guy said gloomily. "The space program was taken over by the military during the Bush era."

"What nonsense." The short, stocky woman with short-clipped gray hair looked familiar. Zoe racked her brain for a minute before identifying her as Ann Carrick, political science department. "NASA is still . . ."

"You know perfectly well NASA is nothing but a military front," a girl in a black tank top interrupted.

"It's always impressive to see how well undergraduates can draw conclusions without the bother of actual data to confuse them," the older woman replied.

"Oh, and I suppose your definition of 'data' is whatever the government tells you," the young guy retorted. "I'll bet you . . ."

The triangle of lights overhead blazed and seemed to expand. Zoe jumped backward involuntarily, and as if in sympathy, the arc lights that studded the parking lot flickered, dimmed, and then blazed in their turn before finally going totally black. Blinded, she instinctively squeezed her eyes shut, but not before the image of the lights imprinted itself on her retinas. She blinked quickly two or three times, trying to clear her vision, before risking a sidelong glance upward once more.

The triangle of lights was gone.

"Holy shit," she whispered to herself in the inky darkness.

"What was—"

"Jesus, did you see that?"

The babble of voices stopped abruptly as the arc lights came back on without fanfare. A circle of faces, white under the harsh glare, gaped in stunned amazement. Wow, Zoe thought. And wow again.

"You people all right?" A tall, skinny man in the uniform of University security raced toward them from a low building on the west side of the parking lot. The huddled group stared at him, stared at each other. A couple of them shook their heads, not in response to his question but experimentally, as though testing their state of consciousness.

Zoe was the one who spoke first. "Do you know what that was?" she asked.

"Me? No." The security guard shook his head. "I thought the lights had blown." He peered up at one of the light poles, frowned, scratched his head. "They're back on now, though." He looked puzzled.

"Where were you?" Zoe reached to pull notebook and pen from her bookbag before realizing she'd left it in the Thunderbird. She swore silently. She didn't want to give him time to think up an explanation; she wanted his first impressions.

"Me?" The guard answered question with question.

"Over in the security building. Why?" His nameplate read Joseph DiMarco; Zoe filed the name in her memory, praying that she'd remember everything without taking notes.

"Did you see the three lights that were hovering over the stadium?" she asked him.

"What lights? When? There isn't supposed to be nothing over the stadium." The guard looked at her suspiciously.

He was obviously hopeless. Zoe turned her attention to the person most likely to theorize. "Professor Carrick?" She fought her journalistic conscience for a moment, then identified herself. "I'm Zoe Kaplan, from the *Michigan Daily*. Do you have any idea what just happened?"

"Not a clue." Carrick shook her head. "Not even an hypothesis."

"Has to be military," the young guy in the torn jeans reiterated.

"Professor Cochrane?" Zoe turned to the assistant dean. "Is it military or government, do you think?"

"Good Lord, how would I know?" He ran a hand through untidy hair, looking annoyed. "More likely a plant department malfunction, I should think."

"Well, that might explain the lights in the parking lot, but not the lights over the stadium." Zoe waited, but the tactic didn't work. Cochrane merely shrugged.

"Sorry." He turned and headed toward a small line of cars at the edge of the parking lot; a few of the others began to do the same. Carrick was already gone.

"Did you report this?" Zoe asked the security guard.

"Not yet." He turned slowly, a full 360 degrees, then shook his head. "Don't see nothing *to* report," he announced. "You kids better get yourselves back home. I don't want no more trouble, okay?"

"But—" Zoe stopped. What was the point? "Thanks anyway, Mr. DiMarco. Ready to go, Jenna?"

"Better believe I am." Jenna still looked pale, although it could have been the lighting.

"Okay, let's roll. Would you drop me at the *Daily*? And can I hang on to your camera until morning?"

"No problem. Think you got anything?"

"Damned if I know." Zoe threw herself into the passenger seat. "I'm dying to find out myself."

TWO

$\bullet$ $\bullet$ $\bullet$ $\bullet$ $\bullet$ $\bullet$

Every window in the huge city room was flung wide, but there was no breeze outside to do any good. Zoe looked around the room, saw nobody, and trotted down the back stairs. She gasped with relief when she entered the air-conditioned production room.

"So this is why you agreed to be summer editor," she accused Gabriel Marcus.

"Yep, rank hath its privileges." He swiveled from the computer screen and grinned at her. "Come by to get out of the heat?"

"No. I've got something."

"I thought the sports page was done." Zoe, in the absence of anyone else who'd wanted it, was summer sports editor, a job that carried a small stipend and virtually no responsibility. The summer *Daily* was a once-a-week tabloid, with a single sports page drawn almost exclusively from wire services. She'd already thanked the journalism gods that this was Tuesday night, with publication the next day.

"It is," she said. "This isn't about sports."

"Oh?" He shook his head dubiously. "Unless it's really major, it'll have to wait. The pages are already locked; I was just about to send it to press."

"If it waits, it's dead."

"Okay, what've you got?"

"It's—" Zoe stopped. What did she have, exactly? "—a sighting, I guess you'd call it."

"A what?"

"Lights. There were these weird lights, hovering over the stadium." Even as she said it, Zoe realized how feeble it sounded. "Well, they were. Weird, I mean," she added defensively. "And then they sort of blazed up and disappeared. And all the lights in the parking lot went out."

Gabriel cocked his head and stared at her. "You're not pulling a Morton Oliver on me, are you?"

"Dammit, Gabriel, you know me better than that." Nothing could have stung Zoe more.

Morton Oliver had been a sophomore beat reporter covering the University libraries back in the early eighties, on the day that the head of the grad library received an unmarked package. It was wrapped in brown paper and plastered with far too many stamps, and the librarian took one look at it and yelled for security. Security yelled for the cops. The cops opened the package, found a clockwork device nestled in wood shavings, and yelled for the feds.

Morton Oliver picked up the story and ran with it. For days his byline was featured on the front page; for days he was the Man on the Spot, covering the biggest story of the year. By the time the feds declared the package a nonexplosive hoax rather than the work of the Unabomber, Morton Oliver was semi-famous around campus.

Zoe wasn't sure when or how the *Daily* editors found out that Morton Oliver himself had sent the package—it was long enough ago that everyone who'd been there was now gone, but not quite long enough to have passed into folklore. Oliver had never been arrested, or even questioned, as far as she knew. But his byline never appeared in the *Daily* again, and his name had become a kind of shibboleth, a synonym for journalistic sleaze.

"Sorry. Lousy joke," Gabriel said. "Did anyone else see these lights?"

"Yes." Zoe felt on firmer ground. "There was a whole group of people there, including Gerald Cochrane and Ann Carrick, from political science."

"Quotes from them?"

"Enough to validate the sighting. Nothing substantive. Oh, and by the way." She dug into her bookbag and brought out Jenna's camera. "I *may* have photographs."

"Really." Gabriel eyebrows rose as he reached for the camera.

"I said 'may'," Zoe warned him. "I'm not much of a photographer, and the conditions were pretty bad. Is there anyone around who can develop the film?"

"Probably. Let me go see." He disappeared for a while, and Zoe chewed anxiously on a fingernail until he returned. "Barney McCormack was in the computer room. He said he'd do it."

"Good." Zoe sighed with relief. "So how much do I get?"

"Depends on what you've got." Gabriel thought for a minute. "First thing, you'd better check with the police and find out if they got any calls about it."

"Right." Zoe crossed to an empty desk, sat down, and dialed. When the police dispatcher answered, she said: "Hi, this is Zoe Kaplan, *Michigan Daily*. I just wanted to get a late update on the total number of calls about the UFO." She pronounced the three letters with amusement in her voice. "Have you got a final tally handy? Oh, good. Thanks." She wrote *107* on the pad in front of her and directed a thumbs-up sign at Gabriel. "One more thing," she said into the receiver. "Can you patch me over to—I think Brad Weinmann is in charge of this one, isn't he?" She scribbled again on her pad. "Oh, that's right, sorry, it is Wes Kramer, isn't it? Could you put me through? Thanks."

She'd never heard of Detective Wesley Kramer, but when he came on the line, sounding harried, she made her voice as friendly as possible.

"Hi, Detective Kramer. Zoe Kaplan, *Michigan Daily*. Sorry to bother you—I've only got a couple of questions and then I'll get out of your hair. I assume the military spokespeople said they didn't know anything about it?" She made it one long, verbal run-on sentence.

"That's correct." The voice on the other end of the phone was abrupt and cautious.

"Yeah, that's what I figured." Zoe kept it light. "And no joy from the National Weather Service, either?"

"They've said there were no weather balloons in the area," Kramer replied.

"Right. Any ideas what it was?"

"Not at this time," Kramer said, speaking formally. "We're still investigating."

"Sure, I understand. Thanks for your time." She hung up the phone and turned to Gabriel.

"The usual. No military exercises, no weather balloons, they're investigating, et cetera, et cetera." She gnawed her lower lip. "I really should go down there and check out the actual reports."

"You don't have time." Gabriel jerked his head toward the clock on the wall. "You can describe the actual event yourself, after all, and you've got reliable witnesses to back you up. There are other things that are more important."

"What've you got in mind?"

"Well, for one thing, you said the lights in the parking lot went out," Gabriel pointed out. "You ought to check with the plant department."

She nodded and dialed, but got only a recorded message directing emergency calls to University security, and she already knew she wouldn't get anything useful from them.

"Nobody home." She turned to the computer. "Guess I better go with what I've got." She stared at the screen. "Wish I could give it more sex appeal."

Gabriel snapped his fingers. "Ed Stempel."

"Who?"

"Professor Thomas Edison Stempel, history department. The University's resident expert on UFOs."

"Resident expert on *what?*"

"You mean you don't know about Ed Stempel?" Gabriel leaned back in his chair, grinning widely. "Ed Stempel teaches a course called 'History of Spirituality,' and another called 'History of Historicity,' which is basically antihistory. Or at least antihistorians. He's one of the anti–Dominant Paradigm people."

"Oh, shit." Zoe groaned. "And what's his idea of the New Paradigm? Little green men controlling American society?"

"Well, it's hard to say." Gabriel steepled his fingers. "He talks in such ultra-scientific jargon that sometimes it's hard to tell. Basically, he insists that the hegemony of the Dominant Paradigm has made it impossible to seriously study what he calls 'alternative science,' including the possibility of alien visitation, and that therefore we have no data on which to make an informed judgment. What he wants is for the University to establish a UFO research center."

"Oh sure, that'll happen." Zoe snickered. "Like, the U is really going to spend money on something like that."

"He's not asking for money." Gabriel shook his head. "He says he can raise the money from outside sources, and he means it. There's a lot of UFO money out there."

"Are they seriously considering it?"

"Not as far as I know. From what I've heard, the history department would give its front teeth to get rid of him, but of course he's got tenure. Besides," Gabriel made a face, "his classes are pretty popular."

"That figures." Zoe reached for the faculty directory. "Well, he sounds like he'll be worth a couple of good quotes, anyway." She dialed the number, and when a male voice answered, said: "Professor Stempel?"

"This is Professor Stempel." The voice was low and beautifully modulated, an actor's voice—or that of a great lecturer. Probably one reason his classes were so popular, Zoe thought.

"Professor Stempel, this is Zoe Kaplan, from the *Michigan Daily*. Have you heard about the sighting tonight?"

"Yes, in fact I have." He sounded amused. "Several people have already called me about it."

"Do you believe it was a UFO?" she asked.

"Of course it was." He chuckled. "It was clearly a flying object, and so far it remains unidentified. Therefore, it was a UFO."

"Yes, sure." Zoe laughed weakly. "But do you think there's a chance it was a—some sort of flying saucer?"

"Not unless someone has attached a motor to a piece of crockery," he said. "Now, I assume what you're really asking, young lady, is whether I believe it was an alien craft of some sort. Is that right?"

"Yes, I—yes." Somehow he was making her feel like *she* was the goofy one. It wasn't a feeling she enjoyed. "Do you think that's what it was?"

"Now how could I possibly know that? First of all, I did not personally see the object. Second, even if I had, there would be no way to make such a determination without further investigation."

"But you do think it's possible?" she pressed.

"I think a number of things are *possible*, including the existence of a reporter who asked intelligent questions. Unfortunately, in the absence of scientifically valid proof, I withhold judgment."

"You referred to 'further investigation.' " Zoe gritted her teeth and plowed ahead. "Are you planning to investigate this particular sighting?"

"Not an entirely silly question." She could almost hear Stempel nod his head in approval. "Since it occurred more or less on my doorstep, as it were, I will probably at least consider it. But you should know that night sightings are fairly common, and far less interesting than other manifestations."

"What sort of manifestations?"

"Physical evidence is always preferred, of course. Evidence of an actual landing, for instance—something like traces on the ground, or low-level radiation. Even a photograph would be of some help, although they are far too easy to falsify."

"What about the lights in the parking lot going out? Does that qualify as physical evidence?" She didn't mention the photographs she'd taken. Let the bastard see them in the *Daily*.

"The lights going out?" Stempel was suddenly alert. "I wasn't told about that. Are you sure?"

"Oh, I'm sure," Zoe said loftily. "At the moment that the . . . object blazed up and disappeared, all the arc lights right under it blacked out."

"You were there?"

"That's right."

"I see. That does make it somewhat more meaningful." Stempel's voice had returned to its original smug tone, but Zoe thought she heard an undercurrent of interest.

"So you are going to investigate?"

"Probably so," he said. "Probably so. Now, if you have no more questions . . . ?"

"Not at the moment, but would it be all right if I got back to you tomorrow?" She would have preferred to throttle him, but she also smelled an ongoing story.

"Yes, you may. Depending," he added, "on the accuracy of the story you write tonight."

"Okay." She fought the urge to slam the receiver in his

ear. "Thank you, Professor Stempel." She replaced the receiver gently and turned to Gabriel. "I may have something going here," she told him. "I'm going to stick with this guy, for a couple of days anyway. And then," she announced, "I'm pretty sure I'm going to kill him."

THREE

$\bullet$ $\bullet$ $\bullet$ $\bullet$ $\bullet$ $\bullet$

"Zoe! Over here!"

Zoe added a jelly doughnut to the bowl of Cheerios on her breakfast tray and steered across the East Quad cafeteria toward the little group at the corner table. Ben Holmes greeted her arrival by raising both arms upward and sweeping them down in a gesture of obeisance.

"All hail the Queen of the Aliens."

"Da *daaaaaa*, da da da daaa, da." Narique Washington caroled the *Star Trek* theme.

"Sub*mit*ted for your ap*prov*al." Barry Statler spoke portentously over Nique's musical accompaniment, happily mixing science fiction references. "*Some*thing in the night sky, over a sleepy college town somewhere in the American midwest. Just what—or *who*—did ace reporter Zoe

Kaplan see?" He waved a circuit board at her before shoving it into his pocket.

"You guys are a real hoot." Zoe dropped her tray on the table and sat down.

"They've been at it ever since they sat down." Jenna shook her head, with its tidy cap of short, auburn hair. Everything about Jenna was tidy, Zoe thought enviously. Even the plain navy-blue T-shirt she wore.

"You don't *iron* your T-shirts, do you?" Zoe blurted.

"What? Of course not." Jenna looked puzzled. "I just smooth them out as soon as the dryer's finished. Why?"

"No reason." Zoe slurped Cheerios and milk.

"Maybe she doesn't have to." This time Ben dropped his voice into plummy horror-movie tones. "Maybe . . . it's . . . really . . . her . . . *skin.*"

"Let me guess." Zoe looked up at him and made a face. "In high school you were voted Class Clown, right?"

"Wrong." His freckled face split into an easy grin. "I was voted Most Outrageous Dude."

"So tell us," Barry said, "did the High Command tell you when the invasion's going to begin?" He rustled the newspaper in his hand, and Zoe caught a glimpse of blue over the masthead.

"Hey, that's not the *Daily.*" She looked again. "Are you telling me I made *USA Today?*"

"Sure." Barry's long, pointed nose twitched. "Weirdness sells, y'know?"

Zoe snatched the paper from him and scanned it greedily. Yes! It was her story—well, a chunk of it, anyway. It was only four paragraphs in the NationLine column on page three, but it was the top story, under the headline

UFOS SIGHTED OVER ANN ARBOR? And it did at least credit the *Michigan Daily* for the story.

"How'd they get it?" Barry asked. "Did you send it to them?"

"Uh-uh. We did send it out to the Associated Press, though. They must've picked it up off the wire."

"They allowed to do that?" Nique asked.

"Yeah. The AP's a kind of member organization. Any newspaper that's a member is allowed to use stuff from any other member paper, as long as they attribute it."

"But they didn't credit you," he pointed out.

"No, but I still get credit for it down the line. It's sort of like when you get an assist on a tackle—it's not a stat anyone keeps officially, but it's there on the film and the coaches know about it."

"Yeah." He nodded. "I've got a batch of those on my highlight film."

"How's that going, anyway?" Zoe asked. "Any nibbles yet?"

"A couple three teams've kind of offered to let me come into camp in July, but none of 'em sound like they really want me." He shrugged. "They all say the same thing—'if you were only a few inches taller'."

"You're good, Nique. Something'll break for you." She hoped it was true—Nique was a good guy—but she knew the odds were against him.

He'd had a fine four-year career as a cornerback for Michigan, including eight interceptions—three of them returned for touchdowns—so even at five-nine he'd figured to make the pros. But when the last name of the last round of the NFL draft had been called, Narique Washington hadn't been one of the Chosen. The wide receivers he'd be expected to cover were simply getting too big.

Still, cornerback was a position of scarcity in the NFL— there just weren't enough six-foot corners to go around. Zoe knew he'd sent a highlight tape to all 28 teams, and the odds were at least a couple of them would give him a tryout when summer training camps began. So maybe Nique still had a shot.

"Well, you'll be finished with your degree in June, won't you?" Jenna said. "So at least it's not like you don't have other options."

"Sure. I know that." He shrugged, and Zoe intercepted the quick glance between him and Ben, the understanding they shared. Jenna doesn't get it, she thought. For these guys, not playing football would be a little bit like dying.

Barry Statler did get it, though; his sharp little eyes darted from Nique to Ben, and there was an odd expression on his face. Envy? Sadness? Zoe wasn't sure.

Barry was the odd man out in the little group, an engineering student with the tall, wiry frame of the dedicated runner. Zoe had been surprised that Ben and Nique had accepted his friendship so easily; football players tended to be self-protective, wary of "jock sniffers," those people who wanted to hang out with athletes, to bask in their reflected glory. But that wasn't what Barry was about; he just happened to be across the hall in Cooley House, and it seemed never to have occurred to him that Narique Washington and (especially) Ben Holmes were famous campus jocks. He was clever and funny in his own right, and after a period of caution, he'd simply become one of the guys.

It was an odd group anyway, Zoe mused, pushing aside her empty cereal bowl and taking a bite of the jelly doughnut. Two football players, a history major, an engineer, and a student journalist—exactly what she loved about dorm living.

"You're in bus ad, aren't you?" she asked Nique.

"Yeah. How about you—you decide on a major yet?"

"No, not really."

"Don't you have to declare this fall?" Jenna asked.

"I can put it off a semester," Zoe said, licking jelly off her fingers. "And anyway, I can change majors later if I want to." It was a question she'd been worrying at for two years; given a choice, she'd have preferred not to major in anything, but just take courses as her interests moved her. After all, writers needed to know a little bit about everything, didn't they? Unfortunately, the University was unmoved by this argument. In the fall, at the beginning of her junior year, she was required to make a decision.

"It's too bad they did away with the journalism department," Barry said.

"Not really." Zoe shook her head. "I get a lot better training at the *Daily* than I would in a j-school. I just hate to waste time taking stuff I don't want, when there's so much stuff I do want."

"Yeah, I feel the same way," Ben agreed. "There's still so much I need to learn—I'm shaky on reading defenses, and I really need to work on my footwork, and meanwhile I'm spending all my time memorizing some stupid poetry."

"That's not exactly the same thing." But even as the words were out of her mouth, Zoe thought: Isn't it? She looked up into Ben's good-looking face and saw his blue eyes laughing at her. "Okay, okay." She threw up her hands. "You made your point." There was general laughter around the table. All but Jenna—her face was stony as she raised her coffee cup to her mouth.

FOUR

· · · · · ·

"I still wish we could have managed August." Anneke Haagen shivered slightly in her light gauze shirt. Cold air poured out of the duct in the converted dining room that served as her home office in the old Burns Park house, and she considered briefly raising the thermostat to lower the air-conditioning. No, hot air rises, she reminded herself; by evening, the bedroom upstairs would be too hot for sleeping. She wondered briefly how much time Michiganders actually spent planning, thinking about, and coping with climate control in the course of a year.

"There's no way I could get away." Karl Genesko, perched on a corner of Anneke's desk, shook his head. "Summer rotation was locked back in May."

"I thought you were taking this as comp time instead of vacation time."

"I am. But I can't take time off when so many other people will be gone. The town may feel empty in August, but we still need a full complement of police. And you're too busy in September."

"I know." She made a face. "September is the crazy month. New staff, new clients—every September, at least a dozen companies suddenly discover that they need to install their entire sales catalog on the internet, or add sixteen different capabilities to their database applications, or—oh, hell." She threw the pen down on her desk. "Why didn't we plan this six months ago?"

"Because six months ago you didn't want to get married, remember?"

"That's right, blame it all on me." She threw a paper clip at him, and he caught it neatly in midair. "Look, are you really sure you don't just want to have a nice, small ceremony on a Saturday sometime in August, go back to work Monday, and plan a trip around the end of the year, when things are slower for both of us? I mean, it's not as though we're kids; and after all, we've been living together for nearly a year."

"Nope." He shook his head. "This is my last wedding. I intend to get it right." He stood up and came around behind her desk to look over her shoulder, his six-five, 250-pound frame looming over her. The linen of his shirt brushed her cheek, and she leaned against him and wondered why on earth she'd hesitated, even for a moment.

Well, she'd been flat-out scared. She'd already screwed up one marriage and too many relationships, and at the age of fifty she'd concluded that she was better off single. She'd had her own home, her own computer consulting business, her own well-ordered, emotion-free life. Karl

Genesko, former Pittsburgh Steeler, now Ann Arbor police lieutenant, simply hadn't fit into her plans.

"All right," she said. "October first it is, and on your head be it. Just don't complain to me because it conflicts with the football season."

"We can squeeze it in between Notre Dame and Penn State." He grinned at her. "Are you ready to go? I think we have time to stop at Zingerman's for breakfast on the way."

Anneke slung her briefcase over her shoulder and followed him through the kitchen to the back door, pausing on the way to grab a handful of peanuts from a bowl on the counter. As they stepped out onto the back porch, a small furry body exploded out of the overhanging tree branches.

"Easy, Swannee." Anneke took a step backward, laughing. The squirrel landed on the porch rail and stood upright, chittering eagerly. She tossed a peanut toward him, and the squirrel made a grabbing catch, stuffed the peanut into its cheek, shell and all, and held up his forepaws expectantly. Anneke repeated the game with three more peanuts before holding up her hands, palms out.

"All gone, Swannee." The squirrel cocked his head at her and chittered again. "No, that's all there is, you greedy little thing." The squirrel settled back on his haunches, extracted a peanut from his cheek, and went to work cracking the shell. Anneke reached out and stroked the top of his head with a finger, and the squirrel fixed an eye on her but accepted the brief caress.

"Kid's got great hands," Karl said.

"He's got the wide receiver's personality, too. Why do you think I named him Swannee?"

She followed Karl up the driveway to his Land Rover,

glancing mournfully at the empty space where her Firebird should have been. It hadn't seemed like much of an accident at the time—just your normal sixteen-year-old driver running a stop sign—but the Firebird had come out of it with a bent frame that was going to take a week to repair. With a sigh, she climbed into the Land Rover.

They drove to Zingerman's in companionable silence. As they headed toward the door, Anneke was busily running potential wedding sites through her mind, so she didn't realize that Karl had gone ahead of her until she heard him laugh out loud.

"What's so funny?" She caught up with him at the corner, standing next to a *Michigan Daily* distribution box. Instead of answering, he handed her a copy of the *Daily*, a broad smile on his face.

"What is it? Oh, good grief."

The black tabloid headline read: THEY'RE BAAAACK . . . with a subhead that said: DOZENS REPORT STRANGE LIGHTS OVER CRISLER ARENA.

Directly below it was a grainy photograph that might have been a nebula viewed through a kaleidoscope, or a reversed photo of a connect-the-dots game, or a group of fireflies mating.

The byline, to Anneke's total lack of surprise, read: ©*The Michigan Daily*, by Zoe Kaplan.

"It would have to be Zoe, wouldn't it?"

She scanned the story quickly. It was a perfectly straightforward description, complete with quotes from corroborating witnesses, written without any apparent hint of mockery. So why did Anneke find herself giggling as she read?

She was still giggling as she got coffee and inch-thick

raisin toast and carried them outside to the patio. "How *does* Zoe do it?" she asked, settling at one of the big picnic tables. "I swear, she must have some sort of built-in weirdness detector."

"Well, thank God this one has nothing to do with murder." Karl took a bite of his sesame bagel.

"Which means, I hope, that it also has nothing to do with you."

"Not unless they find the body of an alien hanging from a goalpost." He turned the paper to the sports page, and Anneke returned to the front page. Near the bottom of Zoe's story, she read:

"This isn't the first time Ann Arbor has been the site of unknown lights in the sky," it said. "Thirty years ago, the city was ground zero for one of the most famous UFO cluster sightings ever recorded. The case was officially closed when Northwestern University professor J. Allen Hynek announced that the sightings were merely 'swamp gas,' but many people refused to accept that verdict."

Anneke tried to recall that spring and summer of '66. She'd been finishing her sophomore year, trying to decide whether she dared major in math, and if so, what she could possibly do with it when she graduated. Teacher? Bookkeeper? Housewife? Immersed in her own life, she had let the great and small events of the 1960s in Ann Arbor wash over her nearly unobserved. If she'd noted the UFO excitement at the time, she couldn't recall it now.

"Do you remember any UFO sightings in 1966?" she asked Karl.

"Only vaguely." He looked up from the paper. "I think we were into spring practice, and a couple of the guys wanted to go out and drive around hunting for flying saucers." He grinned. "I was more interested in learning to read O-line movements."

Anneke reread the story once more. She had a high regard for Zoe's journalistic skills; if she presented something as fact, Anneke was prepared to accept it. Still . . .

Well, Ann Carrick and Gerald Cochrane were pretty reliable witnesses. Besides, from the way it was written, it appeared that Zoe had actually been an eyewitness herself. "I wonder what it was they saw," she said aloud.

"I imagine there are half a dozen cops at City Hall tearing their hair out over that very question." Karl sounded amused. "I wonder who drew this one?"

"Well, at least it wasn't you."

FIVE

· · · · · ·

They finished their breakfast and returned to the Land Rover, heading for City Hall. Anneke's business was upstairs at the city clerk's office, but when they got to the lobby she turned with Karl toward the police entrance, drawn by pure curiosity.

"I bet you're looking for Wes, aren't you?" Desk sergeant Linda Postelli was a large, soft, motherly-looking woman with unruly grayish hair twisted into a bun at the back of her neck. Her resemblance to a third-grade teacher had made her invaluable in sorting out domestic disturbances, until the night an enraged husband had sliced through her thigh with a hunting knife and left her with a permanent limp.

"Why Wes?"

"You mean you aren't volunteering to help search for little green men?"

"Is he the one who got stuck with it?"

"Got it in one." She jerked her head toward the end of the corridor, a wide grin on her face. "That popping sound you hear is Wes's blood vessels bursting." Karl returned her grin and headed down the corridor, with Anneke following along.

They heard the noise as soon as they turned the corner. Not shouting, exactly; more like loud grunts, punctuated by erratic exclamations and the occasional thump. Karl lengthened his stride and reached inside his jacket, but then suddenly halted at a door near the end of the hall. Anneke, staying well behind him and out of the way, saw his face break into a broad smile. She covered the remaining yards and peered around him into the room.

It was the standard office, too small and crammed with too much furniture—two desks, several filing cabinets, very little floor space. And at the moment, most of the available floor space was taken up by two men, both of them in business suits, rolling around on the floor grunting and flailing at each other. Sheets of paper crackled under and around them. Behind one of the desks, a broad, solid man remained seated, watching the activity with a gloomy expression on his face.

"Let me guess," Karl said from the doorway. "Each of them wants to be named ambassador to Mars?"

"Get *off* me, you buffoon!" a voice from the floor shouted.

"Very funny," Wes Kramer replied to Karl, ignoring the men on the floor. "He must be a laugh-riot around the house," he said to Anneke.

"Keeps me in stitches." She smiled at Wes without expecting an answering smile; Wes Kramer never smiled. "Shouldn't you . . ." She gestured at the floor.

"Nah."

"Let *go*, you idiot. You're tearing my jacket." One of the men on the floor yanked his arm free and hitched himself sideways. The other man made a grab for some of the papers, and the first man grabbed for some of the others. With a final series of grunts they heaved themselves apart and scrambled to their feet, both of them equally red-faced.

"Unpardonable," the smaller of the two said, in an unexpectedly resonant voice. "Detective Kramer, please accept my apologies." He brushed and pulled at his clothes, patting and straightening. Anneke noted automatically that the suit was certainly Italian and certainly expensive. "I'm afraid this is precisely the sort of thing that gives ufology a bad name among intelligent people." He pronounced the word *u-f-ology*.

"He thinks that sticking an *-ology* onto a term will automatically make it a science," the other man said. He was a large, soft figure—not chubby exactly but doughy-looking under his rumpled suit. A receding patch of straw-colored hair topped a pale, round face that looked like it was meant to be cheerful but instead was sharply intelligent and aware. He tugged at his jacket, which had twisted itself sideways; one sleeve rode up to the elbow and the collar had worked its way around under his chin.

"And *he* thinks that anything he can't examine under his microscope doesn't exist." The smaller man ran one hand over his hair, smoothing the thick brown waves back into order. He was, Anneke realized, quite remarkably handsome—almost too pretty, in fact, with the sort of precise, classic features more usually seen on a television sitcom. He was only about five-four, and slightly-built as well, yet he somehow managed to be a more commanding presence than the larger man.

"Save it for your TV-audience yahoos," the other man said. "Pomposity and Armani suits won't buy you intellectual credibility."

"What exactly is going on here?" Karl took a step forward into the office.

"You don't want to know," Wes Kramer said glumly, reaching for the coffee mug with the *Semper Fidelis* motto on it. He still wore the buzz cut acquired during his Marine days, but it seemed to be the only Marine habit he'd kept. Instead of an erect posture, Wes's shoulders held a permanent slump; instead of military neatness, his side of the small office overflowed with crumpled paper, half-empty cardboard coffee cups, and oddments of clothing. His ugly tweed jacket had a rip in one pocket, and there was a large stain on the polyester tie that hung sideways over his wrinkled shirt. Anneke was very fond of him.

"This guy"—he motioned at the smaller man—"is *Professor* Edison Stempel, who says he's researching flying saucers."

"I *said* I was studying reports of unexplained phenomena." He turned toward Karl, standing high on the balls of his feet. "And you are . . . ?"

"Lieutenant Karl Genesko."

"Yes, of course." Stempel nodded as if confirming something to himself.

"And this other guy—" Wes jerked his head toward the

large blond man—"is *Professor* Conrad deLeeuw. He says he's here to prove the whole thing is a fraud perpetrated by Professor Stempel. Both of 'em want to go through the reports of the sighting from last night, and both of 'em want it first." He shrugged. "I was just lettin' 'em work it out themselves."

"It hardly seems worth fighting over," Karl commented.

"We were *not* fighting," Stempel contradicted sharply. "Please understand that, Lieutenant. We simply reached for the papers at the same time, and more or less tripped over each other." He turned to deLeeuw, who nodded confirmation, the first time the two men had looked directly at each other.

"I see." Karl kept his grin in check. "You're with the University?" he asked Stempel.

"That's right. History department."

"History department. Isn't it a stretch from history to UFOs?"

"That depends"—Stempel cocked his head—"on how rigid your thinking is."

"In other words," deLeeuw interrupted, "if you're sufficiently gullible you can believe anything is a part of anything else."

"You're Professor deLeeuw?" Karl turned to him.

"Yes. I'm in biochemistry."

"And you think Professor Stempel is responsible for last night's . . . events?"

"Oh, please, of course he is. I mean, a big, flashy sighting right in his own back yard? How much coincidence does he expect people to swallow? Although I guess the fact that anyone listens to him at all proves that there are people these days who'll believe anything."

"And you intend to investigate this?" Karl asked.

"You bet I do. Actually, I'm on sabbatical at Johns Hopkins this year. The only reason I'm in town is for a biogenetics conference. It's just pure luck that I was here when Ed decided to pull his stunt."

"In other words, a coincidence," Wes said dryly. DeLeeuw nodded, missing the irony in Wes's voice. He also missed the hint of suspicion, Anneke thought. She knew enough about the police mind to understand how darkly they viewed coincidence.

"That's right. And that's why I have to see those reports. This time there'll be an objective observer on top of events from the very beginning. Someone familiar with UFO hoaxes."

"An objective observer," Wes repeated. "And that'd be you."

"Right." DeLeeuw nodded several times, once more missing Wes's sardonic tone.

Stempel had listened to the exchange with cool patience. "And just why, my dear Connie," he said finally, "do you suggest I committed this elaborate escapade?"

"Because you're being upstaged," deLeeuw shot back. "Newer and crazier people keep coming along. Your books aren't selling as well as they used to. You must have been furious when Jack Fuhrman got hired as technical advisor on *Starseed*, weren't you?"

"*Starseed?*" Wes asked.

"It's a TV show. One of those pseudoscience things—you know, were the ancient Egyptians really travellers from another galaxy? Is Albert Einstein's brain really operating our defense system? The answer's always 'yes,' of course. That's what the technical advisor is for—to give them enough fake jargon to make the yahoos feel like they're really getting something 'scientific.' "

"Which is precisely why I turned it down when they *did* ask me," Stempel said.

"Yeah, right. Do you really think anyone is going to believe you'd turn down television exposure?" deLeeuw sneered.

"I don't expect *you* to believe anything," Stempel replied. "After all, isn't disbelief the primary tenet of your existence?"

"How like you to confuse 'rationalist' with 'atheist'," deLeeuw said. "But then, intellectual precision isn't exactly at the top of your to-do list, is it?"

"Professor deLeeuw," Karl said, "you say you're familiar with UFO hoaxes? In what context?"

"I'm a member of the Society for Logical Rationalism," deLeeuw replied. "We're dedicated to exposing all kinds of charlatans, especially psychics, UFOs, that sort of thing. Think of us as a kind of truth squad."

"I think," Stempel said, "that this is where I say 'you can't handle the truth.' " His Jack Nicholson imitation was credible enough to bring a smile to Anneke's face.

"Why?" Wes asked deLeeuw. "I mean, what's it to you if people want to believe in little green men?"

"The same thing it should be to you, and to everyone else who cares about where our society is going," deLeeuw snapped. "These people aren't just random lunatics. They've declared war on the very logic our culture is based on. I'm a scientist. If scientists don't defend the scientific worldview, who will?"

"Ah, yes." Stempel smiled. "From those wonderful folks who brought you the hole in the ozone layer. . . ."

"You guys finished?" Wes leaned back in his chair.

"Yes. Sorry." DeLeeuw made a face. "Look, why don't we split up the reports. We'll each go through half of them, and then swap. I don't mind waiting while Ed sounds out the words."

"And I'll manage to put up with Connie's grunting and snuffling." They favored each other with brilliant smiles.

"Fine. Now, as you guys know, police reports are public record, so you got the right to see them. Well, there they are." Wes waved a hand at the clutter of papers still scattered across the floor. "You can pick 'em up and sort 'em out however you want. And then you can use the interview room across the hall. And when you're done you can return 'em to me. And in between, if you want to haul out your phasers and set 'em on kill, you're welcome to do it, as long as you don't bother me about it. Got it?"

"Got it." deLeeuw grinned unexpectedly and began collecting up the papers from the floor.

"So what have you got on last night?" Karl asked when the two men had gone, still squabbling about which papers each would peruse first. He pulled over a second chair for Anneke before sitting down in front of Wes's desk.

Instead of answering, Wes shoved an untidy mass of papers across the desk.

"You mean you had a second set all along?" Anneke laughed aloud.

"Wanted to see them in action," Wes said. "Besides, I don't trust either of them not to swipe something."

Karl scanned the reports quickly, passing them to Anneke as he finished.

"Hmm." Anneke hadn't realized she'd made the sound aloud until she saw both men looking at her. "Virginia Hardesty." She tapped the sheet of paper in front of her, which contained a long list of names. "She was one of the callers?"

"Yeah." Wes managed to look even glummer than before. "You know her?"

"I've met her a few times. My company did a piece of the council's computer system." Virginia Hardesty was in her third term as fourth ward councilwoman. "I'm not crazy about her politics, but the one thing I can say about her is that she may be the least imaginative woman I've ever met. If she says she saw something, she certainly saw *something*."

"Oh, everybody saw something." Wes waved a hand at the list. "Most of 'em just called to find out what it was. But Hardesty said she wanted to make sure there wasn't an explosion or some sort of city emergency. Insisted on talking to the watch commander, too. He said she sounded kind of disappointed that there wasn't a nice, juicy crisis. Politicians." He spat out the last word like a bad-tasting bug.

"A lot of these reports are very circumstantial," Anneke noted.

"Yeah, I know," Wes said. "And a lot of them match up with each other, too, which is apparently unusual for this sort of thing. Three lights, in a kind of triangle, hovering over the athletic campus for about fifteen minutes. Then there was a brilliant flare of some kind, and the triangle disappeared."

"Any leads yet?" Karl asked.

"Leads to what? And for what?" He scrabbled through the papers, which Karl and Anneke between them had sorted into a neat stack, returning them to a chaotic mass. "You can see the reports yourself. NOAA swears there were no weather balloons aloft. The military swears it didn't have anything in the area. None of the research labs were doing anything, *they* say. Radar at Willow Run didn't pick up anything; neither did Metro. Even the observatory says it didn't spot any anomalies. And any single one of them could be lying through their teeth."

"I wonder what it was." Anneke reread one of the descriptions.

"Probably fireworks. Some sort of student prank." Wes shook his head dismissively. "Could of been anything like that."

"Who else is working on it?" Karl asked.

"You're looking at the whole task force," Wes said with angry sarcasm. "Trouble is, since there's no actual crime, they don't want to tie up a lot of manpower on it. And believe me, there aren't a whole lot of volunteers."

"Well, you should be able to wrap it up this morning." Karl's mouth twitched, but he managed to suppress the grin. "Just write everything up, and dump it in the f-and-f file."

"F-and-f?" Anneke asked.

"File and forget." This time Karl did grin. "You issue a statement that 'the investigation is continuing,' and by the next day everyone has moved on to something else. After all," he spoke to Wes, "as you said, there hasn't actually been a crime committed."

"Don't I wish." Wes squeezed his eyes shut, reopened them, and glared around him. "You can f-and-f a tire-slashing, even a purse-snatch—after all, nobody expects us to solve *those*." This time his sarcasm was tinged with bitterness. "But if something is loony enough for the nuts to get their teeth into, watch out."

To Anneke's surprise, Karl nodded with every evidence of agreement.

SIX

• • • • • •

The *Daily* was still an oven. Zoe slogged up the stairs and trudged the length of the aisle between the long oak cabinets. She could hear a murmur of voices from inside the (air-conditioned) business office, but only one other person was in the city room. That was summer editorial director Mary Cannell, and even from the other end of the room, Zoe could see she was pissed off about something.

"Jesus, Kaplan, where the hell've you been?" Mary glared at her from behind the news desk and waved the telephone receiver at her. "Here, take this, will you?" Her brown hair was pulled back into a tight ponytail, and she swiped at the sweat that beaded her forehead.

"What's going on?" Puzzled, Zoe dumped her bookbag

on the desk and accepted the phone. "Hello, this is Zoe Kaplan."

"Great, great, just the girl I've been trying to reach." The voice on the other end of the line jittered with enthusiasm. "This is Cole Franklin, from the *National Searchlight*. *Great* stuff you came up with last night, just *great*."

"Thanks." Zoe held the receiver away from her ear and made a face at it. Wonderful; just what she'd always wanted—a testimonial from a sleazy supermarket tabloid.

"Listen," the voice went on. "We think you're onto something that'd be perfect for us. We'll pay you one thousand dollars for an exclusive on your flying saucers plus the photos you shot. Don't worry about the quality of the photos, either. We'll take care of that."

"What? No." Zoe felt her nose wrinkle in disgust.

"Ha. I told them you wouldn't bite." Franklin sounded positively delighted by her refusal. "You're as bright as I figured, young lady. Okay, two thousand. But that's as high as we go. And let me tell you, that's even more than we paid for the half-alligator, half-woman."

"Are you—" Zoe sputtered, her tongue tripping over half a dozen enraged responses. "Never mind. Goodbye, Mr. Franklin." Holding the receiver between thumb and forefinger, she let it drop back into its cradle with a thump.

Where it promptly began ringing again. In fact, Zoe noticed for the first time that two other lines were also lit up. With a shrug, she started to walk away, but Mary stopped her.

"Uh-uh. Come on, Kaplan, you answer them. I'm tired

of taking messages for you." Mary waved a handful of pink While-You-Were-Out slips at her.

"What the hell's going on?" Zoe took the slips from her, frowned at them and picked up the phone. "Hello, *Michigan Daily*."

"Yes, hello, I need to speak to Zoe Kaplan." The voice was breathless and female, and pronounced her name *Zo*—one syllable—instead of the correct *Zo-ee*. "I have to tell her about the aliens. I have messages from them for her—they're very anxious to let earth know about the war."

Zoe refused to ask which war. "Sorry, she's not here. She won't be back until next week." She hung up and looked at Mary in disbelief. "That was someone with a message for me from the aliens. Do you believe it?"

"Why not?" Mary pointed to the collection of message slips. "You've already got one from a guy who wants you to warn everyone to stay indoors on June twenty-seventh, because that's the day the aliens plan to sterilize all human beings. And there's another one that wants you to tell people that the aliens won't abduct anyone who's wearing a copper band around their heads. And *then*," she said acidly, "they *really* get weird."

"Oh, shit." Zoe glared at the mass of pink paper, then transferred the glare to the telephone, which was ringing once more. "Hello, *Michigan Daily*," she rapped out.

"May I speak to Zoe Kaplan, please?"

At least this one pronounced her name correctly. "Sorry, she's out of town until next week."

"Damn. Look, this is Leon Kaminsky, from the Associated Press office in Detroit. If you hear from her, would you ask her to give me a call?"

Zoe did a quick mental about-face. Leon Kaminsky was

AP's southeast Michigan bureau chief, and a thoroughly respected newsman.

"This is Zoe Kaplan, Mr. Kaminsky. Sorry, but I've been getting so many nut calls I'm sort of hiding out till it blows over."

"Doesn't surprise me." Kaminsky's gentle voice sounded amused. "Still, you handled last night's story very well. Thanks for filing it with us. Did you happen to notice that you made *USA Today?*"

"Yes, I did, thanks." This was praise from a source she appreciated. "But I've gotta tell you, I'm beginning to wonder if I'm glad or sorry."

"Not to worry. You handled it just right—nice and factual and straightforward."

"So I'm not going to suddenly become famous as a nut writer?" She was relieved that he understood what she was worried about.

"Not as long as you just keep handling it as straight news. Which I'm sure you'll do. In fact, the reason I'm calling is to ask you to file tonight's story with us."

"Damn." Disappointment filled her. "I won't be writing one tonight. Unfortunately, the *Summer Daily*'s just a weekly."

"In that case," Kaminsky said at once, "how would you like to string it for us?"

"Sure!" This offer she didn't have to think twice about.

"We don't pay much," he warned.

"That's okay. It'll be great experience." Not to mention that it would look good on a résumé later on. "Besides," she said, laughing, "I just turned down two thou from the *National Searchlight.*"

"Ugh." She could almost hear Kaminsky shudder.

"Okay then, we'll sign you on. Now, how about your pictures? Can you transmit them from there, or do we need to arrange a courier?"

"No, that's okay, we can transmit," she said, proud of the *Daily*'s technology. "I'll send them out right away. What's your deadline on copy?"

"It doesn't work that way. On breaking news, you file it as it happens, then pull it all together for the final story."

"I don't . . ." She hesitated. "I'm not sure there's going to *be* any more breaking news, unless the cops actually figure out what it was. Which, frankly, I'm guessing they won't because they don't really give a shit."

"In that sense, you're probably right. There'll be some sort of update, but that'll probably be all." Kaminsky paused. "Okay, let's do this. You file a second-day lead by, say, six o'clock. Interviews with the police, maybe some of the original witnesses, whatever looks good—I'll leave that to your own judgment."

"Okay."

"Then, in addition to that, give us a fairly good-size backgrounder on the 1966 sightings. I assume you have a morgue?"

"Yes." Well, not exactly. "But isn't that strictly feature stuff?"

"Of course." He laughed gently. "Did you think AP never filed features? We do, you know—they're some of our most popular items."

"Sure, I knew that." Well, she had, sort of, she just hadn't really thought about it. "Okay, then. I'll have the news update by six. I'll try to have the backgrounder in by then too, but that one may be a little later."

"Give it to me by eight. I'll flag it so editors know it's coming. Any questions?"

"Well, there is one thing."

"What's that?" He sounded wary.

"Well, I know you don't pay much, so I thought . . ." She took a deep breath. "I'd like a byline."

To her relief he didn't laugh, although there was amusement in his voice. "I guess we can do that. As long as your stuff is as good as I expect it to be."

She hung up and sat perched on the desk for a minute, thinking. Mary Cannell had left, after a venomous glance at the phone, and the cavernous city room was empty. Zoe checked her watch—just past two o'clock. So plenty of time. Out of habit she settled herself at the sports desk, where she pulled a pad and pen from her bookbag and began scribbling. The phones on the city desk continued to ring, but she ignored them.

For the second-day update: talk to that cop, Wesley Kramer, in person this time; a couple of University experts—maybe someone in meteorology, and maybe a psychologist who could give her a few grafs on mass delusion and superstition. She'd have to get back to Ed Stempel again, too.

The 1966 retrospective would be strictly document research. The *Daily* didn't have a morgue in the true sense of the word, but it did have a library which contained bound volumes of all one hundred and eight years of past *Daily*s, as well as a complete set of microfilm.

Looking good, she thought, scribbling a last line in her pad. Only . . . She looked up from her notes, but the city room remained empty. Now if she could just find someone to tell her *how* to file material over the wire. After a moment she headed down the back stairs to the computer room.

"Hooray." She stepped inside the messy room and closed the door behind her, holding her arms out from her sides to let the air-conditioning dry her sweat-damp shirt. "Finally, signs of sentient life."

"Hey, Kaplan, take a look." Barney McCormack, the *Daily*'s resident computer wonk, seemed unsurprised to see her. He pointed to the big monitor screen, where the logo of the *OnLine Daily* identified the paper's Internet site. This was the news page, listing each of the day's stories in underlined blue text. Barney clicked on the headline that read THEY'RE BAAAACK. . . and brought up her story.

"What about it?" she asked.

"There. See?" His skinny legs, in shredded denim cut-offs and even more shredded sneakers, pushed against the computer desk, shoving his chair back to give her room. He pointed again. "I've annotated it."

"What do you mean?" She peered at the screen more closely, and finally spotted it: Sprinkled throughout her text were occasional words and phrases in underlined blue. Each of them, she knew, were links to other Internet sites—click on them, and you'd be instantly whisked to somewhere else in cyberspace.

"Watch." Barney clicked on the word *hover*. The monitor went white, then black; a white graphic bloomed, of a narrow, triangular face with huge slanted eyes and a slash of a mouth. Beneath it, in an ugly, twisted typeface, were the words *Aliens Among Us.*

Barney clicked the right mouse button, and her own story reappeared. He clicked again, on the underlined blue words *military authorities*. This time the screen was filled with a photograph of a desert landscape, reddish-colored and ominous, a few buildings barely visible in the distance.

"Area Fifty-one," Barney said. Once more he clicked back to Zoe's story. "That one links to an alien abduction site," he pointed, "and I think *police* goes to one of the big conspiracy sites." He grinned at her. "Isn't it cool?"

"Cool? *Cool?*" She heard her voice squeak with outrage, and took a deep breath. "Barney, you've got to undo that," she said as calmly as she could manage. "Please."

"Why? I thought you'd like it." His long, narrow face, pale even in summer, looked hurt.

"Barney, if it were any other story, I'd absolutely adore it. But I'm already up to my eyeballs in bad jokes and random lunatics over this story. If I'm not careful, people are gonna start calling me 'saucer chick,' which is not what I had in mind as a career move."

"Oh, come on, Kaplan. You are definitely overreacting."

Was she? "Maybe." She shrugged. "But I'd rather not risk it, okay? Besides, I've already got freakazoids coming out of the woodwork—I've got one message telling me to stay away from them because they'll only talk to virgins."

Barney laughed loudly. "In that case, why are they even wasting their time around this campus?"

"Beats me." She grinned. "But you see what I'm dealing with? I'd really like to low-profile it on this, okay?"

"Yeah, I guess I see your point." He swiveled back to the computer, brought up a file of text, and clicked away for a couple of minutes. When the monitor once more displayed Zoe's story, she saw with relief that the blue text was gone.

"Thanks, Barney. I'll tell you this, though—the next time I come up with a good one, I'm gonna be all over you begging to be annotated."

"Hey, I like the sound of that." He leered at her cheerfully. "Especially the all-over-me part."

"Figure of speech, pal. Strictly a figure of speech."

"Maybe we've come up with a whole new euphemism— what'd'ya say, honey, you want to get together and annotate?"

"Not tonight, dear, I have a chip-ache," she retorted.

"Shit, I figured it'd be something like that." He grinned. "So what else can I do to make your day?"

"You can show me how to transmit stuff to the AP."

"Not exactly what I had in mind, but what the hell—it's a start."

SEVEN

· · · · · ·

There were a couple of people over in the business-staff area when she got back upstairs, but city side was still deserted. She sat at the sports desk again, picking a spot out of the sun and throwing open the windows behind her.

She called around until she located a meteorologist willing to be quoted, although all he said was that he could think of no atmospheric activity that would produce last night's reported effect. The psychologist was unexpectedly more difficult; the guy she wanted was out of town for the summer, as was her second choice. She was mulling over the faculty list of Michigan's enormous psych department when she heard her name.

"Excuse me. Can you tell me if Zoe Kaplan is here?"

The man stood diffidently in front of the sports desk.

He was big and rumpled, with one of those pale complexions that turn an unbecoming shade of pink in the heat. The pink flush surrounded pale blue eyes and rose past his forehead to his scalp, where it mixed with thinning straw-colored hair. The combination produced an interesting pastel effect, Zoe thought, kind of like a stuffed toy Easter bunny.

She started to tell him that Zoe Kaplan had left campus for an extended stay in an ashram, then abruptly changed her mind. She was used to making snap judgments about people, and there was something about this guy that interested her.

"I'm Zoe Kaplan," she said.

"Oh, good." He sat down in a chair next to the desk, reached into his jacket pocket and withdrew a business card, damp and crumpled from the heat. "I'm Conrad deLeeuw."

"Conrad deLeeuw, chemistry department," she read aloud off the card.

"Oh, sorry. This is the one that's relevant." He snatched the card from her hand, shoved it back into his pocket and withdrew a different one, equally damp and crumpled. This time it identified him as the vice chairman of something called the Society for Logical Rationalism.

"What's the Society for Logical Rationalism?" she asked.

"It's an organization of people—scientists mostly—dedicated to debunking pseudoscience."

"You mean things like flying saucers?"

"Exactly. I read your story this morning. I thought you handled it well—up to a point."

"Oh?" Zoe raised an eyebrow.

"Yes." He plowed ahead eagerly. "You printed the facts as you saw them, I grant you. What you didn't include was the real context of the whole UFO hysteria. Oh, I understand that that wasn't your purpose." He held up a hand as if to forestall an objection. "But when you get older, you'll understand the ramifications of so-called 'value-neutral' reporting."

"I will." Zoe kept her voice flat, refusing to argue journalistic theory with this pompous pudding of a man. Eventually, she figured, he'd get to the point.

"You see, by giving every crackpot idea equal weight, equal coverage, you give them equal validity," deLeeuw continued. "But because the media are the information gateway in our society, they have a responsibility to be selective—to help the public distinguish scientifically valid ideas from garbage."

Sheesh, like this was an issue that journalists didn't argue endlessly among themselves, Zoe thought disgustedly. Aloud, she said, "And you think I should have written—what, exactly?"

"I think you have a chance to do something important here." DeLeeuw leaned forward over the desk. "I'd like you to help me expose a hoax."

"You think those lights last night were some sort of prank?" This was more like it; maybe the guy knew something.

"No, not a prank." DeLeeuw shook his head. "I don't think it was just a lark, or a joke. I believe it was a deliberate hoax, intended to be taken seriously. And I think you can help me prove it."

An idea popped into Zoe's head. "You think you know who did it?"

"I'm positive of it." deLeeuw paused. "This has to be off the record, of course. I don't have any proof yet, so you can't print it or it would be libelous."

"Right." Zoe stifled a sigh. If she could get this guy past the elementary journalism lessons, he might just have something for her.

"I believe—no, let's say I'm hypothesizing—that those lights were a hoax perpetrated by Professor Edison Stempel."

Bingo. "Do you have any evidence?"

"Not yet. But I have a fair amount of experience investigating UFO hoaxes—I've been with SLR for more than five years. And I intend to get the evidence, I promise you. Are you willing to help investigate?"

"Let me ask you something." Zoe bypassed his question. "For the sake of argument, how can you be so sure it's *not* some sort of alien spacecraft? I mean, granted, there's no proof that aliens have visited earth, but after all, there's no proof they haven't, either, is there?"

"Oh, Lord, the Snorg Hypothesis." DeLeeuw rolled his eyes upward.

"The what?"

"The Snorg Hypothesis. It's a term that kind of represents the basic UFO logical fallacy, because by definition it lacks falsifiability."

Zoe leaned back in her chair and shook her head. "You want to run any of that by me a second time?"

"You say it's possible that there are alien visitors on earth because I can't prove there aren't. That's perfectly true. It's also possible that an invisible snorg is sitting at that computer terminal over there right this minute. I can't prove that isn't true, either."

He leaned forward, sawing air with one hand. "Look, one of the basic elements to any truly scientific theory is what's called *falsifiability*. What I mean is, there has to be some test or experiment that could *dis*prove your theory. For instance, let's hypothesize that the boiling temperature of water is two hundred and ten degrees Fahrenheit. We can test that by heating water to two hundred and ten degrees; if it doesn't boil, we've proved the hypothesis false.

"Now in fact, if you try to boil water in Denver, you'll find that it *is* false. So you have to alter your hypothesis to state that the boiling point of water *at sea level* is two hundred and ten degrees. That's the way the scientific method of inquiry operates—you keep experimenting, and you keep adapting your theory to the results of the experiments.

"But now let's hypothesize that water turns purple in the presence of a creature from Betelgeuse. Since we can't produce such a creature, we can't produce the experimental condition. So the hypothesis can't be proven false, the way the boiling-temperature hypothesis can.

"That's what's wrong with the Snorg Hypothesis—if you can't prove it's false, you can't test it, so it doesn't qualify as scientific theory.

"On the other hand, the *Negative* Snorg Hypothesis *is* scientifically valid. The statement that 'there's no such thing as an invisible snorg' *can* be proved false—all you have to do is produce your Snorg. The same thing is true of aliens from Zeta Reticula, or abominable snowmen, or people who can set things on fire by staring at them."

"Except for one thing." The new voice was a squeaky tenor, and Zoe jumped a foot. "Every time we *do* give you evidence to disprove your 'Negative Snorg Hypothesis,' you pretend the evidence itself doesn't exist."

The newcomer was tall and thin and stoop-shouldered, wearing a military camouflage shirt with an embroidered shoulder patch. He had a narrow, ascetic-looking face that Zoe found unexpectedly interesting. There was intelligence there, but there was also a lot of anger, combined with a kind of taut intensity that reminded her of a Christian martyr in a Renaissance painting. An uncomfortable face, she thought.

DeLeeuw didn't seem impressed. "Hello, Jarvis. I should have expected you to show up. I suppose you're going to try to convince her that those 'alien autopsy' photos aren't rubber mock-ups."

"I'm going to offer her evidence." The newcomer set a worn, bulging briefcase on the desk with a thump. "You're Zoe Kaplan?"

"That's right." It was too late for the ashram story, although this was the kind of person she'd have used it on if she could. "And you are . . . ?"

"Jarvis McCray. I'm with ARAA—the Agency for Research on Alien Activity. We analyze alien actions and behaviors, and prepare contingency plans for the coming war."

"When you say alien, I'm assuming you don't mean Mexican border jumpers."

"No." McCray didn't smile. "I'm talking about off-earth beings." deLeeuw snorted loudly. McCray turned and stared deeply at him for several seconds. "I don't have energy to waste getting into arguments with Rationalists."

"You two know each other?" Zoe said.

"Yeah, we know each other," McCray said briefly.

"I believe the last time we met was at that conference in Muskegon. When you were trying to convince people that the *Challenger* explosion was the work of an alien missile." deLeeuw snickered. McCray turned his back on him and faced Zoe once more.

"The evidence you want is in here." He rapped the briefcase. "We don't expect much from the mainstream media, but we don't want you to be able to say nobody offered you the facts."

"Facts!" deLeeuw snorted again. McCray continued to ignore him.

"Here." McCray pulled a stapled sheaf of papers from the briefcase and slapped it on the desk in front of her. "This is information about Hangar Eighteen. And this—" he slapped down another document "—is the most current data we have on Area Fifty-one. This is a backgrounder on the original Roswell crash, in case you aren't familiar with it"—*slap*—"and here's a white paper on alien implants"—*slap*—"and this is the best available information on the current membership of Majestic Twelve." *Slap*. "There are also copies of the more important relevant photographs"—*slap*—"including the alien autopsy." He flicked the smallest glance at deLeeuw, whose face held an expression of deep disgust.

Zoe stared at the massive pile of documents in confused amazement, emotions she tried to keep from showing on her face. She searched for an appropriate question to get her to the center of this tangle.

McCray must have read her confusion. "You don't know anything about the alien conspiracy, do you?"

"No." Zoe decided on frankness. "I've never paid much attention to the whole flying saucer thing."

"Please don't use that term," McCray rapped out. "We're not talking about some *War of the Worlds* joke here. What I've just given you is evidence of the greatest crisis in the history of earth—a conspiracy that reaches into the very highest levels of government." He regarded her intently. "If you're truly ignorant of the entire situation, there's just a chance you might actually have an open mind. Do you?"

It was a have-you-stopped-beating-your-wife-type question; who would admit to being closed-minded? Instead of answering, Zoe asked the question she should have come up with immediately.

"Do you believe last night's sighting was an alien spaceship?"

"Not a spacecraft." Zoe noted the altered terminology. "Those aren't designed for use in atmospheric conditions. What you saw last night was a lander, used for planetary exploration. *They're* preparing for the coming war, even if America isn't."

"You think it was here for a kind of military reconnaissance?" Zoe was fascinated in spite of herself. Out of the corner of her eye, she saw that deLeeuw looked even more disgusted than before, and she gave him points for letting McCray rave instead of arguing with him.

"We're not sure." For the first time, McCray seemed hesitant. "We don't think this is a likely location for them to initiate a major military action—for one thing, it's too far from their supply base. But there's obviously something important about the Ann Arbor area. Thirty years ago they spent more than two weeks reconnoitering this area; the fact that they've returned now must mean something. That's the reason I'm here—to try to find out what."

"Are you going to try to make contact?"

"Not exactly." He tightened his lips to a narrow line. "You have to understand, these aren't your lovable *Close Encounters*–type aliens. These are highly dangerous beings who have their own agenda—one we admittedly don't fully understand yet—and it is extremely risky to get in their way. But for once we'll have one of our own people on site from the very beginning to make sure the authorities aren't allowed to cover up the truth."

"What authorities do you mean?"

"All of them. The military, the government, the local police—even your precious University is very likely involved. You probably believe the University doesn't do classified research anymore, don't you? Of course—that's what they want you to believe." He sliced the air with his hands; short, jagged gestures. "Believe me, the conspiracy isn't just at the highest levels of government; it also has very deep roots. Watch and see the way their so-called 'investigation' will go—the local yokels in the police department will try to tell people it was a weather balloon, or a low-flying plane, like they did in Texas. Or swamp gas. Swamp gas! Well, not this time."

He rapped a fist on the stack of papers. "Read this. Then you'll know the truth, and you'll be able to tell people what's really going on."

"I'll read them, I promise." McCray had begun as a kind of interesting nutcase, but now he was beginning to creep her out. She noted with relief that Barney McCormack had come up the back stairs and was lounging against the old dumbwaiter shaft. She stood up and held out her hand to McCray. "Thanks for the stuff. I'll be in touch if I have any questions."

His frantic intensity had disappeared as abruptly as it had begun. "No you won't," he said. "Never mind. It was worth a try. Read it anyway. You'll learn something even if you don't believe it." Ignoring her outstretched hand, ignoring deLeeuw, he picked up his briefcase (now considerably less bulging) and stalked away down the long aisle.

"Sheesh." Zoe waited until she heard McCray's footsteps clicking down the slate staircase before dropping back into her chair.

"Now you have some idea of what we're up against," deLeeuw said with apparent satisfaction.

"Oh, come on. Why get worked up about a random crackpot?"

"We wouldn't, if that's all he was," deLeeuw insisted. "But that organization of his—ARAA—has more than three hundred members. And it's only one of dozens of them, all of them spouting variations of the same insane party line, and all of them sucking in more and more people. Especially young people—it's every bit as bad as any religious cult. In fact, it wouldn't be too extreme to categorize this mania as an intellectual health crisis."

He paused and wiped at the sweat trickling down the side of his face. "That's why it's so important to expose this particular hoax—because Ed Stempel has infected more people than most of the crazies, and he'll keep spreading his contagion until someone stops him. So will you help me get the proof we need?"

"I'll keep investigating." She spoke as carefully to him

as she had to McCray. "And if you have any information, any facts, I'll be delighted to print them."

"Ready to go, Zoe?" Barney McCormack strolled around behind her and dropped a casual hand on her shoulder.

"Yeah, I think so." Zoe stood up once more and began gathering up McCray's papers.

"All right." DeLeeuw reluctantly got to his feet as well. "I'll keep in touch, I promise."

"Good, good. Let me know if you come up with anything." Zoe stuffed the papers into her bookbag. "All set, Barney." She nodded to deLeeuw and followed Barney down the back stairs.

"Holy shit." Once they were inside the computer room, with the door firmly shut, Zoe flopped into a chair and shook her head. "Thanks, Barney. I owe you big-time. My God," she burst out, "are they *all* fucking nuts?"

"Hell, these two are practically sane compared to what's out there." He motioned toward the computer. "You should see some of what's on the Internet."

"No, I shouldn't." She picked up a can of Coke sitting on the desk, shook it experimentally, and drank off the contents. "Y'know, the anti-UFO guy is actually just as obsessed as the other one. Maybe having anything at all to do with this shit softens your brain." She reached into her bookbag and pulled out a sheet of paper at random. "You think if I read this I'll start seeing invisible Snorgs?"

"Invisible what?"

"Never mind. How about if I buy you a pizza?"

"Sure." He grinned at her. "But you'll still owe me."

EIGHT

• • • • • •

"Holy shit." Zoe looked up from the smeary page and stared at Barney across the red-and-white-checked table-cloth. "Do they actually believe this?"

"Lots of them do, yes," Barney said from around a mouthful of pepperoni and mushroom.

"Fucking nuts," she repeated, taking a bite of pizza and returning to the document. It was headed:

BRIEF CHRONOLOGY OF THE
AMERICAN-ALIEN CONSPIRACY

July 2, 1947: Alien craft crash-lands at Roswell, New Mexico.

Sept. 24, 1947: President Harry S. Truman

establishes Majestic 12, a top-secret committee to handle all elements of the alien situation. Original members included Nelson Rockefeller, future CIA Director Allen Dulles, John Foster Dulles, Averill Harriman, Dean Acheson, George Kennan, J. Edgar Hoover, and Admiral Arthur Radford.

1949: A live alien is recovered from a downed craft. Named EBE, for Extraterrestrial Biological Entity. EBE was imprisoned and studied by government scientists until his death in mid-1952.

1954: First Alien-American Treaty signed. Under this treaty, the grey aliens are given the right to abduct humans for medical and experimental purposes; in exchange, the American government will receive advanced extraterrestrial technology. The treaty also permits the aliens to construct underground bases in various locations throughout the United States and on the moon.

1957: The Greys begin a concerted campaign to weaken the American people to facilitate the takeover of earth. With the help of the CIA, they provide access to military weapons among the civilian population, foment race wars, and develop and distribute drugs to our cities. They also selectively introduce environmentally damaging elements and diseases, including, but not limited to, AIDS.

1963: President John Kennedy discovers the

alien link to the drug trade and tells Majestic 12 he intends to inform the American people of the Greys' presence. He is assassinated by CIA agents in Dallas to prevent this from happening.

1963 (?): The Greys go beyond their agreed-upon use of human abductees, and begin implanting them with mind-control devices. It is estimated that as of today, approximately 40% of the human population currently carries these devices. At around this same time, the number of sightings of alien craft increases, with confirmed sightings in Michigan in 1966, the Hudson River valley beginning in 1983, and continuously in the Groom Lake area of Nevada known as Area 51 (Dreamland). It is believed that the aliens are growing either careless or confident.

1969: 66 people are killed in a confrontation between human and alien scientists at an underground lab at Dulce.

1972 (?): A dozen scientists and researchers, all with high-level security clearances, form The Aviary to coordinate information about the alien presence.

"Barney, this is stone nuts!" Zoe blurted when she reached the end. "I mean, this is . . . it's *The X-Files*, for pete's sake."

"Sure it is, a lot of it." He munched pizza, unperturbed. "This is like a new mythology, you know? It's been floating around out there for a long time; it's just beginning to coalesce, that's all. *The X-Files* just sort of tapped into it all."

"Yeah, but these people *believe* it."

"Well, Americans always love a good conspiracy theory, and this stuff gives them the biggest, baddest conspiracy theory you can come up with."

"I know, but . . ." Zoe shifted the slice of pizza to her other hand and shuffled through McCray's papers. "Did you see this one? The one that's supposed to be a photograph of an alien autopsy?" She held up the grainy reproduction. The thing depicted on the table looked more like a piece of carved salami than an alien.

"Well, yeah, that one's kind of suspect, even among the more committed UFO troops. In fact, there are some people who think it's a major piece of disinformation."

"Disinformation?"

"That's stuff that's been planted by the CIA or MJ-Twelve, either to confuse the real UFO researchers, or sometimes to set them up. You know, they introduce some real juicy item, everyone bites on it, and then they come up with proof that it's phony and make all the UFO people look like jerks."

"That doesn't sound like too tough an assignment," Zoe said with a snort.

They finished their pizza and headed back to the *Daily*. "How come you know so much about this stuff?" Zoe asked on the way.

"Mostly from the Internet. You can't spend as much time online as I do without bumping into it. It's a great medium of communication for people who are widely spread out. They post information about sightings, and government documents, you have abductees posting descriptions of their experiences, you have UFO research papers online—it's all there."

"Sheesh. The Internet has a lot to answer for."

"Well, whether we like it or not, that's the way information is going to be transmitted from now on. You think of the *OnLine Daily* as a kind of adjunct to the 'real' newspaper. And at the moment, of course, it is. But five years from now—maybe even a lot sooner—it'll be the hard copy that's the adjunct."

"I don't know." Zoe pondered the notion. "After all, people can't read their computers over coffee at the Union."

"Sure they can, or anyway, they will. All they need is a palmtop computer with a cellular modem—and most phone lines'll be cellular pretty soon. You'll carry your computer around with you as automatically as you carry your wallet."

"Maybe. But I think there'll always be a place for print media."

"But it *is* print media," Barney insisted. "It'll still be the same written words as always. All we're really talking about is black marks on a white background, and what difference does it make if those black marks are on mashed-up trees or an electronic readout?"

"That's true, isn't it?"

"And on a Web site, there's effectively no limit on space. No more cutting your best quotes because some other story ran too long. No more having to choose between three or four great photographs—run 'em all. No more beating yourself up trying to paraphrase a whole document—include the whole thing for people who want all of it. And if someone wants more detail on a subject, or if they missed some earlier story they want to go back and read, one mouse click and it's right there in front of them. You can link in anything you want."

"I guess I never thought about it that way." Zoe was particularly taken with the infinite-space idea; she always seemed to have more to write than space to put it in.

Back at the *Daily*, Barney returned to his computer while Zoe grabbed her bike and pedaled to City Hall. There was a brief statement from the police about the UFO investigation, but she couldn't get in to see Kramer. She thought about calling Genesko, but it felt like an imposition, and she didn't think he'd know anything about this anyway.

She rode back to the *Daily* and started working the phones. Stempel wasn't in his office or at home, but she managed to get hold of a city official who was willing to express confidence in the police, and a physicist who talked for a while about the impossibility of interplanetary travel. She wrote up what she had, included a reprise of the original sighting, and sent it in, hoping it would do.

A couple of people had shown up, studying or pounding keyboards. Gabriel Marcus arrived while she wrote, sitting at the sports desk with a battered textbook in front of him.

"Anything new?" he asked.

"Uh-uh. I'm just doing a couple of follow-ups. Guess what, Gabriel? I'm stringing it for AP."

"Hey, great. Good for you. Got anything juicy?"

"Unfortunately, not really." She made a face. "I filed

the update, but there really wasn't anything except the same old same old. But they also want a backgrounder on those 1966 sightings."

"That could be good. And who knows?" Gabriel grinned at her. "Maybe they'll come back tonight for an encore."

Barney had downloaded a piece about the 1966 sightings from an Internet site. Armed with the date of the first report—March 21, 1966—Zoe went to the *Daily* library, hauled out the bound volume for Spring 1966, and confidently dragged it open to the March 22 issue.

There was nothing there.

Well, they probably didn't get on to it until the next day, she figured, flipping pages. But there was nothing on March 23, either. Finally, on the 24th, she found a story—about fifteen inches on the bottom of the front page, headlined: EXPLANATIONS FOR UFO SIGHTINGS GROW.

It was your basic "comment story"—various experts asked about some current event. She ran her eye down the columns quickly. The local congressman suggested various experimental aircraft; an astronomy professor suggested a reflection off the Peach Mountain telescope; a zoology professor suggested "will-o'-the-wisps." Like the blind men and the elephant, Zoe thought; they're all extrapolating from their own particular set of knowledge.

On March 26, the famous "swamp gas" report ran second lead, but it was an AP story—the *Daily* apparently hadn't thought it important enough to send a reporter to Detroit to cover the press conference.

She found only two more short pieces, little more than

squibs. One, headed ANGRY DENIALS, quoted the Washtenaw County sheriff insisting that his men "saw some type of vehicle in the sky," coupled with an aeronautical engineer who reported a UFO behind the VA hospital.

And finally, on March 30, the *Daily* reported that the Ann Arbor police had received over fifty new reports of sightings, including one over the county jail seen by half a dozen officers.

After that, nothing.

She closed the bound volume and considered what she'd read—or more to the point, not read. For what had become such a famous UFO event, the *Daily* sure hadn't given it much ink. And what they did give it seemed to focus mostly on the likelihood of government aircraft. There didn't seem to be anyone yelling about alien invasions, or hunting for little grey men from outer space. It just hadn't been much of a story.

Well, it was now. She'd have to do most of the retrospective from Internet sources. And maybe she could interview someone who was around at the time. She picked up Barney's printouts and headed back to her desk to write it up.

Kaminsky hadn't given her a length limit on the 1966 sidebar, but she knew no newspaper was likely to run anything much over a thousand words or so. And if her stuff was going to be cut, she'd rather do it herself. Sighing, she reached for her mouse, wishing this was Barney's brave new world of infinite newspaper space.

"Gabriel?" It struck her finally as she was preparing to delete a graf she particularly liked.

"Yeah?"

"Since we're only a weekly in the summer, what would

you think about putting this stuff on the *Daily* Web site? I know we don't usually update it except with each paper, but this story'll be strictly birdcage liner by then."

"You mean, like a kind of electronic Extra." It took a couple of seconds, but Gabriel's face lit up. "It wouldn't cost us a penny, would it, and we can stay right on top of a big local story. I love it." He banged his textbook shut and swiveled to his computer terminal. "Let me see what you've got."

She saved out two versions of her story—a shorter one for AP, and an all-you-could-eat version for the Web site. Barney trotted upstairs to confer with Gabriel. Zoe called Kaminsky to make sure he didn't object—she was effectively scooping herself online, after all—and they agreed that an AP ligature after her byline would satisfy all parties. Barney dragged out the big bound volume from Spring 1966, and scanned in a couple of old photographs; they would go on the web site along with her article. He also produced a list of UFO-related Internet sites, and the three of them argued furiously about which to include in their links section.

They were downstairs in the computer room, admiring their handiwork, when the first call came in.

"It's for you." Gabriel handed Zoe the phone.

"They're back!" It was a female voice, young and giggly. "The flying saucer's right over the Rock this time. You oughta check it out."

"I see. Thank you for calling," Zoe said sweetly, and after she hung up: "Asshole. That's what I love about the summer session—a whole town full of undergraduates with too much time on their hands."

The phone rang again. Again Gabriel handed it to her.

"Are you collecting reports about the UFOs?" This voice was also female, but adult and brisk.

"Do you have any information?" Zoe asked cautiously.

"I can see them—well, I can see *something*—right now. Outside my living room window."

"Would you describe them?" Beneath her caution, Zoe felt a bubble of excitement.

"Three lights—no, four. Three white lights in a rough triangle, and a fourth light, reddish, either off to the side or above. It's difficult to tell because of the perspective." The woman spoke calmly and precisely.

"Sounds the same as last night." Zoe grabbed a pencil and a scrap of paper. "What's your address?"

"Sorry. I don't want to get involved in this circus. I called you instead of the police in the first place because I don't want to be identified. But at this moment it—or they, or whatever—is almost directly over Tappan. It's moving in a kind of circle, but I'd guess it's heading roughly northwest."

"Got it. And thanks." She jumped to her feet. "They're back," she told Gabriel and Barney. "Over Tappan Junior High. I've gotta get over there. Although by the time I bike all the way, it'll probably be gone."

"I've got a car." Barney uncoiled from his chair. "Come on, I'll drive you."

"Take a camera!" Gabriel shouted as they raced for the door.

"Right." Barney turned back, reached into a desk drawer and pulled out a complicated-looking device bristling with accessories. Zoe followed as he ran for the back door, dragged it open, and pointed to a battered Ford Escort in the parking lot. She yanked open the passenger door and fell inside, shoving aside a wadded-up jacket and shuffling her feet into a welter of cans, crumpled candy wrappers, and other unidentifiable detritus.

They headed down Packard toward Stadium Boulevard, but as they approached Granger Zoe spotted the lights. "Over there!" She pointed to the east, and Barney hung a hard left, ignoring the angry horn of an oncoming car. The lights were ahead of them and off to the right, but as Zoe watched in an agony of impatience, they moved slowly across their line of vision, traveling north. "Turn here," she ordered, and Barney obediently swung left onto Baldwin. "Head for Washtenaw," she said unnecessarily; Barney had already turned right on Hill Street.

The lights were dead ahead as they approached Washtenaw Avenue. "Hurry." She leaned forward tensely, her right foot instinctively pressing against the floorboard. She ignored the crunching sound made as her foot smashed a Styrofoam cup, hoping only that it hadn't squished coffee all over her shoe. She blinked, peering toward the Rock in the distance. As near as she could tell, tonight it was a particularly repellent shade of purple.

The Rock, as its designation implies, is a single piece of granite, about eight feet high and shaped roughly like a four-sided pyramid. It sits on a small, grassy triangle in the middle of the intersection of Washtenaw and Hill Street, where it was originally placed as a memorial to some historical event or figure lost in the mists of history. In contemporary times, however, the Rock has only one function in life—to be painted.

Everyone paints the Rock. Sororities paint it in chapter colors. Visiting football fans paint *Michigan Sucks* on it. High school students paint birthday greetings to each other, an alternative to toilet-papering trees. Whole families make an outing of it, debouching from the family car carrying buckets of leftover paint and thick, stiff brushes that even the smallest child can handle.

It is a local joke that the Rock, under its hundreds of coats of paint, is really only a six-inch pebble.

Tonight the ghastly purple was made even ghastlier by the weird glow from above. The lights were pretty much the same as last night, Zoe concluded. Three of them, arranged in a rough triangle. Only this time she could just pick out the accompanying red light that the woman on the phone had mentioned. She blinked; actually, there were two red lights, smaller and dimmer than the bright white triangle. They were moving in relation to the triangle, too, sometimes above it, sometimes off to the side, flitting around each other in a complicated dance. But the main formation now seemed to be stationary.

"Pull up there. Hurry, while they're not moving." She realized suddenly that Hill Street was lined with cars, motionless against the curb, drivers and passengers gawking upward. A group of people milled around the small triangle of grass that the Rock sat on. There were even a couple of guys perched high in tree branches.

"Just park anywhere. Where's your camera?" Zoe grabbed the door handle in an agony of impatience. Barney rammed the Escort nose-first against a patch of curb, cut the engine, and reached a long arm over the back of the seat for his camera. Zoe, her eyes fixed on the lights overhead, leaped out of the car almost before it came to a stop, slipping as her foot encountered a scrunched-up plastic bag. She grabbed for the edge of the door, regained her balance, and took a step forward.

And the lights overhead exploded into brilliance.

Her eyes squeezed themselves shut. Around her she heard shouts and screams, followed by raucous cheers. When she forced her eyes open again, the entire area was in darkness.

Along Hill and along Washtenaw, for at least a block in each direction, no lights shone from behind windows. The street lights were out. Even the traffic light at the intersection was out. And then, without fanfare, all the lights blinked on again.

There were ironic cheers from the people next to the Rock, and a babble of voices. Overhead, the night sky was clear of everything but unexceptional stars.

"Did you get anything?" she called to Barney.

"Not really." He came around to her side of the car, shaking his head. "The flare-up probably overexposed the film. I did get off a couple of shots of the crowds, and the blackout, for what it's worth."

"Shit, shit, shit. If it had only stayed put two minutes longer. . . . *Hell.*" She looked around; the small crowd was dispersing, laughing and chattering. "Come on, let's go back to the *Daily*. I need to make some phone calls. At least we're going to have some hard news for that online Extra. And besides," she realized with sudden excitement, "I get to file this for the AP, too."

NINE

• • • • • •

"Phmfph." Anneke, sitting up in bed reading, hadn't realized she'd made the sound aloud until she saw Karl raise an interrogative eyebrow at her. "Listen to this." She flipped back a page and read aloud:

" 'The dominant paradigm of our time—a slavish adherence to western linear thinking—is already breaking up. In its place is a new paradigm which offers intellectual independence from old, worn-out concepts and the prevailing climate of denial. This new paradigm comes not from the scientific establishment, not from a few members of a self-proclaimed scientific elite, but from the shifting worldview of the masses of people who are willing to see more, to consider more, to open their minds to more possibilities, than have ever before been laid before us. We are seeing the beginning of a true scientific revolution—not a revolution *of* scientists, but a revolution by the people *against* the scientists themselves, against those rigid minds which tell us what is impossible, instead of joining with us in a search for what is possible.' "

She slammed the book down on the bed. "Would you believe that?"

"Who wrote it?"

"Believe it or not, it's from the introduction to a book by Professor Thomas Edison Stempel, B.A., M.A., Ph.D., and something called Sp.L., which is no academic degree I've ever heard of. It's just . . . just *babble*."

"You're the only person I know who's more offended by illogic than by pornography."

"No, but honestly, he talks about this 'new paradigm' as though it's just something you can take a vote on. I mean, a Kuhnian paradigm shift begins with a *discovery*—a real conceptual breakthrough that turns existing theory on its head because it produces empirical evidence that conflicts with the current paradigm. It doesn't happen because a gaggle of New Age airheads get together and decide, hey, let's all believe the speed of light *isn't* one hundred eighty-six thousand miles per second." She heard her voice rising from annoyed to shrill. "Sorry. I guess I do consider illogic the eighth deadly sin. Do you know, the girl at the bookstore said this was on the *New York Times* best-seller list?"

". . . visitors to Ann Arbor?" The voice from the television speaker, unbearably perky, broke into her consciousness. "We'll tell you about it, after these messages."

"Hang on, here it comes." She turned toward the screen. On Detroit television newscasts, nearly every report from Ann Arbor was handled with imbecilic cuteness. She could only imagine how they'd cover a UFO sighting.

"Is Ann Arbor about to become a landing platform for aliens from outer space?" The woman on the screen smirked into the camera. "Last night, *something* was sighted hovering over the stadium, described by several people as a group of lights that were definitely not your average airplane. And then tonight, a similar . . . something . . . was sighted over an exclusive faculty neighborhood. For more details, we go to Jerry Singleton in Ann Arbor for this exclusive report."

"Oh, good grief. Again?" Anneke groaned, then stared in horror as the screen broke to a shot of a youngish man with a toothy grin standing in front of the Rock. "My God, is that where it was? That's only a few blocks away from us."

"Poor Wes. This is all he needs." Karl sounded both sympathetic and amused.

The man on camera managed to grin even more widely. "Liz, we're in Ann Arbor, where hundreds of people swamped the police switchboard for the second night in a row with reports of strange lights in the sky." Anneke and Karl listened as the voice offered half a dozen different descriptions of the "sighting," ranging from an ominously silent platoon of aircraft to a full-scale explosion.

"Among those reporting the sighting last night," Singleton went on, "was Ann Arbor city councilwoman Virginia Hardesty. Ms. Hardesty declined to speak to our reporter, but according to the police report, she witnessed, and I quote, 'a brilliant flash of light' in the area of the stadium as she was driving home from a committee meeting. And then tonight, more than a hundred people, many of them respected University faculty members, reported another sighting, this time over the Burns Park area just south of the campus."

"Good God." Anneke rolled her eyes. "Please tell me we're not going to have television crews tramping all over the neighborhood."

"Liz, we were lucky enough to get an interview with Professor Edison Stempel, of the University of Michigan history department. Professor Stempel is an acknowledged authority on unidentified flying objects." The scene cut to Stempel himself, sitting at a handsome oak desk in front of a wall of books.

"The reason sightings of this sort are called UFOs," he said to the camera, "is precisely because they are unidentified. I realize you want me to tell you that aliens have landed, but at the moment I can't do that. An investigation of this sort takes time."

"Professor," the off-camera voice of Singleton spoke, "just how do you investigate something like this?"

"Carefully." Stempel chuckled at his own joke. "Seriously, Jerry, we're only now beginning to develop the sort of analytical devices that may tell us what these anomalies really are. I've been working on something myself that may help, especially since I'm right here on the spot, as it were."

"Did you yourself see this object?" Singleton asked.

"Unfortunately, no." Stempel shook his head, and Anneke thought he looked angry. "In fact, I'd like to ask anyone who sees these lights again to call me at once. I believe that if I can be on site when they are actually present, I can provide a kind of analysis that's never been done before. I can always be reached through my office phone number." He recited the number.

The screen shifted to Singleton and the Rock. "Maybe Professor Stempel will get that call tomorrow night," the reporter said to the camera. "Until then, Liz, that's the story from Ann Arbor."

"Jerry?" The anchorwoman said. "Do the police have any theories about what these lights are?"

"No, they don't, Liz. They seem to be as baffled as everyone else." Karl made a noise halfway between a snarl and a snort. "We can tell you that spokesmen for both the air force and the National Weather Service have denied any activity that could account for these sightings."

"Well, keep us informed, Jerry." The grinning face of the anchorwoman returned to the screen. "After all, it *is* the tourist season in Ann Arbor." She snickered daintily. "Next up, we'll tell you which low-fat cookies flunked our taste test, after these messages."

Anneke reached for the remote and hit the mute button. "This city has absolutely *got* to get its own television station," she said.

"Poor Wes." Karl repeated the words Thursday morning over breakfast, as they watched a different Detroit television station run a very similar story.

"Poor us, if we get overrun by UFO hunters," Anneke said. "And poor Zoe," she added.

"Why poor Zoe?"

"Because the *Daily*'s only a weekly in the summer." She laughed. "All this excitement going on, and nowhere to write it for."

"Knowing Zoe, she's probably writing it for the *New York Times*." Karl grinned. "And in the absence of that, she'll have it Xeroxed and distribute it around campus herself."

"I wouldn't put it past her. She'll find an outlet or die trying. In fact . . ." She picked up her coffee cup and stood. "I want to take a look at something." She carried her cup across the hall to her office, where she booted up her computer. "Yes," she called a moment later. "Come look."

"So she did find an outlet." Karl, carrying his own coffee cup, looked over her shoulder at the monitor which displayed the words *OnLine Michigan Daily*, in a mix of traditional Old English masthead and modern red lettering. Blazoned across the screen was a headline that read: UNIDENTIFIED LIGHTS ROLL TO THE ROCK. "What does the story say?" he asked.

"Actually, there are two stories." Anneke reached for her mouse. "Let me print them out." She waited for the whine of the laser printer, then logged off, and together they returned to the breakfast table to read the morning news with their coffee and bagels. It's no different from any other morning newspaper, Anneke thought; only the delivery system is different. She handed Karl the main story, and she took the other, laughing aloud at the headline.

1966 AND ALL THAT

It began in darkness at Hillsdale College on March 21, 1966. It ended in a blaze of publicity and horselaughs at the Detroit Press Club five days later. The "Michigan Sightings" became one of the most famous cases in all the UFO annals.

The first report came from a Hillsdale dormitory, about 40 miles southwest of Ann Arbor, where a student reported that she and several of her friends, as well as a college security guard, had seen "a football-shaped object," complete with pulsating red, green, and white lights, hovering near the dorm.

Their report was circumstantial enough that the U.S. Air Force dispatched Prof. J. Allen Hynek, an astronomer from Northwestern University, to investigate. Prof. Hynek was at the time a consultant to Project Blue Book, the official Air Force operation to investigate and explain unidentified flying objects.

The next night, several people reportedly saw another football-shaped object, this time hovering over a swamp near Dexter about five miles west of Ann Arbor.

Over the next few days, UFOs in various sizes, shapes, and configurations were reported in Scio Township; in Jackson; in Ypsilanti; and in Saugatuck. Not to be outdone by Michigan, reports also came in from Ohio, Indiana, and Illinois. And while some of the reports came from college students, several also came from police and sheriff's deputies.

On March 25, 1966, Prof. Hynek announced the results of his investigation before a packed house at the Detroit Press Club.

"Swamp gas," he said.

Ann Arbor, as well as the rest of the nation, howled with laughter. Michigan became "the Swamp Gas State." Then-Congressman Gerald R. Ford '37 (R-Grand Rapids) demanded a full-scale Congressional probe of the Air Force's investigative procedures.

A year later, Operation Blue Book was quietly shut down and the U.S. military got out of the flying saucer business for good.

Prof. Whitley J. Canfield of the psychology department said that he recalled the sightings, but that "nobody took them very seriously, except as more proof that the government was lying to us.

"You have to remember," he said, "that this was in the middle of the Vietnam war. And this is all going on about ninety miles from Selfridge Air Force Base. I can't remember anyone really seriously talking about aliens or flying saucers, except as a joke—everyone just assumed that it was some sort of military thing.

"The one thing we were all absolutely positive about," he said, "was that it was *not* swamp gas."

She was still giggling when she finished. She handed Karl the backgrounder, took the lead story, and read through Zoe's report of last night's sighting. It was more straightforward—and certainly more mature—than the television coverage, but it really didn't add anything. Except for the location of the lights, and the crowd of spectators, it was basically identical to Tuesday night's events. No weather balloons in the area; no low-flying airplanes or hovering helicopters; no blips on airport radar screens. The police are investigating, et cetera, et cetera.

No, there was one difference—this time there were additional reports of sightings from rural areas out in the county.

"Martin and Phyllis Schilling, from Salem Township, reported seeing a circle of lights spinning over their barn at shortly after midnight. According to Martin, 'there were two riding lights underneath it, kind of like one of them gyroscopes'."

Anneke dropped the printout onto the table and took a long, soothing drink of coffee. "My God, the silly season really has arrived, hasn't it?"

"Believe it." Karl rolled his eyes. "Poor Wes," he said for the third time.

At the Nickels Arcade offices of Haagen/Scheede: Computer Solutions, Anneke found two of her part-time student programmers—the only kind she hired—engaged in a spirited discussion of the sightings.

"Phosphorous," Calvin Streeter stated.

"Too volatile." Marcia Rosenthal shook her head. "You'd need pounds of it to get that kind of flare-up."

"And anyway, how would you set it off?" Calvin tilted his head, thinking.

"You could . . . how about a really long, slow-burning fuse?" Marcia suggested. "And if you used a balloon," she said excitedly, "the whole thing would disintegrate when it blew, so you wouldn't even leave any residue."

"Uh-uh." Ken Scheede, Anneke's young partner, jumped into the discussion. "You couldn't manage a fuse that long. These sightings have had a very long visibility curve." He grinned at Anneke.

"So will Don Werner, if we don't finish that millennium fix for him." Anneke returned his grin.

"Too right." Ken jerked his head toward the main desk. "And we've got two more millennium-bomb requests in the mail. What's more," he said ominously, "one of them is in COBOL."

"Are you kidding? Good grief." She looked at Calvin and Marcia. "Do either of you do COBOL?"

"Not in this lifetime." Marcia shook her head; so did Calvin.

"What about you?" Ken asked, grinning again.

"Don't even think about it. If you think I'm going to log a couple of dozen hours drudging around with that . . . honestly." She threw up her hands. "Could these people possibly have put it off any longer? Everyone's been warning them about the millennium bomb for nearly ten *years*, for God's sake."

The millennium bomb. Early computer programs were written to save then-precious memory space, so dates were given in two digits, 1984 being simply 84, for instance. But when the calendar clicks over to the big 2-0-0-0, date-specific calculations are going to go into orbit. Questions like how long an invoice has been unpaid, or whether an employee has worked for your company long enough to be vested in your pension plan, or even how old someone will be in 2004, are going to produce answers that are rich and strange and utterly disastrous.

"Tell the COBOL people to go—well, just tell them we can't handle it," Anneke said. "I'll take a look at the other one." She picked up her mail and took it to her private office, where she handled paperwork for half an hour, then logged on to the Internet to check her E-mail. When she'd downloaded it all, she opened the *Daily* Web site once more, curious to see if they were updating it.

They were. Directly under the masthead was an announcement:

"Ann Arbor police chief Sheldon Spector has called a press conference for 11:00 A.M. today to discuss the recent sightings of unidentified lights over Ann Arbor. The *On-Line Daily* will carry a complete report of the press conference as soon as it is completed."

Anneke logged off, looked at her calendar, checked her project management profile. Then she stood and picked up her briefcase. She did need to check out that reported glitch in the police department's statistical reporting program, after all.

TEN

• • • • • •

"Oh, please, it's absolute garbage. It's just . . . just *histobabble*." Jenna Lenski's face was screwed into a scowl so ferocious that even Ben Holmes looked alarmed.

"How's that?" Zoe set her breakfast tray on the table and sank into a chair.

"This—this piece of crap." Jenna shoved a newspaper across the table toward Zoe, who recognized it as one of the Detroit dailies. She also recognized the man in the photograph on the front page of the Your Life section: Professor Thomas Edison Stempel, identified in the caption as "in the vanguard of alternative science."

"Histobabble—like psychobabble." Zoe grinned. "I like it. In fact, I may even steal it." She scanned the story quickly. It was a perfectly respectable, and perfectly boring, interview, in which the reporter had asked a bunch of leading questions, Stempel had gone on at length about each of them, and the reporter had printed the results almost verbatim. There was a lot about the Dominant Paradigm—how western science contrived to stifle creativity if it didn't fit into a preconceived research mold. And there was a lot about how Alternative Science could light the way down newly-discovered pathways (he really talked like that). There didn't seem to be anything about things that Alternative Science had actually *produced*, barring a couple of sentences about acupuncture.

"As far as I can tell—which isn't much," Zoe admitted, "it's a lot of crap. But why do you care?"

"Because I hate his guts, that's why." Jenna bit savagely into a piece of toast.

"How come? I know you're a history major, but they don't let him teach any required courses, do they?"

"No, but I . . . well, I had a kind of a run-in with him. Last year." Jenna looked both angry and embarrassed. "I signed up for his course in The New History. I was just a sophomore," she said defensively. "I didn't know who he was—*what* he was. It sounded interesting."

"What happened? He flunk you?"

"No such luck. That I could have filed a grievance over. No, five weeks into the semester, after it was too late to get into another class, the son of a bitch kicked me out."

"Can he do that? What grounds?"

"He said I had let myself become 'an intellectual prisoner of the western dominant paradigm'." She spit the words out like a bad-tasting bug. "He called me an 'intellectual anchor' holding back the progress of the rest of the class, and 'a slave to the left brain' who would never be able to do anything but 'regurgitate the tired old theories of tired old cultures.'" She quoted the words as if they were branded into her brain cells, which Zoe thought they probably were.

"Of course," Ben interjected mildly, "you *had* just pointed out to the whole class that if the U-2 spy plane was really such unique technology, how come the Russians were able to shoot it down?"

"Well?" Jenna glared at him. Narique Washington chuckled, and Jenna widened the glare to include him as well. "He didn't have an answer for it, did he? The man was an absolute asshole," she declared. "Every scientific breakthrough was supposed to be a 'suspicious circumstance, requiring extraordinary examination'—" she mimicked Stempel's deep voice "—as if human beings were such incompetent idiots that they couldn't invent the wheel if you gave them the spokes and the axle."

"Sounds like quite a scene." Barry Statler grinned at her over the tangle of multicolored wires that he was busily unsnarling. "Wish I'd been there to see it."

"I wish you had, too," Jenna said grimly. "I could have used some support. The rest of the class just sat there like crash-test dummies, writing down the Great Man's words. Talk about regurgitating. And now, after all this—this latest stuff going on, the bastard is even more of a celebrity than he was before." She glared at the newspaper with loathing.

"How come you didn't have anything from Stempel in this morning's story?" Barry asked. He had a printout in front of him, and Zoe could see her byline from the *On-Line Daily*.

"I couldn't get hold of him. And anyway, he hasn't seen the thing. Maybe I'll get something from him after the next sighting," she said. "Of course, I don't even know if there'll be another one."

"Probably will," Ben said. "Don't these things always come in threes?"

"That's celebrity deaths," Nique said, laughing.

"Or plane crashes."

"Or bad Bruce Willis movies."

"Or . . ."

Zoe took a last gulp of coffee and left them to it. At least Jenna didn't look like she wanted to commit murder anymore.

ELEVEN

● ● ● ● ● ●

There were half a dozen TV trucks in the City Hall parking lot, and a chattering crowd of over-coiffed people inside. Anneke let herself be carried along up the stairs to the second floor, where the doors to the conference room stood open. On a table beside the door were stacks of papers in various colors, and Anneke, following the lead of the reporters ahead of her, took one from each stack before entering the room, which was already nearly full. Anneke slid into a seat in the back row just as Sheldon Spector began to speak.

"Good morning. I'm Sheldon Spector." He motioned to a handsome, middle-aged woman on his left. "This is Nina Belasco, the department's public information officer. And on my right is Detective Wesley Kramer, who is in charge of the investigation. I have a prepared statement, and then we'll answer any questions when I'm finished." He rustled papers on the table, the bald spot in the center of his close-cropped hair gleaming in the television lights. Sheldon Spector looked like what he was—a strong, stocky, no-nonsense career cop who'd worked his way up from the ranks.

His statement was brief and to the point, full of the same negatives that had been endlessly reported. Not weather balloons; not aircraft or helicopters; not a University research project. Looking around the room for the first time, Anneke spotted Karl sitting quietly in a rear corner, and Zoe's curly black head in the front row.

"Now, if you have any questions about the investigation—" Spector seemed to emphasize the word "—I'll be happy to try to answer them."

There was a babble of shouts and a forest of waving arms. A woman in the front row called out loudly: "Do you think these manifestations pose any danger to the people of Ann Arbor?"

"So far there has been no suggestion that they pose any threat, no." Spector pointed to another waving arm.

"Have you found any physical evidence at the site?" a short, chubby man asked.

"No, we haven't."

"But you have done a thorough crime-scene analysis?" the man pressed.

"If you mean, did we do a microscopic examination of the areas, no, we didn't."

"Why not?" The question came from half a dozen directions at once.

"There are a lot of answers to that," Spector replied, "but the shortest one is that, to the best of our knowledge, no crime has been committed."

"That's not necessarily true." The challenge whipped across the room; the speaker, Anneke saw, was Conrad deLeeuw. He was on his feet, his big body looming over the audience. "A hoax of this sort almost certainly involves at least one and probably several criminal offenses," he charged. "For instance, if an explosive device was used to produce the flare-up effect, that's a crime. So is violation of air space. So is criminal trespass on University property. So is filing a false police report." He stabbed the air with a forefinger as he enumerated each point. "Believe me, I have a great deal of experience dealing with UFO hoaxes—that's why I've volunteered to help with the police investigation."

"You're Conrad deLeeuw?" A short, pretty redhead stood up and waved at a cameraman on the far side of the room. The camera swiveled toward deLeeuw. The redhead waved a piece of beige-colored paper. "Your handout says you believe it's a hoax and you want to prove it. Do you know who's responsible for the hoax?"

"I have suspicions based on sound hypotheses," deLeeuw said, squirming a bit under the glare of the cameras, "but I'm not yet in a position to publicly name names."

The redhead turned back toward the front of the room. "Chief Spector, can you tell us why you've turned down Mr. deLeeuw's offer of help?"

"You've gotten other offers of help, too, haven't you?" A small man with a sharp little nose and sharp little eyes popped up from his chair in the second row, waving a sheet of blue paper aloft. "Didn't Professor Edison Stempel also offer to help?"

Anneke rifled quickly through the papers she'd picked up outside the room; the beige one was indeed a statement from deLeeuw, the blue one from Stempel. Both of them offered their services, gratis, to the AAPD. She scanned the room, but if Stempel was present she couldn't locate him.

A blond woman in a bright-red power suit—Liz Epstein, from Detroit's Channel 3—called out: "Yes, you have a world-famous UFO researcher right here on the faculty at the University of Michigan. Can you tell us why you don't want to use him to help in your investigation?"

"Ladies and gentlemen, if you please." Spector held up a hand. "We've had *dozens* of offers of help. We've had psychics, and astrologers, and channelers, and people calling themselves u-ef-ologists, and telepaths, and pyramidologists, and shamans. Unfortunately, this sort of event brings out every nut in a ten-state area."

Nina Belasco winced visibly and touched Spector's arm, but the damage was already done.

"Are you calling Professor Stempel a nut?" Epstein asked. There was a predatory smile on her face.

"No, I'm not." Spector plowed ahead. "I'm only telling you who we've had contact us."

"Then are you going to accept Professor Stempel's help?" the sharp man persisted.

deLeeuw was still standing, Anneke noted, but now he was being ignored. Interesting; they'd been offered help by both a UFO "expert" and a UFO debunker, but it was only the "expert" that the media were excited about.

"If Professor Stempel, or this gentleman, or anyone else,

has information about these events," Spector raised his voice above the hubbub, "we'll be very glad to receive it."

"But you won't involve Professor Stempel in your investigation," the man said in an accusing voice.

"We will not involve civilians of any sort, regardless of their particular . . . expertise . . . in internal police operations, no." Spector bit the bullet and spit out the refusal. Around the room, reporters scribbled busily.

"In other words, you're perfectly willing to exploit the UFO community, but you're not willing to give them access to official reports." The speaker was tall and thin, with a mop of brown hair falling over his face. "I'm Jarvis McCray," he announced. "I'm a field investigator for ARAA—the Agency for Research on Alien Activity. If you people—" he waved at the assembled media "—really want to know the truth behind these sightings, I've provided a White Paper which will explain the whole background of alien activity in the United States."

Everyone shuffled papers once more. McCray's White Paper—which was printed on yellow stock—was a thick sheaf held together with an industrial-strength staple, headed *Fifty Years of Betrayal*. In the upper right-hand corner was a boomerang-shaped device that looked vaguely familiar; Anneke stared at it, then started to giggle when she realized it was nearly identical to the *Star Trek* logo.

Spector tried to ignore him. "Are there any other questions about our investigation?" he asked.

"I have a question, Mr. Spector." McCray spoke loudly; the media representatives, scenting a photo op, didn't interrupt. "Tell me this—if I brought you information about the origin of these lights, what would you do with it?"

"That would depend on the nature of the information."

"Of course it would!" McCray pounced on this response. "In other words, if I proved it was a hoax, you'd announce it to the world. But if I gave you evidence proving alien activity, you'd turn it over to your friends in the military and officially pretend it didn't exist. Isn't that right, Mr. Spector?"

"Mr. . . . McCray, is it?" Spector spoke in tones of deep disgust. "Look, you bring me evidence—real evidence—of anything, and I'll announce it to the whole goddamn world. If you can get hold of one of your little green men, you trot him out here and I'll call another press conference and we can all ask him if the moon is really made of green cheese. Okay? But until then, the AAPD will conduct this investigation by the book."

"What book is that? The CIA code?" All the cameras were aimed at McCray now. "Isn't it true, Mr. Spector, that you're under orders from the Pentagon *not* to investigate these sightings?"

"What? Of course not."

"So you're saying your pet investigator there—" he pointed to Wes Kramer "—has *not* been in touch with the military about this?"

"Of course he has," Spector said angrily. "On both occasions—"

"Why not let him speak for himself?" McCray interrupted. "What about it, Sergeant Kramer? Haven't you been in constant contact with your military bosses?"

Wes looked at Spector, who shrugged and nodded, tight lipped. "Sure I've been in touch with the military," Wes agreed. "I talked to them on both nights, to ask them if they had anything in the air that could have been the cause of these whatevers."

"And they said no." McCray's upper lip curled scornfully. "Surprise, surprise. You have a military background yourself, don't you, Sergeant Kramer?"

"Sure." Wes twisted in his chair, visibly uncomfortable under the media attention. "Most cops do."

"What exactly was your military experience?"

"Twelve years in the United States Marines," Wes snapped. His shoulders straightened and he glared out at the audience. "Including five years with navy intelligence."

"Navy intelligence!" McCray's eyes widened with surprise and delight. "So *that's* where this particular cover-up is coming from. You're still attached to intelligence, aren't you, Sergeant? Aren't you still taking orders from your superiors in Washington? And haven't they told you to make sure you *don't* find any evidence of alien activity here? That's really what's going on here, isn't it, Sergeant?"

"Yeah, right." Wes made a noise like a growl, and his eyes narrowed. "Actually, the boys in the Pentagon wanted to tell the whole truth, but they're all under the hypnotic control of the Grand High Chancellor of Centauri Prime, see? And since they all got six eyes, they've got real strong hypnotic powers."

A lot of people laughed; to Anneke's surprise, a lot of people didn't. Epstein, dominant in the bright red suit, stepped forward. "I get the feeling you don't take this very seriously, do you, Sergeant?"

"No, ma'am, I do not." Wes remained unapologetic. "I think the police have more important things to do with their time than waste it investigating a student prank."

"In other words, you've already made up your mind." She turned toward Spector, and her camera obediently swiveled with her. "Chief Spector, do you feel that Sergeant Kramer can do a proper investigative job if he isn't willing to be open-minded?"

Spector looked at her, then looked toward the camera, then threw up his hands. "Ms. Epstein, I don't think you could find anyone on this force who doesn't believe this is a student prank. And I don't think this is a case that warrants calling in the state police. And as for the military connection," he added craftily, "I don't believe we have a single cop above patrol level who doesn't have at least some military experience."

"With respect, Chief Spector, yes you do." Liz Epstein pointed toward the back of the room. The feeling of horror that Anneke felt was nothing compared to the look on Karl's face as the lights and the camera and the faces throughout the room focused directly on him. "And you have to admit," Liz Epstein went on inexorably, "that putting your top investigator on this case would at least signal to the community that you are taking this matter seriously."

He couldn't, Anneke thought; he wouldn't waste Karl on something like this. But there weren't any major investigations going on at the moment. Still . . . But when she turned back toward Spector she saw the hesitation on his face; saw him look toward Karl speculatively; and saw something she didn't think she'd ever seen before. Wes Kramer, leaning back in his chair, with a broad and happy smile on his face.

TWELVE

• • • • • •

Given the look on Karl's face as the press conference broke up, Anneke had just about decided to leave as quietly as she'd arrived when she saw Zoe waving wildly to her.

"I didn't expect to see you here." Zoe fetched up next to her, gasping slightly after plowing and pummeling her way through the media crush. "Wow. He looks like he's ready to find a quarterback to sack." She grinned. "If you need a place to hide out for a few days, give a yell."

"It's not funny." Anneke returned Zoe's grin in spite of herself. "He must be wild." She looked around, but Karl was already gone.

"I can only imagine. Come on." Zoe bounced impatiently. "I want to go talk to him for a minute. Oh, I forgot to tell you—I'm stringing this stuff for the Associated

Press. And we're running hour-by-hour coverage on the *Daily* Web site."

"I saw the Web site. And congratulations on the AP job. But I don't think we ought to bother Karl right now."

"I won't be long. Besides," Zoe pointed out shrewdly, "he'll probably be glad to have someone he can vent to."

"And besides *that*, if you're with me you'll have a much better chance of getting to see him. Never mind." Anneke laughed at the offended look on Zoe's face. "I know you wouldn't do that. All right, let's go commiserate."

Downstairs, they squeezed past clamoring media to Linda Postelli's desk. Linda let them through with an evil grin that Anneke knew was the least Karl would have to put up with in the next few days.

His office door was firmly shut, and when they knocked, he called out: "Who is it?" instead of his customary "Come in." When they'd identified themselves and opened the door, they found him sitting behind his desk, a stack of papers squared up neatly in front of him, his face so utterly expressionless that Anneke felt her stomach lurch.

"God, I'm sorry." She gulped slightly, unnerved by his stillness. Zoe was apparently less affected; after a second, the girl broke into a cascade of giggles.

"Sorry, Lieutenant. Honestly. It's just . . . Sorry." She waved her hands in the air.

"Never mind." Karl moved finally, and Anneke was relieved to see his mouth twitch in what was almost a smile. "I suppose I'd better get used to it. I'm just as glad you're here," he said to Zoe. "I want to ask you some questions."

"Ditto." She dropped into one of the chairs in front of his desk. "Shoot."

"All right. Now, first—" He stopped as the phone on the desk buzzed. "No, I can't right now," he said into the receiver, then, "Wait. Yes, send him through." He hung up. "Professor Stempel is here."

"Would you like us to leave?" Anneke asked.

"No, I rather think I'd like you both to stay. Come in," he called in response to the knock on the door.

"Thank you for seeing me, Lieutenant Genesko." Stempel paused in the doorway, looking handsome and self-assured, with only the briefest flicker of his eyes toward the two women.

"Why don't you sit here, Professor Stempel." Anneke stood up and moved to a chair in the corner, and Stempel nodded and slipped into the vacated seat.

"This is Anneke Haagen, a consultant with the police department," Karl introduced her, "and this is Zoe Kaplan, of the *Michigan Daily*."

"Indeed. I was intending to contact you today," he said to Zoe, "but I don't think this is the proper time or place, if you don't mind."

"If you have questions for Ms. Kaplan," Karl said, "why don't you ask them now? I know from experience that she's often difficult to get hold of."

"Perhaps you're right." Stempel nodded abruptly. "All right, Ms. Kaplan, why don't we begin at the beginning." He drew a leather-bound notebook and gold pen from his pocket.

"To start with, can you tell me at what time you first saw the lights?" he asked.

"A little after ten o'clock."

"Can you be any more specific?"

"Not really. Say ten-fifteen, give or take a few minutes either way."

"Where were you at that time?"

"We were heading to State Street for ice cream."

"Where you were going is entirely irrelevant, Miss Kaplan. I need to know your exact physical location, if you please."

No, I don't please, you arrogant little dweeb, Zoe thought. Out loud, she said: "I was on William, between State and Thompson. The lights were southwest of us." As she spoke she pulled over a blank sheet of paper and picked up a pen. "Is this a sort of standard questionnaire you use for people who say they've seen a UFO?"

"More or less. As you drove toward the lights, did they seem to get larger?"

"You mean, like we were getting closer to them?" Leading question, Zoe thought—he should have just asked if I'd noticed any changes in the lights. This way, he plants the suggestion in my mind. Just bad interviewing technique, or purposeful? She wrote *general questions*, then scribbled the question itself while shaking her head. "I don't recall that they seemed to get any bigger, but it seems to me that they got *brighter* as we got closer. Would that indicate that they were stationary as we drove toward them?"

"Possibly. Now, would you describe exactly what you saw from the parking lot?"

"It's all in my story." Zoe wrote the words: brighter possibly means UFO stationary? before picking up a copy of the *Daily* and holding it out to him.

Stempel ignored the newspaper. "I am engaged in research, Miss Kaplan, not storytelling. Now, can you estimate the height of the object?"

"Not really. I'm not real good at that sort of thing anyway, and there wasn't anything to use as a frame of reference."

"Was it above the level of Crisler Arena?"

"Oh, sure. It was higher than anything else around. Wait a minute. We could see it when we hit the top of the Stadium Boulevard overpass and that's lined with trees. So we must have been looking up at a fairly steep angle."

"Good." Stempel nodded approval. "Now, when you were standing under it, what sounds can you remember hearing?"

"Hmph, I never thought about that." Zoe cocked her head. "I don't remember anything unusual, though; people were talking to each other, and I could hear cars going by out on Stadium, but that's about it. No whirring or beeping or anything."

"What about smell? Did you notice any particular odor?"

"Nope." This time she sounded positive. "The commuter bus had just gone by, and the only thing you could smell were the exhaust fumes."

"All right. Now you say the lights went out?" His sonorous voice was very quiet.

"Right."

"Which lights?"

"All of them. I mean, all the arc lights in the parking lot." She hesitated. "And the lights along the walkway to Crisler. And I think the lights in the security building—at least, when the security guy came out, he said something about the lights in his office going out."

"I see." Stempel made another entry in the notebook.

"What about the street lights along Stadium?" Karl asked.

"No. They stayed on." Zoe sounded suddenly positive.

"Good." Karl seemed unaccountably pleased, and Stempel looked at him sharply before proceeding.

"Now," Stempel asked, "you also saw the object again last night, is that right?"

"Yes, but only for a couple of minutes."

"That may be sufficient. I want you to fix both events in your mind, and try to tell me if there were any differences between them."

Zoe squeezed her eyes shut. "Only the red lights," she said finally, opening her eyes. "The thing over Crisler was just a set of white lights, but last night there were a couple of red lights with them."

"Otherwise, they were identical? Same size, same configuration, same brightness?"

"I'm pretty sure, yes. There was one thing, though," she said suddenly. "They moved differently."

"What do you mean?"

"Well, the first one did a lot more swooping, I think. It sort of zigged and zagged, and then it'd zoom upward and zoom back down again, but it stayed more or less right over Crisler the whole time. The one last night was jigging around a little, but it was moving pretty steadily across the sky. It only stopped over the Rock for a couple of minutes before it flared out."

"I'll take that into account. One more question—could you see stars *between* the lights?"

"Between the lights," Zoe repeated. "No. Whatever the thing was, it was opaque."

"I think that will be all, Ms. Kaplan." Stempel closed the notebook and returned it and the pen to his pocket. "Thank you for your time." He looked pointedly from Zoe to the door.

"No problem." Zoe ignored the hint, reached into her bookbag and dragged out her own battered notebook and pen. "Can you tell me, was this the standard questioning you use for everyone who's seen a UFO?"

"More or less. If you'll excuse us now, Ms. Kaplan?"

"No, stay put, Zoe," Karl said, although the girl had shown no indication of leaving. "I may need you further."

Stempel looked from Karl to Zoe and back. "You really don't understand in the slightest, do you?" he said finally to Karl. "Ms. Kaplan," he snapped. "Everything I am about to say is off the record—permanently off the record. Is that understood?"

"Got it." To demonstrate agreement, Zoe ostentatiously closed her notebook and dropped it into her bookbag. Stempel watched without comment.

"Lieutenant, you haven't the smallest idea of what you're getting into," he went on. "The UFO community includes some excellent researchers, but it also includes an unfortunate number of charlatans, and an even larger number of people whom one can only refer to charitably as emotionally unstable. If you ever want to get to the truth of these events—more importantly, if you ever want these people to *believe* that you've gotten to the truth—it is imperative that you proceed along scientifically valid lines of inquiry. But even more to the point, it is equally important that the UFO community *perceives* that that inquiry is valid. I have the means to offer you a totally new investigative tool, one I have been developing myself for nearly two years. Moreover, my presence in this investigation will virtually assure you that the vast majority of the UFO world will accept the published results, and will therefore cause you no further trouble once your investigation is concluded."

"In other words," Karl said, "you're offering me the means to prove that these . . . manifestations, are in fact alien visitors?"

"No, that is not what I'm offering," Stempel said with a flash of temper. "As a matter of fact," he said more slowly, "I rather think we'll find that these particular sightings are a very sophisticated hoax."

"I see. In that case, Professor Stempel, wouldn't I be better off bringing in Professor deLeeuw, who has a great deal of experience exposing just this sort of hoax?" Karl wore an odd expression that Anneke couldn't quite identify.

To her surprise, Stempel's face broke into a smile of genuine amusement. "I cannot imagine a more foolish move, Lieutenant."

"For the record," Karl smiled in his turn, "why is that?"

"Consider." Stempel spread his hands. "Without me, you're in a lose-lose situation. Whatever the result of your investigation, the people you need to convince of the truth are the masses who absolutely believe in the existence of alien spacecraft. Your problem is, these are precisely the people who also believe, just as implicitly, that the government is aware of these aliens and is covering up the truth. Now," he smiled gently, "as a Rationalist, Professor deLeeuw is the sworn enemy of these people. No matter what he says, they will refuse to believe him. Whereas I have a reputation for scientific objectivity that gives me a certain credibility within the field. If I tell them it is a hoax—with credible evidence, of course—they will believe me."

"I see." Karl looked at him without speaking for several moments. "That isn't your only reason, is it?"

"Very good. No, it is not. Would you care to tell me what my other reason is?"

"If you like. You believe that Professor deLeeuw engineered this hoax himself, in order to suck you in and then discredit you. Isn't that correct?"

"I would not like to make such a statement publicly." Stempel's eyes flicked toward Zoe. "But I find it curious that Professor deLeeuw makes much of the 'coincidence' of my presence, here on my own campus. I am forced to wonder about the extraordinary fortuitous coincidence of *his* presence in Ann Arbor at this particular moment in time. I am making no accusation, mind you; but you do understand now why my involvement in this investigation is so very crucial."

"In fact, I'm afraid it's precisely why your involvement in this investigation is impossible," Karl replied. Stempel's head jerked up. "You must see," he went on before Stempel could speak, "that we cannot allow a possible principal in a case—whether as victim or perpetrator—to become enmeshed in the actual investigation. To do so would put the entire investigation at risk. I'm sure that, as a researcher yourself, you understand my position."

Anneke, who had been listening to the whole comic-opera conversation with increasing amusement, suppressed a laugh at the sight of Stempel's baffled face.

"Yes, of course, under controlled research conditions.

But—" He had the intelligence and self-discipline to know when he'd lost the battle, Anneke thought, but his face was harsh with suppressed anger. "Very well. I assume, of course, that you have no objection to my working on my own."

"None in the world," Karl said gravely.

"In that case . . ." Stempel started to rise.

"Professor Stempel?" Zoe broke in. "Can I ask you one question *on* the record?"

He looked at her for a moment, as though an idea had occurred to him, before resuming his seat. "Go ahead, Ms. Kaplan."

"How come there's so much interest in this particular sighting? Aren't there reports of UFO sightings all the time?"

"Yes, there are. But most of them are unconfirmed reports by single individuals in rural settings. They're not the most . . . reliable of reports. What is unique about this is the quality of the witnesses, and, especially after last night, the level of confirmation. In this case there can be no question that something was there. And that something remains unexplained. Now," he continued, "let me ask you something, Ms. Kaplan. I've read your reports, and I find them adequately objective. Would you be interested in what I believe you call a scoop, when I uncover this hoax?"

"Sure I'd be interested." Anneke detected a note of caution in the girl's voice, and something else that she could almost swear was amusement.

"Good. I imagine you've been receiving calls about the sighting at the *Daily?*"

"Yes. That's how I got to the Rock in time last night."

"So I imagined. Now, if you will call me as soon as you get another report, and if I can get to the site while the object is still visible, I may be able to provide substantive evidence about this matter. If that is the case, I will inform you of the results of my investigation as soon as I have conclusive evidence."

"Sure, no problem," Zoe agreed.

"Very well." Stempel stood, extracted a business card from inside his jacket, and handed it to her. "This has my home number on it. Please do not give that number to anyone else. Thank you for your time, Lieutenant."

Almost before the door had closed behind him, Zoe began to giggle. "I don't believe it," she said. "That's two of them."

"Two of who?" Karl asked.

"Just this afternoon, that deLeeuw guy came to the *Daily* to get me to help him prove that *Stempel* was behind the hoax. Now Stempel wants me to help him pin it on deLeeuw. Sheesh, what a pair. I wonder who else is going to crawl out of the woodwork before this is all over?"

"I'm afraid to think about it," Anneke said. "With this much media attention, every lunatic in ten states could turn up here. And I still can't quite understand why there *is* so much media interest."

"Probably because it's Ann Arbor, and it's weirdness," Zoe said, shrugging. "And also because of the 1966 sightings, which are pretty famous among UFO freaks. Besides," she pointed out, "a lot of those people today weren't real press. There were people there from the tabloids, and I think even from some UFO magazines, and God knows what else. Stempel's right about one thing," she said. "These people won't believe you if you tell them it's a weather balloon or something."

"Yes, Professor Stempel had a lot to say, one way and the other." Karl looked at Anneke. "What was your impression?"

"I think," she said slowly, "the word that comes to mind first is 'overanxious.' Underneath all that preening pomposity, he seems just a bit desperate."

"I agree." Karl nodded. "But just what is he so desperate about?"

"Well, I imagine it would be quite a coup if he could be the one to uncover the hoax."

"Yeah. Hey, how about this? Suppose he's the one who's behind the hoax in the first place? Maybe he set it all up himself, and he's planning to frame deLeeuw."

"But then why would he ask you to notify him about the next sighting?" Anneke asked. "If he's behind it, he'd know where and when the next one will be."

"Misdirection," Zoe said promptly. "So you'd ask exactly that question, and then you'd figure it couldn't be him."

"It's possible," Anneke conceded. "Anyone whose mind is fuzzy enough to write that book of his is capable of any kind of mental convolution."

"Can I ask a couple of questions?" Zoe had her pen poised above her notebook.

"Can I stop you?" Karl growled.

"Nope. The first thing I wanted to know is how come you were never in the military."

"Four-F. You'll find that most college football players would be. Not many of them get to the end of their college careers without at least one or two serious injuries that disqualify them. In my case, they had to put a pin in my shoulder after my sophomore season, and after that the army didn't have any interest in me."

"Lucky you," Zoe said. "So about the investigation—are you going to focus on the likelihood of a hoax?"

"For the record," Karl stated, "I intend to investigate all possible sources of these manifestations."

"Hell, is that all I'm gonna get?" Zoe grinned at him. "Okay, how about this—are you planning a really serious, in-depth investigation?"

"You may write," he said with absolute solemnity, "that I intend to give this investigation every bit of the attention and effort that it deserves."

THIRTEEN

· · · · · ·

There was a shoulder-high sandwich board in the middle of the Arcade, blocking Anneke's path to her office. She stepped around it, muttering to herself about advertising blight. Then she stopped and turned back for another look.

MADDALENA MAESTRA
Author of
TerraGenesis

RUDY GIAMBRA
Author of
The O(mega) Files

**THE SIGHTINGS:
ARE THEY THE BEGINNING OR THE END?**

The sandwich board stood in front of a plate glass window painted in transparent rainbow colors, so that you looked through it into a pastel world of pearly light. Silver letters, painted in an arc, read: LightSource. Behind the glass, crystals of various shapes and colors were scattered on glass display shelves, along with ceramic unicorns, pewter elves and witches, bulbous candles, and rows of books in bright primary colors.

The store was clearly thriving; it had recently expanded from a single to a double storefront, adding not only more bookshelf space but a meeting area as well. Peering through the misty window, Anneke could see that rows of folding chairs had been set up across every available inch of floor space. Nearly all of them were filled.

Beside the sandwich board, the door to the store was open, and chill, air-conditioned air wafted out into the stuffy Arcade. So did voices; one of them, throaty and un-mistakeably female, said: "Camellia, you can *not* expect me to share a platform with someone who is fomenting hatred toward the very Beings who are our only link to Enlightenment. Not to mention," the lovely voice lowered to an acid-tinged mutter, "having to listen to someone with a voice like a vaccuum cleaner on speed."

"Good one, babe." The male voice that replied was a rough baritone from the streets of New York. "A little bitchy, maybe, but still pretty good. Gotta admit, Camellia, I'm not too thrilled sharing the stage with Lady Air-head here."

Fascinated in spite of herself, Anneke shifted position so she could see around the sandwich board. Three people huddled in the doorway, out of earshot of the chattering audience. One of the women—Maddalena Maestra?—was short and plump, with graying light-brown hair in a long braid down her back. She was swathed in yards of brightly-patterned fabric, and when she moved, bells jingled on her wrists and ankles.

The other woman was elegantly beautiful in a dark reddish suit, carefully made up, her heavy auburn hair swept back in a sophisticated French knot. The man, in contrast, was stocky and dark and muscular, wearing black pants and a black T-shirt stretched tight over bulging biceps and a broad chest. He lounged against the edge of the doorway, hands in his pockets and a broad grin on his face, looking more like a longshoreman than a psychic or whatever he was.

"But I didn't know what else to *do*," the plump woman wailed, bells jingling as she waved her hands helplessly. "I mean, first Maddalena called, and then you called, Rudy, and you're both so *wonderful*, I didn't want to disappoint either of you, and I thought, well, it would be so *interesting* to have both your viewpoints, because after all, what's important is that you're both *believers*, so I thought that, well . . . "

"Never mind, Camellia." Rudy Giambra patted her on the hand. "Okay, what about it, babe?" he asked the elegant auburn-haired woman, who must, Anneke realized with surprise, be Maddalena Maestra. "Ready for some *mano a mano?*"

"Poor Camellia's gone to so much trouble that it wouldn't be fair for us to put our own feelings first, would it?" Maddalena smiled at the plump little woman.

"Not to mention," Rudy pointed out in his gravelly voice, "that there's a store full of book buyers in there."

"No, of course *you* wouldn't want to mention that, would you, Rudy dear? All right, Camellia, let's do it."

"Oh, *thank* you both. Didn't I *say* how wonderful you

both are?" Camellia scuttled, jingling, to the front of the audience, and Anneke could have sworn she saw a flash of triumph on the doughy face. She trotted around behind a long table covered in a red-and-black cloth that clashed painfully with her own wildly-patterned wrappings. Along the length of the table were scattered artifacts of crystal and amethyst and silver-colored metal. Camellia picked up a padded mallet and struck a small silvery gong. The audience—nearly fifty people, Anneke figured after a quick count—obediently shuffled into silence.

"Ladies and gentlemen," Camellia announced in her girlish voice, "we have *such* an amazing treat for you today. Two of the foremost experts in the field of alien studies are going to talk to us about the events going on right here in Ann Arbor. First, the *wonderful* Maddalena Maestra, author of *TerraGenesis*, and who has actually *channeled* the Greys." Maddalena strode to the table and slipped gracefully into the chair to Camellia's left, to excited applause from the audience.

"And of course I'm sure you all know Rudy Giambra," Camellia went on, "the man who uncovered the Omega papers that warn us of the alien wars going on right now." She glanced upward fearfully, as if expecting an alien attack at any moment. "Rudy is a former president of the UFO Research Federation, and he's had *years* of experience studying alien sightings." Rudy waved his hand in an abrupt motion as he sat down on Camellia's right, to a round of applause slightly less enthusiastic than Maddalena's. "Rudy's book is *The (O)mega Papers*," Camellia announced, "and I'm sure you'll *all* want to read it."

"Don't push 'em, Camellia," Rudy said. "*Omega*'s not for everyone. There're people who'd just as soon not know about the war. If you're more comfortable pretending everything's all right, you may as well just keep doin' it for as long as you can."

He planted his thick, blunt hands, palms down, flat on the table in front of him. "But if you wanna be prepared for it, then you better start gettin' ready now. Because there's a war goin' on, folks. It's happening right over our heads, and most people don't even know about it. What's more, it's been going on for almost fifty years. And what scares the hell out of me is that, even though humans are officially noncombatants, Earth is gonna be ground zero for the final battle." He paused. "Yeah, I said scared—and believe me, I don't scare easy."

Anneke believed that last part, at least; Rudy Giambra looked like a man who'd learned how to protect himself at an early age. She'd slipped into the store to listen for a few minutes, lurking behind a revolving rack of greeting cards featuring dyspeptic-looking angels with soulful eyes and oversized wings. Now she listened as Rudy described the cosmic conflict to come.

There were five or six, or perhaps eleven or twelve, different alien races involved—Anneke couldn't quite keep it all straight. The one thing that Rudy was clear about was that the Greys were the Bad Guys.

According to Rudy, they had first appeared in 1947, scaring the United States government nearly to death and forcing them into a series of extraordinary security measures. A group called Majestic 12 was formed, and a treaty was signed with the Greys, and underground bases were built—*for* the Greys, Rudy seemed to be saying, rather than as a defensive position for humans. And all of it, Rudy maintained, was a desperate attempt at a delaying action while the government cast around for a way to protect humanity.

"Majestic Twelve's gotten a real bad rap," he said soberly. "I know Americans get suspicious any time they think the government's runnin' a game on them. But in wartime, we know we need to keep some things under wraps. And that's what you gotta understand." He rapped a fist on the table. "There's a war on, the biggest war this planet's ever seen. An' if they tell us their strategies, they'd be tellin' the enemy, too."

He wasn't remotely what Anneke would have expected to see in a New Age store—he was rough-looking, and coarse, and his voice lacked even the slightest vestige of hypnotic quality. But his very earthiness seemed to give him a believability that a more polished speaker might have lacked. I'm just a regular guy, he seemed to be saying, not some phony who's out to bamboozle you.

The government's holding action worked, Rudy went on. In 1971, Majestic 12 made contact with another alien race, this one from a planet orbiting a star near Betelgeuse. He called them the Blues; they were part of an alliance of alien races called, oddly enough, the Federation of Humans.

"So now we finally got ourselves allies with some muscle," he said. "The trouble is, it's pushed up the Greys' timetable. That's why we had to publish the Omega documents now—because it's finally time for the American people to start preparing." He'd been given the documents, he said, by the Federation itself, and at a great deal of personal danger. "But the real heroes," he insisted, "are the people at Wellfort Publishing, who managed to keep this secret right up until it hit the bookstores. By then it was too late for the Greys to suppress it."

When Rudy was finished, there was prolonged applause from the mostly-female audience. Maddalena joined in, a polite smile on her face.

"Well done, Rudy," she said when the applause ended. "You certainly know how to use fear as a blunt instrument, don't you?" Her smile became sad and sweet. "It's tragic that so many people fear enlightenment, that they cling so desperately to their ancient, atavistic prejudices."

Her voice became deeper. "It's so much easier to fear than it is to understand. And tragically, it's much easier to manipulate people through fear than it is to enlighten them with the truth." She fixed large, dark eyes on the audience. "I'd be lying to you if I told you that enlightenment is going to be easy. It isn't. In its way, the enlightenment of humanity will cause as much dislocation, as much upheaval, as any war would have. But when it has finally been completed, Earth will be a place to rejoice in, not a place to fear."

Maddalena's Greys—"they're unhappy with that word, because they're actually more of a misty bluish-gray in our reality"—were in every way diametrically opposite to Rudy's. In Maddalena's cosmology, when the Greys first arrived on Earth in 1947, their mission was to save humankind from its own self-destructive instincts.

"When I first channeled K'Tel, I'll admit to you that I didn't believe her. In fact, I didn't believe *in* her." Maddalena held out her hands, palms upward, the long, tapering fingers tipped in dark red polish exactly matching her suit. "I mean, would you have? It's one thing to join minds with a twelfth-century Druid priestess, but a creature from outer space? I don't mind telling you, at first I thought I'd gone around the bend." Maddalena laughed, a charming tinkle of self-mockery that the audience echoed with fond chuckles. Only Rudy remained stone-faced; Anneke had the sudden notion that he'd heard this exact speech before, right down to the tinkling laugh.

The Greys—to use the common parlance, Maddalena said—were making progress. Enlightenment was spreading, slowly to be sure, but steadily nonetheless. "Look at all of you here," she said, smiling at the rapt audience. "Twenty years ago, even ten years ago, you wouldn't even have known enough to seek enlightenment. But today, people are beginning to seek their place in the cosmos, to expand their consciousness beyond their own physical boundaries. I feel very blessed to be one of the conduits of this expansion."

Even the least promising of subjects, the secrecy-obsessed Majestic 12, weren't beyond help, Maddalena said with another tinkling laugh. "They mean well, of course—well, most of them do. We'll get through to them eventually," she assured the audience. "Look," she said at last, "if the Greys are the evil demons Mr. Giambra—for whatever reason—wants you to think they are, why didn't they simply destroy humanity as soon as they arrived? The one thing we both agree on is that they have the power to do so—and yet they've been here for fifty years and have not used that power yet." She held out her hands palms-upward once again. "And I can personally promise you, through K'Tel, that they never will."

She was good, very good indeed, Anneke decided, watching from behind the angel greeting cards. She had a sense of humor that Rudy lacked, and the advantages of gender. But more than that, hers was a far more attractive message than his. Given a choice, who wouldn't choose joy and rapture over fear and loathing? Especially if the joy and rapture could be achieved by simply "opening your heart and mind" and letting a group of benign alien creatures do all the hard work for you?

FOURTEEN

· · · · · ·

"What a crock." Rudy's harsh voice was a shock after Maddalena's smooth, soothing tones. "The Greys don't want to *destroy* humanity; they're busy *using* it. Until the Blues showed up, earth was their own little barnyard, full of animals they could milk for DNA, and human tissue, and fetuses. Not to mention an easy source of experimental lab animals. Or do you think they've been abducting humans just to give them a ride on a spaceship?"

"Oh, dear." Maddalena sighed deeply. "Not that old canard. My dear Rudy, as you know perfectly well, those so-called abductions are really rescue missions. They are *saving* those souls, not destroying them." She turned from him to the audience. "And those 'alien implants' I'm sure he's about to bring up are not 'mind-control devices,' as he'd have you believe, but a kind of metaphysical construct that poor Rudy is simply not enlightened enough to fully understand."

Rudy started to reply, but Camellia jumped in hastily. "I'm sure we've all got *lots* of questions for our guests. Who'd like to start out?"

"I've got a question." Jarvis McCray climbed to his feet, his camouflage shirt a sharp contrast to the rest of the mostly pastel audience. "How much money have you made on your Omega fraud so far, Giambra?"

There were indrawn breaths from the audience, and Camellia cringed. Rudy, however, merely chuckled.

"I was wondering how long it'd take you, Jarvis." His tone was almost friendly. "And I'll tell you the same thing I told you, and everyone else, at the Ufornia Conference in Santa Barbara—if I thought the Omega documents were phony, I'd not only be sleepin' a whole lot better, I'd be back home writin' novels, like I was before. And believe me, I make more on my novels than I ever will on Omega."

"Oh, I believe you," Jarvis said. "But haven't sales of your spy and terrorist crap about tripled since Omega was published?"

So that's why Rudy Giambra's name had seemed vaguely familiar, Anneke thought. She'd never read any of his books—thrillers weren't her interest—but she'd seen them recently in bookstore displays, the kind that stand in the doorway holding dozens of copies of books by a single author. Clearly, Rudy was a hot property at the moment.

"Beats me." Rudy shrugged off Jarvis's question. "I've been too busy with Omega to track sales. My agent takes care of all that."

"Yeah, right. Tell us this, Giambra—just exactly how

did you get hold of the Omega documents? How were you contacted? Who was the intermediary? And most of all, why you?"

Rudy threw back his head and laughed aloud. "That's what's really stuck in your gullet, ain't it, Jarvis? That the Blues contacted me instead of you. Well, there's a couple of easy answers to that. First, because I've been working in the UFO field for nearly twenty years. They know who I am, and they know I can be trusted. And second, they won't go near you or your kind of group because they know you're a batch of loose cannons. The last thing they need is a troop of out-of-control paramilitary loonies tramping through the woods shooting at everything that moves. What's needed is organized military action, not a bunch of crazed vigilantes."

" 'Organized military action.' " Jarvis quoted the words as though they tasted bitter. "In other words, disarm everyone but the government. That's exactly what your CIA and MJ Twelve bosses want, isn't it?"

"Knock it off, Jarvis." Finally, Rudy displayed anger. "I've told you before—you wanna argue about the Omega papers, fine. But calling me a CIA mole is actionable, and I won't let you get away with it."

"So sue me," Jarvis sneered. "Or maybe that's what they're really after—is that it? They *want* you to be exposed, don't they?" Jarvis appeared struck by his own words. "Of course. It's the classic disinformation scam, isn't it? They set up a phony 'report,' or some other piece of fake crap, wait for it to make a big splash, and then they come up with proof that it's all a fake. And bingo—they've discredited the whole UFO movement again. Of course, that means you'll get hung out to dry, doesn't it, Rudy?

But then, MJ Twelve never did worry much about who gets hurt, as long as it isn't one of themselves."

"Jarvis, if you don't shut your mouth, I'll do it for you." Rudy was on his feet, hands clenched into fists. Anneke saw Jarvis's right hand stray toward his pocket. She opened her mouth, then shut it again, not sure what to do—not sure, for that matter, just how concerned to be.

"Oh, my dears, this is a place of peace." Camellia scuttled out from behind the table and placed herself directly in front of Rudy. "I'm afraid I have to ask you to leave for the time being," she said to Jarvis. "You're emitting the *most* disturbing vibrations, it's positively *painful* to those of us who are at all sensitive." She moved toward him, still talking, and grasped him firmly by the arm. "And I know it can't be good for *you*, either, my dear, you really *must* practice controlling your negative ion flux, and when you do I'd *love* to have you come back." She led him toward the door. "I'm sure you have such *interesting* things to contribute, and I'm sure we all want to hear what you have to say as soon as you can say it through a more *positive* energy force." She ushered him out of the store, smiling and beaming at him, and shut the door behind him. "And I know," she said trotting back to the table, "that some of you still have questions for Maddalena, and don't we all want to hear about her latest session with K'Tel?" she finished at last, cocking her head in Maddalena's direction.

It was an absolutely bravura performance; Anneke had to stifle an urge to applaud. From the corner of her eye she could see Jarvis McCray's camouflage-clad form, standing still in the middle of the Arcade as though trying to figure out what had just happened. The audience, equally unsure, muttered uneasily, throwing occasional glances toward the door. Rudy had sunk back into his chair, his face still tight with anger.

"Yes, Beryl?" Camellia smiled and pointed to an up-raised hand in the center of the audience. "I was hoping you'd want to join in." She turned toward Maddalena. "Beryl is one of Ann Arbor's most *convergent* minds, she's been such a beacon for us."

"I know about Beryl, of course." Maddalena smiled toward the audience. "We've corresponded frequently. I'm delighted we're finally getting a chance to meet."

Beryl. Anneke knew the name, but she'd never seen her in person. Beryl was one of those locals who seemed to be visible—and audible—on every issue. When bicycle activists tied up traffic for two hours riding a continuous circle around central campus, Beryl was there. When a group demanded that the school board turn a neighborhood elementary school into a homeless shelter, Beryl was there confronting outraged parents. When a student organization demanded that the University serve only organic foods in dorm cafeterias, Beryl was there. She used no last name; Beryl, she said, was her "karmic name."

There was a mumbled reply that Anneke couldn't make out. "I'm sorry, dear," Camellia said, "but could you please speak up a bit so we can all hear you?"

". . . really believe . . . enlightenment . . . the Greys . . . matter . . ." Anneke still couldn't understand what she was saying. Maddalena seemed to be having the same trouble; she leaned forward in an attitude of attention, fixing her large, dark eyes on the speaker.

"I'm sorry," Maddalena said. "Are you asking whether there are levels of enlightenment? Yes, in a sense. Enlightenment isn't a single moment of epiphany—it's a process. So we all . . ."

". . . mean everyone . . . same level . . . no matter . . . life they live or . . . do to . . ." The woman's voice was as low as before, but the audience had stilled, making her marginally more audible. The normal shuffling and muttering of any sizeable group had died away as everyone craned to hear; the result was a kind of rapt attention to the speaker.

"Do you mean, will different people reach different levels of enlightenment at different times?" Maddalena was getting irritated, whether by the questions themselves, or by the difficult nature of the exchange Anneke couldn't tell. "As I explain in my book . . . What?"

"So you believe that nobody is better than anyone else, that we'll all be equal no matter what we've done in this life?" The voice was no louder than it had been before, but now the room was so still that Anneke could hear her own heartbeat.

"If you truly receive enlightenment, yes." Maddalena beamed, getting a grip on the conversation at last. "Of course, if your karmic balance is very negative, the process will be longer and more difficult. But I promise you, no matter what you've done, you too will have the chance to be equal in enlightment."

"What *I've* done? What about you, with your fancy sweatshop clothes, and makeup that cost the lives of innocent animals, and your book that tells lies about the Greys?" Beryl's voice was clear at last. "The Greys aren't going to give people like you full enlightenment—you have to earn it, to sacrifice for it. You preach equality, but evil has to be punished, otherwise why will people seek out the light? It's people like you who'll be in service to the greater beings."

The silence now was half attention, half breathless expectation. The audience was certainly getting its money's worth, Anneke thought. Like everyone else, she waited for Maddalena's response.

"Oh, my poor child." Maddalena's voice was low and infinitely sad. "How blighted your life must be, to need such a painful fantasy. But this isn't a cult, where only the chosen few are admitted to the light. The Greys aren't asking us to reject the world around us. On the contrary, they offer us both spiritual *and* physical joy. I promise you, if you can open your heart to true enlightenment, you will be able to be happy on both planes. And now," she said rather briskly, "I think the lady in the back row has a question?"

"Uh, yes." The lady in the back row looked abashed as heads swiveled toward her. "Did K'Tel give you any specific details about the Third Water Level? It seems awfully difficult."

"Yes, she did." Maddalena nodded smoothly. "Of course, water is one of the four Elementals," she said. "And you must understand . . ."

Anneke, deciding there were some things she definitely must *not* understand, quietly opened the shop door and slipped outside.

"But that wasn't the really weird thing about it," Anneke said.

"Oh?" Karl raised one eyebrow over his coffee cup, and Anneke laughed. She had described the bookstore scene to him over dinner; now she shook her head in remembered disbelief.

"No, really. What got to me was that everyone in that room seemed to be operating from the same belief system. There were a lot of . . . I guess *factions* is the best word for it. But every single person there absolutely believed in the existence of these Greys. Their arguments were only about why they were here, and what it all meant."

"In other words, a series of power struggles among believers."

"Right. Like the internal squabbles within a political party—they may disagree on details, but the basic tenets are accepted by everyone."

"More like a religious war, I think," Karl said. "Political partisans can agree to disagree, compromise for a larger goal, but religious zealots believe that every element of their belief system is equally important. That's what makes them so dangerous." He sipped coffee. "You said that everyone there was a true believer. Does that include the two authors?"

"That's a good question." Anneke pondered for a few moments. "I'd have to say I'm not sure. But I will say this—they both took it very seriously, at least. Of course, they would, wouldn't they? Belief or not, it's their livelihood."

"And a very lucrative one, I'd bet."

"Well, remember what somebody-or-other said." Anneke finished her coffee and stood up to clear the table. "Nobody ever went broke underestimating the American public."

FIFTEEN

. . . . . .

Barney McCormack was having the time of his life.

"Look at this one," he crowed, pointing to the monitor. On screen, a hugely brilliant eye, its iris an improbable purple, shot rays of light out into the cosmos. Underneath were thick, twisting letters that spelled out the words *Alien Armaggedon*. As Zoe watched, the letters faded from glowing red to pale lime green, brightened to a rich blue and slowly shifted back to red.

"Awesome work," Barney said happily, clicking his mouse. "There." The screen now displayed the *Michigan Daily* logo reversed out against a black background. The main heading, also in white, said: *Ann Arbor's UFO Central*. Other text, variously colored in yellow or white or pale blue, provided links to Zoe's stories, to photos, and to bits and pieces Barney had discovered and posted. Further down the page was another heading that announced: *Explore the world of UFOs on the Internet.*

"That makes forty-three links," Barney said proudly, adding *Alien Armaggedon* in its proper alphabetical position.

"This is getting out of hand." Gabriel Marcus glared uneasily at the screen. "Even online, we have to remember that we're a newspaper. This stuff is . . . it makes us look like we're buying into this crap."

"Oh, come on," Barney protested. "It's just fun and games, that's all. We're not saying we take it seriously."

"How it mostly makes us look is solvent." Pete Garcia, the summer business manager, pointed to the top of the screen, where a helicopter dragged a tiny figure across an advertising banner that proclaimed: *Bruce Willis IS The Imposter.* Along the side, a Jeep Cherokee climbed a long, steep mountain road over and over. "That's real advertising dollars you're looking at," Pete said.

"Do you realize we're averaging over five thousand hits an hour?" Barney said. "We're also a featured site on Yahoo Internet Life, the Cool Site of the Week, a Top Five Percent Site, and half a dozen other awards besides."

"I know, I know." Gabriel gnawed his lower lip. "What's that about?" He pointed to a link beneath Zoe's 1966 backgrounder.

"That's a great piece," Barney enthused. He clicked his mouse and brought up a text article. "See?"

UFO DO'S AND DON'T'S

DO stay calm, and pay attention. Try to notice as many details as possible.

DO write down what you see as you see it instead of trusting to your memory.

DO photograph what you're seeing if you have a camera, but don't use a flash attachment, which could reveal your presence to the UFO.

DO record the following details: the exact time you first spotted the UFO, and the exact time it disappeared; size, shape, color of the craft; color of lights; any unusual sounds or odors.

DO look for other effects that occur while the craft is visible. UFO spotters have reported lights and computers malfunctioning, automobile engines stopping, and radios broadcasting strange sounds. Note also any other effects like wind blowing, trees or dust being blown, a feeling of heat or cold, etc.

DO examine the site for physical traces like burn marks, tracks, dug-up earth, etc. But also, DO wait until the craft has left before beginning a close examination.

DO report your sighting to one of the many reputable UFO organizations, instead of to police or military authorities (whose only purpose is to prove there are no such things as UFOs). Keep your notes until you can talk to an experienced UFO field investigator.

DON'T panic. Keep your wits about you at all times.

DON'T approach the craft, even if it seems to be perfectly safe. Some people have suffered severe radiation burns and other serious effects from contact with a craft.

DON'T make overtures to any occupants inside the craft. Your "friendly" gesture may be misinterpreted as a threat.

DON'T touch anything at the site unless it's absolutely necessary (for instance, an object you think will be removed by other people). UFOlogists or field investigators have special expertise, and you may damage possible important evidence.

"Isn't it great?" Barney said, grinning.

"Get that thing *out of my newspaper*," Gabriel exploded. "Lunatic links are bad enough, but this makes it look like we're actually *publishing* this garbage."

"But it's a riot." Barney was wounded. "Besides," he added slyly, "it's a public service piece, isn't it?"

"Get rid of it!" Gabriel roared.

"But—"

Zoe decided it was time to get out of the crossfire. "I'm going to check on the phones," she said, backing out of the computer room. Of course Gabriel was right, she thought as she trotted up the back stairs, but she hated to hurt Barney's feelings.

Upstairs, it was finally cooler, thanks to a line of thunderstorms that had come through around dinnertime. The phones were ringing off the hook, as they had been almost steadily since dusk. Two regular-term staffers who weren't officially working during the sumer had been pressed into service to take calls; Zoe looked from one to the other, but both shook their heads.

"Nothing here in town yet." Katie Sparrow grinned, her red hair a bright tangle. "So far I've got a couple of them from out past Dexter, four from different parts of Lenawee County, and a couple from Flushing."

"Flushing? Where the hell is that?"

"Outside Flint."

"Flint? Jeez, they're calling us from all over the state."

"I've got a better one than that." Joe Bolling held up a pink While-You-Were-Out slip. "Three calls from Romulus reporting white lights going by overhead at high speeds."

"Romulus?" Zoe burst out laughing; Romulus was the site of Detroit Metropolitan Airport. "You'd think people who live next to an airport would be able to recognize a plane when they saw one. Do any of the reports sound like our UFO?"

"Not mine," Katie replied. "I've got three spinning disks, a couple of bright lights zooming overhead, and an exploding red light."

"An exploding red light?"

"Don't ask." Katie shook her head.

"Where are they?" Joe, phone receiver to his ear, was semaphoring to Zoe.

She grabbed for the phone. "This is Zoe Kaplan. Have you got a UFO to report?"

"Well, yeah, I think so." The voice was male and hesitant. "See, I was just driving home, going up State Street, y'know? And there were these lights. Three of them, way up there, and at first I thought it was just stars, y'know? But they moved, only they stayed together, if you know what I mean?"

"Exactly where were they?" Zoe asked as patiently as she could manage.

"Well, that's the thing." The man paused, and Zoe gritted her teeth to keep from screaming at him. "See, they were sort of over the Union, only they kind of drifted, y'know? So then they were over the Diag. And then I had to turn off State Street, so I sort of lost them."

"Okay, thanks. I'll check it." Zoe slammed down the phone. Every light on it was now lit up. She raced to the window behind the sports desk and leaned out over the sill, peered upward, then backed up so quickly she slammed her head against the top of the window. "Shit, they're right out there over the Diag."

She raced downstairs and flung open the door to the computer room. "It's showtime. Let's go, Barney—the damn thing is practically right outside our window."

"Where?" Gabriel jumped to his feet.

"Out over the Diag. Come on. Oh, wait." Zoe grabbed for the phone, punched a lit button at random, lifted the receiver, replaced it, and quickly picked it up again, neatly disconnecting the caller. She yanked a crumpled business card from her bookbag and punched in the number.

"Damn." Instead of Professor Stempel, she heard the tinny sound of an answering machine. She hopped up and down impatiently until it finally beeped, then said quickly: "Professor Stempel, it's Zoe Kaplan, *Michigan Daily*. Time is nine thirty-eight. Sighting over the Diag, drifting, probably heading northeast." She flung the receiver back into its cradle. "Let's go, Barney," she said, as though he was the one holding her up.

"Wouldn't we be better off on foot?" Barney asked as they raced for the back door.

"Uh uh." Zoe had already considered the idea and discarded it. "The thing's moving around. We need to be able to follow it."

"Right." They hurled themselves into the Escort and Barney roared out of the parking lot with a clash of gears.

"There!" Zoe pointed as they turned onto William and stopped at the State Street light. The lights seemed to be directly over Angell Hall, but she thought it might be a trick of perspective. They seemed higher this time, not as bright somehow; they were kind of drifting, making long, slow arcs in the sky. As she watched, the triangle of lights slipped quietly behind the Haven Hall tower and reappeared several seconds later on the other side. Out of the corner of her eye, she could make out a few pedestrians on the dark sidewalk craning their necks upward.

"Drive around to North U," she directed Barney, who obediently steered the Escort along the north edge of central campus. The lights hung high overhead, still drifting, still apparently heading northeast. They weren't the only ones following its path; people trotted along on the sidewalks, gesturing and pointing, and as they turned left onto Washtenaw other cars followed them. "Thank God it's summer," Zoe said. "Imagine what this scene would be like if all the students were in town."

"The mind boggles." Barney slithered the Escort into an opening between a huge, ancient Plymouth and a Taurus station wagon. The driver of the Taurus honked in outrage. Barney ignored him. "Seems to be heading for the medical center." He wove his way through the tangle of streets on the north side; when he emerged out behind the hospital, the lights were still just ahead of them, tantalizingly close.

"Shit, I think they're crossing the river." Zoe pointed. "No, maybe not. I think they're stopping. Pull into that parking lot." She tumbled out of the car almost before it stopped, and Barney grabbed his camera and followed her.

"Let's see if we can get some pictures before they start moving again," he said.

The lights had led them around almost in a circle. They were at the edge of a wide expanse of grass; ahead of her, and to right and left, Zoe could see the glint of water that she surmised was the Huron River. When she stepped forward, her feet sank deeply into soggy turf.

"Where the hell are we?" Zoe looked around in confusion, legs pumping to keep up with Barney's long strides.

"Fuller Park. It's mostly soccer fields." Barney slowed and pointed eastward. "That's North Campus over there, right across the river."

The lights were drifting high overhead, but they seemed to be making a wide, circular sweep over the park. Ahead of them, near the edge of the river, two or three small groups of people clustered. Zoe saw a clutch of half a dozen or so guys in military camouflage and headed toward them, scenting an angle.

". . . still too high," one of them was saying as she approached.

"Yeah, but they're starting to get careless," another said. He seemed to be the leader of the group; the others clustered around him, almost at attention. As she got closer and her eyes adjusted to the darkness, Zoe recognized Jarvis McCray.

"It's the nutcase from the police press conference," she

whispered to Barney. Striding forward with an air of confidence, she called out: "Are you here to try to make contact?"

He looked at her contemptuously. "We're here to gather evidence they can't ignore."

"What kind of evidence?" She didn't bother asking who "they" were.

"Don't get in our way," he said. His hand strayed to the pocket stitched to the leg of his military-style pants. "This isn't a kid's game." He turned his back on her and muttered something to the guy next to him, a short, pudgy adolescent with a bad case of zits. He wasn't any worse-looking than the rest of them, Zoe decided as they all turned toward her, stony-faced, arranging themselves in a kind of ragged phalanx. She stood her ground for a couple of seconds, mostly to prove she wasn't intimidated, then gave a cheerful grin and turned away. Behind her, Barney was openly clicking off pictures of the group.

The lights, the thing overhead, was circling in place, Zoe noted; it drifted back and forth in sweeping arcs. A couple of dozen people had found their way to the park, most of them garbed in the normal Ann Arbor uniform of jeans or shorts and nondescript T-shirts, although there was a fair representation of old-fashioned tie-dyes and beads and gauzy Indian prints. She scanned the wide expanse of grass, noticing what looked like a purposeful gathering near a stand of trees. Motioning to Barney to follow, she squished across the damp grass.

They fetched up beside a group of people sitting cross-legged on the ground in a rough semicircle, their hands palms-down on the grass at their sides. They were all female, in their late teens to early twenties, and Zoe decided immediately they would be the perfect dates for Jarvis McCray's troops. All of them—about half a dozen—wore mud-colored shifts in varying tones of brown or beige or khaki, over blue jeans and rubbery-looking sandals. They weren't actually dressed in identical clothes, Zoe realized after a moment; it was more as though they shared the same kind of spectacularly bad taste. One of them, roughly at the apex of the semicircle, was muttering something Zoe couldn't hear. She was small and thin with pale hair, pale skin, pale eyes, and a small, pointed chin, totally unprepossessing to Zoe's eyes but apparently fascinating to her followers, who had their eyes glued to her face in rapt attention.

"What's going on?" Zoe asked a young woman standing at a respectful distance.

"That's Beryl."

"Beryl who?"

"Beryl," the young woman repeated. "*You* know, the leader of Greystar."

"Greystar?" Zoe felt completely lost.

The woman made a *tsking* sound at Zoe's ignorance. "It's a spiritual movement—very Gaian." Zoe didn't even bother to ask what Gaian was; if she parroted this woman's words back to her one more time, she was going to start to giggle. "Beryl is wonderful—she's the one who's trying to get the vegetarian bill passed."

"*That* Beryl?" Memory clicked in. Zoe recalled reading about a particularly hilarious City Council meeting at which a group of people had demanded legislation requiring all restaurants in Ann Arbor to set aside fifty percent of their seating as no-meat areas. Even her vegetarian friends—well, most of them, anyway—had hooted at that one. "What are they doing?" she asked.

"They're, I guess, communing." The young woman sounded unsure but impressed. She fingered a rough crystal on a cord around her neck. Her nose was pierced, and another crystal glittered next to her right nostril.

"With the whatsit up there?"

"I guess. Beryl must really believe it's the Greys up there." She looked upward and then back to Beryl. "See, it's all about enlightenment. Beryl herself is real special—almost completely enlightened already. Most of the rest of us . . . well, it's real hard, because our whole culture is so screwed up, and it's screwed us up so much that we can't be really good enough." She sounded sad and guilty.

"Are you—" Zoe broke off as the crowd began to *ooh* and *aah*. She looked up; the triangle of lights was brighter than it had been, larger and closer. As she watched, it started to spin, slowly at first and then faster and faster, the lights blurring together into a sparkling corona. And now it was descending, picking up speed, spinning and coruscating as it zoomed downward directly over their heads.

There was a *whoosh!* of sound; shrieks and squeals from the crowds; the thing flashed overhead and on past them, disappearing to the east behind a thick wooded area. There was an explosion of light in the distance that seemed to light up the sky, the trees suddenly silhouetted in sharp relief, and a crack of sound like a sonic boom.

Then total darkness, and a moment of awed silence before the people in the park erupted into shouts and cheers and the nervous hilarity of people who don't quite know what just happened.

"Holy shit." Zoe let out a shaky breath; she'd seen that flareup effect three times now, but this one was vastly more spectacular, like the difference between a sparkler and a Roman candle. She felt a weight on her shoulder and spun around, adrenaline wiring her nerves. A huge, dark form loomed over her, and she leaped backward in sudden panic.

"I'm sorry, Zoe. I didn't mean to frighten you."

"Jeez, Lieutenant." Zoe gasped, feeling her heart race. "Don't *do* that." Behind Genesko, she saw Anneke smothering a laugh. "Very funny. Did you guys see all that?"

"Yes." A pair of powerful-looking binoculars dangled from his hand.

"And?" Zoe dragged out her notebook, as much to signal the on-the-record nature of the question as to write down the answer. "What did you think?"

"Very . . . spectacular."

"And? Oh, come on," she complained when he just smiled and shook his head. "You can give me more than that." He shook his head again, smiling. "Oh, well." She snapped the notebook shut and looked around for Barney. Most of the other spectators had dispersed; only Beryl's group remained, still in their ragged semicircle, pale faces turned upward to the dark sky. "I'd better go file this with the AP before someone else beats me to it."

SIXTEEN

• • • • • •

"It's such an *elaborate* operation." Anneke gnawed on her lower lip. "I mean, you're dealing with three different technical elements just to start with."

"Three?" Karl backed the Land Rover down the long driveway and flipped down the visor to block out the morning sun.

"At least three." Anneke squinted and reached for the visor on the passenger side. "First, there's the object itself—design, control mechanism, visual effects. Then you've got that flareup effect, and the disappearance of the object. And finally, there are the localized electrical outages. All of it done three times now, and in three entirely separate locations."

By the time they'd caught up with the thing last night, after a call from dispatch reporting widely scattered sightings, they'd only had three or four minutes to examine it before its final, whooshing disappearance. It had been exactly as advertised—three bright white lights, two dimmer red ones, in a triangular shape of indeterminate size and features. Even Karl's high-powered binoculars hadn't helped; under magnification the lights seemed to strobe, becoming blurrier rather than clearer.

"Too difficult technically for a group of students with too much time on their hands?"

"Not necessarily." She shook her head. "Not if a couple of them are in engineering, or computer science. It's just that it must have needed so much planning, so much finicky detail. I keep wondering, would a group of students *bother?*" She turned in her seat to look at him. "You really feel that sure that it's a student prank?"

"As opposed to a Visitation, you mean?" He grinned at her as he steered the car onto Washtenaw.

"As opposed to something military or classified," she said, laughing. "Or for that matter, something . . . purposeful, I guess I mean. Something with an underlying motive, anyway."

"It could be," he acknowledged. "We certainly have enough people accusing each other. We'll see."

"Most of these things are never actually solved, you know." She was careful not to sound worried, but she knew this was exactly the sort of nonsense that could be a career-killer for a cop unlucky enough to get tangled up in it.

"I think this one will be." He sounded confident enough, Anneke thought. She was just about to ask him if he thought he knew something when she heard the cheep of his cell phone. He pulled it out of his pocket.

"Genesko." He listened for a couple of minutes, his expression becoming increasingly grim. "On my way."

"What is it?" Anneke grabbed for the dashboard as the Land Rover swung into a hard U.

"A dead body up on North Campus. The guy who reported it recognized the victim—it's Professor Stempel."

"Stempel? Murdered? What—?" She cut herself off; he wouldn't know any more than she did yet.

She was wrong. "There's more," he said. "That's why they called it in by phone instead of putting it out over the radio. According to this same guy, he was killed, and I quote, 'where that flying saucer landed'."

"Good God. It's going to be . . ."

"Yes." He steered the car through the green, rolling expanse of North Campus, which felt even more empty and abandoned than usual with classes out for the summer. Only a few cars dotted the huge parking lots, and there were virtually no pedestrians. A good place for a murder, Anneke thought. Or for a flying saucer to land.

But when the car swung around to the back of the music school building, all sense of isolation disappeared.

There were already a couple of dozen people milling around on the broad sweep of manicured lawn that dipped down to the west, where it ended abruptly at the edge of a densely wooded area. A few of them wore police uniforms, but more of them didn't, and the ones who didn't were pressing against the yellow crime-scene tape that encircled most of the huge lawn.

"Let the circus begin." He smiled at her briefly, without much humor. "You can get a ride back with one of the squad cars. All right?"

He was out of the car before she could reply. She

opened the door and stepped down onto the grass, the sun and the babble of noise hitting her at the same time, both of them already generating far too much heat. It wasn't going to be quite as much of a scorcher as the last few days had been, but it was a long way from cool and the humidity, if anything, felt even worse. As she moved toward the milling crowd at the edge of the crime-scene tape, she began to make out words, chief among which seemed to be *cover-up*.

". . . not this time!" The speaker, she saw, was Jarvis McCray. He pumped a camouflage-clad arm high in the air, drawing ragged cheers from the assemblage. "The Greys and their traitor allies have finally made a mistake that even the government can't cover up." He jabbed a finger in the direction of the woods. "Not only did they murder someone well-known, someone whose death can't be shrugged off, but this time they left real evidence—evidence even the police won't be able to ignore."

There were more cheers. The onlookers were a mixed bag, Anneke noted. Many of them were students or student types—young, in jeans or shorts and the inevitable T-shirts. But she also noted a couple of middle-aged women, an elderly man with a tiny terrier on a leash, and two or three men in denim work shirts. There were also half a dozen young men, in camouflage to match McCray's, their faces taut with excitement. Two of them held high-powered binoculars to their eyes, aimed toward the woods.

McCray opened his mouth to go on, but then stopped and stood still as if waiting for something. Anneke heard the squeal of brakes and a chatter of sound; when she turned, she saw gloomily but without surprise the mobile van decorated with the fist rampant painted on the side, the logo of *Channel 3 Hard-Hitting News*. Liz Epstein, microphone in hand, called out, "Where's the body?" as she plowed through the onlookers toward the yellow tape. The crowd parted for her obediently; a beefy man with a camera atop one shoulder trailed behind her.

"Liz Epstein, Channel Three," she said to one of the patrolmen behind the tape. She added her patented blinding smile, a beat or two late. "How close can we get, officer?"

"This is as far as you can go, ma'am." The patrolman was sweating liberally, tracks of moisture sliding down his face.

"Oh, surely not." Epstein beamed at him. "We must be a hundred feet away. We're always allowed at least to the edge of the crime scene."

"This is the edge of the crime scene, ma'am." He indicated the field with a jerk of his chin.

"But that's—you mean that mark on the grass?" She peered out toward the lawn, motioning to her cameraman to come forward. "What is it?"

"Sorry, ma'am, I have no idea."

Anneke looked out beyond the crime-scene tape for the first time, and her eyes widened as she realized finally why the police had cordoned off such a huge area.

The police activity itself was too far away to see clearly, other than to note the uniformed and plainclothes personnel coming and going, and the dark green Taurus station wagon nearly at the woods line. But what leaped out at her now was a wide, black splotch of scorched and flattened grass about fifteen feet across, near the far end of the lawn—in fact, at just about the point where the cluster of police indicated the location of the body of the late Professor Thomas Edison Stempel, alien researcher.

"I can answer that," McCray announced loudly to Epstein. "I can tell you exactly what that mark is."

Epstein turned toward him. "And you are . . . ?" She moved her hand slightly, and the camera swiveled to follow her.

"Jarvis McCray. Director General of the ARAA—Agency for Research on Alien Activity."

"And you know what made that mark in the grass?"

"Yes, I do." He turned to face the camera lens. "Last night, an unidentified flying object was sighted over Fuller Park, which is about a mile west of here." He jerked his pointed chin back over his shoulder. "After circling the park several times, it flew off in this direction, and disappeared behind those trees right over there. That—" he pointed toward the blackened grass "—is where it came down."

Epstein moved in on McCray, microphone forward. "Are you saying," she asked, "that those are the tracks of a spaceship?"

"Not a spaceship—a planetary reconnaissance craft," McCray corrected her wearily, as though he'd said the same words many times before. "If that landing burn is properly investigated, I believe you'll find that it came down almost vertically, but with a slight eastward skid. Stempel must have arrived while it was still on the ground."

"Stempel—that's Professor T. Edison Stempel, a University of Michigan history professor. Is that the person who was killed?" Epstein was speaking for the camera, squeezing in background.

"That's right."

"And you're saying that he was killed by aliens?" Epstein's voice didn't waver over the question.

"I'm not only saying it, this time we can prove it. See that?" McCray pointed. "When that burned area is analyzed—and it will be, by someone who *isn't* controlled by the traitors in Washington—we will have absolute proof of alien presence, *and* alien murderers.

"This time," McCray announced, "they left tracks. This time they left the body. And this time, by God, we're not going to let them get away with it." He pointed to the two young men with binoculars. "We intend to have someone stationed here throughout the entire investigation, to make sure the police don't destroy or pollute the evidence the way they did at Dulce."

"Or the O.J. trial," a young man in jogging shorts called out. A couple of people snickered.

Epstein pulled a cell phone out of the pocket of her gold jacket, pushed buttons, and spoke urgently for a few moments. Anneke could just make out the word "chopper."

"Christ, Jarvis, you really don't have a clue, do you?" The voice came from behind her; Anneke turned to see Rudy Giambra striding forward. His hands were jammed into the pockets of his black jeans, and his mouth was a tight line. "This is bad—this is much worse than you realize." He spoke not to McCray but to Epstein.

"And you are . . . ?" She aimed her microphone at Rudy, flicking her hand at the cameraman.

"Rudy Giambra. I'm on the board of UFO Research Federation. I'm also the one who released the Omega Papers."

"You're also the author of the best-selling novel *West by South*, aren't you?" Epstein's eyes seemed to brighten. "So you're an expert in the field of UFOs?"

"Not really." Rudy shrugged. "There are no real experts; we just don't know enough. But I can tell you that this murder worries me a lot."

"Why? Just because it was Ed Stempel who bought it?" McCray interrupted. "Hell, this is the first useful thing he ever did for the movement. We finally have *real evidence.*"

"Yeah, real evidence." Rudy scowled, carving deep lines between his heavy black eyebrows. "Jarvis, will you for once in your life crank your brain up to medium, and ask yourself *why* we suddenly have all this wonderful evidence?"

"What do you mean?" Jarvis glared at him suspiciously.

"For fifty years, the Greys have managed to operate without leaving any physical traces for investigators to get a handle on. Now, suddenly, we get this complete scenario." Rudy swept his arm out in a wide arc. "They land, leaving traces even a ten-year-old could recognize. They take out Ed Stempel—and it's worth asking, why Ed Stempel?—and they leave the body for autopsy so that their involvement can be absolutely proved."

"So? They got careless, that's all," McCray retorted. "After all these years of dealing with fools and traitors, they finally got overconfident."

"No!" Rudy barked out the word; heads swiveled in his direction, and a few people stepped backward uneasily.

Anneke had the sense that the entertainment value of the scene had suddenly taken an unwelcome twist.

"The Greys don't get 'careless'," Rudy went on. "And if they do, they make damn sure they go back and clean up after themselves. Only this time, they didn't bother. Why not? Why don't they care anymore if their presence is known? Because something important has changed, that's why. And frankly, it scares the shit out of me." He stopped, wiping perspiration off his forehead, and peered upward as if scanning the skies. Other heads tilted backward, following his gaze. For a moment, Anneke too looked up at the cloudless blue sky.

She snapped her eyes back to earth with a feeling of disbelief. These people really did believe Stempel had been murdered by aliens; there was a terrifying logic to their illogic that crept inside your mind and rattled around there. She noted a few of the spectators drifting off, muttering uneasily.

The camera kept rolling; Epstein was savvy enough to let the two men go at it without interruption. Finally Rudy turned directly toward her.

"Look, I know this must seem unbelievable to you," he said, although Epstein's face wore the same expression of perky interest it always did. "But for once, you have something concrete to show your viewers."

"Like I said—real evidence," McCray insisted.

"Oh, it's real evidence, all right," Rudy agreed, still looking at Epstein. "Let's talk about facts—just the facts." He held up his right hand and folded down the index finger with his left. "Fact—some sort of unidentified craft has been sighted in the sky over Ann Arbor for three consecutive nights. Fact—" he folded down his middle finger

"—something landed in this field last night, something big enough, and hot enough, to burn that mark into the grass. Fact—" another finger "—Professor Edison Stempel, an experienced UFO investigator, is dead on the site of that landing."

He stopped and directed a long stare at Epstein and her camera, then let his eyes move across the crowd. "Something important happened here last night. I think it was something that signaled a new phase in alien activity. And if I'm right, the time for coverups is over." He returned his gaze to the camera. "It's time to let the American people know the truth."

The crowd muttered and shuffled its feet; a girl in a T-shirt that read *The truth is out there* smothered a giggle; a few people turned and walked away, as though the show was over. Impossible to tell who believed what, Anneke thought, or even if they knew what they believed.

The only thing she believed absolutely was that this one had the potential to be the worst mess of Karl's career.

SEVENTEEN

● ● ● ● ● ●

Ben Holmes was passing out printouts of her story when Zoe dropped her breakfast tray on the table.

"Sounds like they really put on a show last night." Barry Statler grinned at her from behind a pile of computer chips he was attaching to a circuit board. "Flashing lights, pinwheels, fiery explosions—everything but a death ray."

" 'At approximately eleven-fifty P.M., just seconds after circling Fuller Park one last time, the object lit up in its customary brilliant flare of light. This time the flare was even brighter, however, and the object then disappeared at high speed behind a stand of woods on the other side of the Huron River.' " Narique Washington read Zoe's words aloud, his sonorous voice making them sound portentous.

"Did you ever think of going into television?" she asked him.

"Yeah, I did sort of." He looked embarrassed. "But you got to've been in the NFL for at least a few years before they'll even look at you."

"Maybe for the networks, but not so much locally," she pressed. "You'd have to be better than the clowns who do the sports reports around here."

"You think?" Nique shrugged. "Maybe so. 'The object made a loud whooshing sound as it passed overhead,' " he read aloud, returning to the printout. "Y'know," he suggested, "it almost sounds like it crashed somewhere."

"What's on the other side of those woods?" Ben asked.

"North Campus." Jenna took a spoonful of some disgustingly healthy-looking cereal.

"Fuller Park." Barry stared upward in thought for a moment. "I think that'd be right across the river from the music school."

"I'm surprised you didn't go check it out," Nique said.

"I think if a spaceship had crashed into the music school, someone would've noticed and called it in." Zoe took a defiant bite of a custard-filled doughnut. "God knows there are already enough nuts bouncing off the walls around here. We've gotten calls from conspiracy theorists, shamans, pyramidologists, karmic healers, people who call themselves starseeds—you name it."

"I thought reporters were supposed to be objective." The voice was behind her; Zoe swiveled her head to confront a small, pudgy girl whom she identified after a moment's thought as Mimi Carter, a sophomore living down the hall from her.

"You should be able to distinguish between flying-saucer nuts and people who are seriously searching for a spiritual dimension to human existence." The sibilants gave the words a hissing, hostile quality.

"Sorry, I guess I'm just an unregenerate left-brain type." The last thing Zoe wanted was for the craziness to spill over into her dorm life. Nor did she want to get into an argument over the old J-theory question about whether it was possible for reporters to be objective, and if not, whether their stories could be.

"You sound like you're proud of it." Mimi waved the sheets of paper in her hand and plowed ahead before Zoe had the chance to announce that, yes, she was proud of it. "Beryl has something important to offer us," she said angrily, "and you make her sound like just another nutcase. Don't you believe that human beings need a spiritual dimension to their lives?"

It was another one of those loaded questions—who would deny the value of a spiritual element? Zoe realized suddenly that she would.

"To begin with—no, I don't," she snapped. "Especially when it's used as a way to avoid confronting real-world issues, which it mostly is. You give people enough to eat, and safe homes to live in, and medical care, and a decent education, and you'll be amazed at how 'spiritually fulfilled' they'll be.

"Besides," she plowed on, ignoring Mimi's outrage, "even if there is any value in some kind of spirituality, we're not going to get it from self-righteous, holier-than-thou loonies like Beryl. And we're sure as *hell* not going to get it from little grey men from Zeta Reticula."

She stopped, out of breath and embarrassed by her own outburst. Out of the corner of her eye, she saw Nique grinning; Barry brought his hands together in silent mock applause.

"Materialists like you think being cynical about everything is just too, too cool." Mimi's mouth was a slash of anger. "Do you really think the human race is so important that we're alone in the universe? Because you're wrong. It may not be Beryl's Greys, but there's *something* out there that's a whole lot greater than we are. Even you can't deny that the human race is desperately sick. You're just too arrogant to believe there's anyone else who can help cure us."

"Millennial fever coupled with racial self-loathing." Jenna was leaning back in her chair and examining Mimi with an air of academic curiosity. "Tell me, are you expecting some major event to occur in the year two thousand?"

"Not necessarily," Mimi protested, looking uncomfortable for the first time.

"But probably." Jenna nodded sagely. "It's a lot like what happened at the end of the tenth century," she explained to her tablemates. "You had a period of religious hysteria because people were convinced the end of the world was coming. And it isn't even only millennial—in 1910, there was hysteria over Halley's comet, only this time people demanded answers from science instead of religion."

"Nowadays its angels or crystals," Zoe said.

"Or computers," Barry offered.

"Or Viagra." That was Ben, grinning widely.

"You think everything can be either intellectualized or laughed off," Mimi said furiously. "It's people like you who are poisoning the earth and turning the human race into animals."

"Animals don't intellectualize; people do," Barry intoned.

Zoe and Jenna laughed aloud as Mimi stood up and flounced away. "Sometimes being a history major pays off," Jenna said.

"What's your area?" Zoe asked.

"Contemporary social history. That's how I got interested in this millennial thing—that and old Stempel's craziness. It's fascinating, but it's also kind of scary. It's the ones like Stempel, who take advantage of people's atavistic fears, that make me furious."

"Maybe Stempel will get caught up in these current sightings, and really step in it big-time," Ben suggested. "Did you talk to him any more?" he asked Zoe. "Does it sound like he's buying into it?"

"I only talked to him for a few minutes." Zoe tried to remember exactly what was on the record. "I think," she hedged, "probably not."

"Damn." Ben slapped the table in annoyance. "Well, maybe last night's sighting'll give him something to get excited about. It sounds like it came pretty close to the ground there at the end."

"Yeah, right." Zoe finished her coffee. "Maybe we'll find a crashed spaceship over behind the music school, with little grey men standing around taking accident-scene photos."

"Who knows?" Barry Statler cocked his head wisely.

"You want the one about 'more things on heaven and earth . . .'?"

"I'd rather have the one about 'what fools these mortals be,'" Jenna said. "I'll tell you this—I'll believe in bug-eyed aliens the day they walk up and bite Ed Stempel on the ass. And maybe not even then."

EIGHTEEN

· · · · · ·

"As near as we can tell, pending the autopsy, he was electrocuted."

"Electrocuted!" Whatever Anneke had been expecting, it wasn't that. "How? By what?"

"I have no idea." Karl spread his hands out over his desktop, palms upward. "There were two burn tracks, about four inches wide and six inches apart, running vertically down his chest. His shirt was burned right into his skin."

"Ugh." Anneke shuddered. "It sounds like napalm. And whatever did it wasn't there?"

He shook his head. "Nothing we've found so far."

"Four inches wide, six inches apart . . ." She held her hands up experimentally. "What could leave marks like that?"

"God only knows. Whatever it was, it carried one hell of a charge." He grimaced. "Maybe it was alien technology unknown to science."

"Don't even joke about it." She laughed uneasily. "Not until you see what's out on the Internet." She held up a thick sheaf of paper. "I don't know if the *truth* is out there, but everything else is."

She'd caught a ride back to City Hall in one of the patrol cars going back and forth, but instead of proceeding on to her own office, she'd used Karl's terminal to log on to the Net. She'd begun by doing an AltaVista search for Stempel himself, and then moved on from there, surfing from link to link wherever she recognized a name. She was still at it when Karl returned from the crime scene late in the morning.

"Stempel really was a major celebrity within the UFO world," she said now. "But so are a number of other people who've turned up in town in the last couple of days." She fanned out the sheaf of paper. "What's most interesting is the way these people link together. They all seem to know each other, and as near as I can tell, they all seem to hate each other. They're all UFO believers—well, all except Conrad deLeeuw—but that's about the only thing they agree on. There's enough factional infighting among them to satisfy an academic department."

"Are they all involved in the Internet?"

"Continuously. The Internet is really the central communication link for the whole UFO phenomenon. Look at this." She consulted a piece of paper. "I started out doing an AltaVista search. If you type in *UFO*, it returns more than *fifty-four thousand* responses. *Area 51* returns more than six thousand, and a combination of *aliens* and

UFO returns nearly twelve thousand. And the people here in town are right in the middle of it all." She looked up from the paper. "It's fascinating, really. You can almost chart their relationships like a sociogram, just from their online activities. Take Rudy Giambra. He's got two linked home pages—one relating to his fiction, another for his activities in the UFO world. He's on the board of a group called UFORF—the UFO Research Federation, which seems to be one of the most prominent of the UFO organizations."

"There are a number of them, I take it?"

"Don't even ask." She shook her head. "Then there's Jarvis McCray. His organization—ARAA, the Agency for Research on Alien Activity—seems to be one of the most controversial of them. There's a lot of argument back and forth about 'military response to the alien threat.' McCray also seems to be linked to the right-wing paramilitary movement, by the way."

"I know." Karl nodded.

"Oh?" She didn't ask for details. "Then there's Conrad deLeeuw. He may be even more famous than Stempel. In fact, deLeeuw is almost the Antichrist in the UFO cosmology. He seems to spend most of his time as a kind of one-man truth squad, a professional debunker. He's the editor of the *Journal of Rational Thought*, he runs a couple of different anti-UFO Web sites; he even shows up at UFO conferences to carry the Rationalist message."

"In fact," Karl commented, "he's as obsessed as the people he's attacking."

"Yes, I think probably so." Anneke knew was he was thinking—that obsession can fuel, because it can justify, any kind of act, including murder. She returned to her papers. "And then there's Maddalena Maestra, who may be the most interesting of them all."

"Oh? Why is that?"

"Well, you see, the mass of alien believers can be charted along a kind of continuum. At one end, you have the Jarvis McCrays and the Rudy Giambras, people who believe in an alien threat by way of advanced technology, weaponry, that sort of thing. At the other end of the continuum, you have the New Age sort of people, who mix aliens with shamanism and Gaia-worship and past-life regression into a kind of spiritualist soup."

"Call them hawks and doves," Karl suggested.

"Exactly!" The old sixties terminology was perfectly apt. "And Maddalena is way over at the dove end of the spectrum—channeling, spiritual rebirth, higher consciousness—all your basic New Age business."

She paused. "The thing is, there's normally very little overlap between the hawks and the doves. Barring a generalized belief in aliens among us, they have so little in common that they don't usually bother to interact except on the most casual level. But Maddalena seems to have gone out of her way to insert herself into the hawk dialogues." She handed him one of the printouts. "That's a . . . treatise, I suppose you'd call it, from her Web site. In the sweetest possible way, she trashes Jarvis McCray's organization, does a number on Rudy Giambra's *(O)mega Files*, and takes on a fairly wide range of UFO researchers, including Stempel himself. She calls him 'that sad little man who can't see over the top of his own ego.' "

"Ouch."

"Definitely ouch. She's very good, is our Maddalena. But it did occur to me to wonder why she bothers. She isn't likely to pick up adherents from these groups, and she's making a fair number of gratuitous enemies." She shuffled to the bottom of the stack of papers. "There's someone else who turned up in some of the newsgroup conversations—Beryl. I don't know her last name, but I assume you do."

"Her legal name is Sarah Berwick." Beryl, Anneke knew, had come to the attention of the police during a demonstration protesting the "exploitation of animals" by the police department's K-9 unit. "I'm surprised she's willing to use the Internet. I'd have figured her for a true neo-Luddite."

"Oh, she is. Except when she isn't." Anneke shook her head again. "Logic doesn't enter into it for Beryl, just . . . here, listen to this. 'The evil is everywhere. It's part of being human. That's why we need their help. But even with it, most humans won't be allowed to reach the Highest Plateau.' "

"It doesn't sound all that different from some of the wilder right-wing religious groups, does it?"

"Not really. The central focus of both of them seems to be a violent objection to human enjoyment. Whether it's sex or sports or food, they figure if it's fun, it must be evil."

"I think I've just been targeted for eternal damnation." He grinned at her.

"Well, at least we'll go together." Her answering grin faded quickly. "In some ways, Beryl is scarier than any of the others, even McCray and his comic-opera brigade. She'd have to be categorized as a dove, but she's the dark side of New Age carried to its ultimate point. There's so much hate there, so much rage. And you know, she's also picking up followers. I found links to her site on more than a dozen other Web pages."

"Including Maddalena's?"

"No. Maddalena's page doesn't have links to other sites. Not all of them do, of course—you may not want to encourage your readers to move on. Beryl does have a link to Maddalena, but it says—wait a minute." She flipped a page. "Here. 'Maddalena Maestra: Some useful information from the Greys themselves, but she lacks a true understanding of the human role in the coming Enlightenment.'"

"So they're not exactly allies, even though they seem to believe the same things."

"No. But then, there are deep factional divisions at all levels, not just between the hawks and the doves."

"Why doesn't that surprise me?"

"I think the most relevant division—relevant to Stempel, that is—is the one that splits along levels of belief. You see, Stempel positioned himself as an objective investigator, an open-minded scientist willing to explore nontraditional science, rather than a true believer. And in order to justify that position, he made a point of shooting down a number of favorite UFO beliefs, in the name of 'legitimizing' UFO research. He was particularly hostile toward alien-implant stories."

"Alien implants?"

"Yes. A lot of people have claimed that they were abducted by aliens and had some sort of mind-control device implanted in their heads." She laughed at the look of disbelief on his face. "The thing is, not only did Stempel refute the implant stories, he really trashed the people involved. He also sneered at the whole Majestic Twelve conspiracy theory, which is really the heart of the alien mythology."

"I'm not even going to ask."

"Better you don't." She grinned. "The important point is that Stempel, while claiming to be on the side of the UFO community, made a career out of attacking some of their most cherished beliefs."

"A good way to make enemies."

"And in this case, some seriously crazy ones. What's more, he seemed to go out of his way to insult and antagonize people—to stir up fights. Here." She handed him a set of pages. "These are some of his newsgroup postings."

Stempel had been nothing if not prolific; she'd found his postings on a dozen different newsgroups, but especially on *alt.sci.alt.research*, which seemed to be his home turf, turf he guarded like an angry Klingon. She'd printed out a couple of samples:

Perquette: It's the basis for the declining birthrate among whites. Check the reports of women who were pregnant before they were abducted, and woke up barren. This has NOT BEEN TAKEN SERIOUSLY.
Stempel: And for a very good reason. Because the sexual fantasies of disturbed women—or trailer-trash racist fantasies, for that matter—do not constitute science. Please take that sort of blither to alt.sex.aliens.
Maddalena Maestra: Poor Ed. You're SO uncomfortable with even the slightest mention of sexuality, aren't you?

WarDog: What about Jenner's study of Mayan crop circles?
Stempel: Prof. Jenner's imbecile scribblings make Von

Daniken sound like Niels Bohr. But what would one expect from a man who got his degree from Matchbook University?

She'd also printed out several other exchanges she thought might be revealing, especially one from *alt.sci.enlightenment:*

Letitia: But channeling isn't a phenomenon, it's a gift. Trying to study it would be like dissecting Pavarotti to try to find out why he sings so beautifully.

Stempel: The difference is, one can actually hear Pavarotti sing; we don't have to take his word for his music. Mad Maddalena, on the other hand, offers neither sound nor sight, just babble. It is, unfortunately, one of the problems with the study of unexplained phenomena, this necessity of chopping one's way through the underbrush of self-aggrandizing charlatans.

Beryl: People like you wouldn't recognize Truth anyway. You can't be happy unless you're destroying something—that's the real definition of Evil.

Maddalena Maestra: Dear, dear. Please don't torment Professor Stempel, children. Think how alone he must feel, trapped inside his own head with only himself for company. Think how surprised he'll be when he achieves Enlightenment and realizes how wrong he's been.

Beryl: But Ed Stempel doesn't deserve Full Enlightenment, because he's poisoning the consciousness of others with his hostility. I know you say that all humans will reach the Light, Maestra, but if we don't punish Evil, we allow it power over others, and that harms THEIR chances for Enlightenment. Besides, if there isn't any punishment for doing evil, why bother living the Profound Life?

There were several other online exchanges as well—between Stempel and Jarvis McCray, between Stempel and Conrad deLeeuw, and between Stempel, McCray, and Rudy Giambra, shortly after the publication of *The (O)mega Files*. Stempel had reviewed the book, calling it "*X-Files* meets *Casablanca*. You can just see the heroic Rudy," he wrote, "muscles flexing beneath tight-fitting T-shirt, Risking All for the survival of Life As We Know It. The fact that he doesn't offer us a single shred of evidence is, of course, irrelevant. In fact, it almost defines the particular heroic mythology he has chosen for himself—the Hero Alone, crying out into the winds of apathy and disbelief. In this case, perhaps pissing into the wind is more apposite."

"He's even more pompous and arrogant online than he was in person—and a good deal nastier." Karl dropped the printouts onto his desk. "Was there anyone he did speak well of?"

"Not that I could find." Anneke shook her head. "In fact, reading his postings, you start wondering why no one murdered him before now. Oh, there's one more thing." She handed him yet another printout. "I also downloaded an article from *Parascience Monthly* that describes and compares other recent clusters of sightings."

"*Parascience Monthly?*"

"It's a 'journal examining the unexamined,' according to its masthead. Stempel was one of their regular contributors. Oh, by the way." She grinned. "Are you aware that you beat the odds by not being born under the Mars Effect?"

"All right, I'll continue my parrot imitation—Mars Effect?"

"Yes. It seems there's a statistically valid correlation between being born during the rise and-or zenith of Mars, and athletic prowess. Just think—if your parents had had more foresight, you could have been a *really good* linebacker."

"So that was my problem." He made a face, half-smile, half-grimace.

"Anyway, I read through some of these reports—for which I deserve combat pay, by the way—and discovered something interesting. Read this—it's a description of sightings in the Hudson Valley, and in Belgium." She handed him the printout, and he read silently for a few moments.

"The Westchester Wing," he said finally, as though the words had an odd taste.

"Yes. Large, triangular, fairly slow-moving, with red riding lights. In fact, almost identical to the thing that's been sighted right here. Which means . . . "

". . . that either the person behind this is familiar with the UFO territory, or . . . "

". . . we'd better start wearing aluminum-foil helmets."

NINETEEN

· · · · · ·

If yesterday's press conference was a media circus, today the parking lot in front of City Hall qualified as a full-scale media riot. Television trucks filled every available space. Cameramen were everywhere, racing back and forth, jostling for position, climbing on, crawling under, squeezing through.

Zoe pushed and shoved her way through the melee, swearing liberally. What a day for her to get religion and actually go to class. "Hey, do you mind? That's my head you nearly took off," she snarled at a short, balding guy in khakis who swung his camera just past her nose.

She'd spent the entire morning in the bowels of Angell Hall listening to a terminally boring lecture on the role of birds in the ecosystem. When she emerged, blinking, into the hot noon sun, she happened to overhear a conversation in which the name "Stempel" was mentioned. She listened more closely, yelped aloud when she heard the word "murder," and raced downtown to City Hall.

When she finally shoved her way to the glass entrance, she found herself part of a clamoring semicircle of people, all shouting questions at a stolid-looking cop who just kept shaking his head.

"There'll be a statement for the media at one o'clock," he said.

"Will Lieutenant Genesko be out to talk to us himself?" a man called out.

"Sorry, I don't know," the cop replied.

"Is it true that the police have hired a UFO expert to work with them?" another voice asked.

"Don't know, ma'am. There'll be a statement for the media at one o'clock," the cop repeated. Zoe guessed he was repeating it for about the two-hundredth time.

She approached the cop wearing her best little-girl smile. "Am I allowed into the building?" she asked.

"You have business in there?"

"I need to get a bike license," she improvised.

"Second floor." He stepped aside, and Zoe slipped past him into the air-conditioned chill of the lobby. First hurdle passed. She strode toward the glassed-in police entrance and stopped at the window, trying to exude an air of confidence.

"I'm looking for Anneke Haagen," she said to the uniformed policewoman behind the glass. The woman, whose nameplate read *Linda Postelli*, was plump and motherly-looking and smiled kindly at Zoe even as she shook her head.

"I'm sorry, but there's no one in the police department by that name."

"She's not actually with the department," Zoe explained. "She's a computer consultant."

"Then I'm sorry, but I wouldn't know anything about her. Was she expecting you?"

"Yes." It was a tricky question; Zoe decided to go with it. "We were supposed to have lunch, but I got held up."

"Well, if she isn't on the force, I wouldn't know where to find her," Postelli said. "Why don't you wait in the lobby? I'm sure if she's expecting you she'll come out to find you."

"The trouble is, I'm so late she probably gave up." Zoe gritted her teeth, trying to decide if Postelli was stubborn, incompetent, or just plain dumb. "She might be in Lieutenant Genesko's office," she said finally. She hadn't wanted to mention Genesko's red-flag name, but she didn't see where she had a choice.

"I see. And you just might get a chance to ask the lieutenant one or two questions, right?" Postelli laughed uproariously, a loud, booming laugh at odds with her cozy appearance. "Nice try, Ms. Kaplan. In fact, one of the better efforts of the day. I'll be sure to tell Lieutenant Genesko all about it—in a couple of days."

"Oh, shit." Zoe grinned feebly. "How'd you know who I was?"

"Considering how often I've seen you go in and out of here, it wasn't hard." Postelli chuckled. "The price of fame, love."

"Great." Zoe made a face. "Would you at least give the lieutenant a message for me?"

"Sure. It'll be message number—" Postelli glanced toward a stack of pink While-You-Were-Out slips "—three hundred seventeen, give or take a few."

"Jeez, that many? All from reporters?" It was more conversation than question, but when Postelli didn't reply Zoe looked at her sharply. "It's not just media, is it? I'll bet you're getting calls from all sorts of flying saucer nuts, right?" Postelli remained silent. "All right, all right." Zoe threw up her hands. "But don't expect to be invited to my next birthday party, Postelli." She grinned amiably at the policewoman; if she couldn't make any progress, she might as well at least make friends.

"I'm crushed, Kaplan." Postelli grinned back at her. "And here I was planning to buy you diamonds. I guess you'll have to settle for this."

She slipped a sheet of paper under the glass, and Zoe grabbed it eagerly, but it was only a bare-bones press release confirming that Prof. Thomas Edison Stempel had been found dead at 6:30 A.M. in the woods behind the music school. And, of course, promising a statement from "a police spokesperson" at one o'clock.

She checked her watch—still half an hour until the fabled statement. She crossed the lobby to the pay phone and called the Associated Press to let them know she was on the story, relieved to find herself talking to a minor functionary. She read him the press release verbatim, and asked him to inform Leon Kaminsky that she'd call in the police statement as soon as it was over. Then she headed back outside to join the rest of the media.

Vans and cars and mobile units were still arriving, each of them dumping more bodies into the mob. People with cameras or microphones or notebooks scurried to and fro, all apparently intent on committing journalism. Zoe took

a deep breath and plunged forward, shamelessly eavesdropping.

". . . fused the lights on Michigan Stadium?"

"Yeah. See, when the UFO took off, all those big arc
lights blazed up and then they blew out. It made a hell of
a bang, believe me." An elderly man spoke into a microphone held by an earnest-looking guy in a dark green
blazer with a breast-pocket patch that read *WWZN-TV*,
call letters Zoe didn't recognize. In front of him, a mini-
cam recorded the elderly man's sixty seconds of fame for
posterity. Zoe bit down hard to keep from giggling aloud;
would someone figure out before the interview aired that
there *were* no lights on Michigan Stadium?

". . . videotape of the sighting over the Rock. If your
people are interested, I think we could work something out."

The speaker was a young guy in ragged cutoffs and a
muscle T-shirt, with a long, complicated tattoo running
the length of his left arm, and bright, aware eyes. The
woman he was speaking to, a brunette in a maroon blazer,
said something Zoe couldn't hear.

" 'Cause I was stoned when I took it." The young guy
shrugged and tried to look innocent. "I didn't realize what
I had. Look, if your outfit isn't interested, I'm sure some
of these other guys will be."

The brunette said something else, pointing toward the
forest of vans. The guy nodded and ambled away. The
brunette watched him go, suspicion and eagerness chasing
themselves across her face.

". . . the kind of expertise the police simply don't have."
The voice was pitched to carry above the generalized
racket of the crowd—a professor's voice. Zoe turned; near

the doorway, the pink, flushed face of Conrad deLeeuw was visible above a large and growing semicircle of reporters.

"I admit it," deLeeuw was saying, "I thought these sightings were engineered by Ed Stempel himself. I believed they were just another publicity device. I was wrong; and if I could apologize to him, I would." DeLeeuw paused and mopped sweat from his flushed face. He looked awful, Zoe thought; not devastated exactly, but badly disturbed. His small, chubby lips were pressed so tightly together they made a narrow slash across his face, and he had developed a tic at the corner of his left eye.

"And if anyone thought that the so-called UFO sightings over the last few days were just another silly prank, well, Ed Stempel's death proves otherwise," deLeeuw went on, as more and more cameras gravitated toward him. "This was an elaborate and vicious hoax designed to cover up a murder. And the only way the police are ever going to solve it is by exposing the hoax itself. The trouble is, the police simply don't have the necessary knowledge to do that."

This time when he paused there was a babble of sound, questions from a dozen different directions. Microphones erupted toward him like heat-seeking missiles. Zoe squeezed forward, ducking under a camera and turning sideways to wiggle between a couple of blazers. She scribbled furiously as deLeeuw fielded questions.

"Weren't you and Professor Stempel deadly enemies?"

"No, we weren't *enemies*," deLeeuw said angrily. "We were . . . antagonists. The conflicts between us were professional, not personal."

"You make it sound like you were just friendly rivals." It

was more accusation than question. "Are you claiming that you're not glad Professor Stempel is gone?"

"Friendly rivals? Of course not. I'm not going to pretend I liked him—he was arrogant, self-important, and mean-spirited. In fact, it's probably fair to say we hated each others' guts. But am I happy that he's dead? No! I . . . no, I'm not." DeLeeuw moved his head from side to side slowly, like a baffled animal. "No, I'm not glad," he repeated, and there was a note of surprise in his voice. Almost like he was going to miss Ed Stempel. Zoe thought suddenly that he probably would.

"Still," someone pressed, "didn't you once call him 'a boil on the University's backside'?"

"Yes I did. So what? All great universities occasionally suffer one or two lunatics; it's the price we pay for academic freedom. But I can tell you this—Ed Stempel is far more dangerous dead than he ever was alive."

There was a burst of interrogation. DeLeeuw gazed out at the throng of reporters and shook his head. Zoe recognized his expression—the deep disgust of a professor at the density of his students.

"You really don't get it, do you?" His tone of voice confirmed Zoe's conjecture. "Look, you've got a famous UFO figure found dead at the location of a 'sighting.' You've got a batch of crazed believers insisting he was killed by aliens. Now think—what happens if the police never solve this murder?" He paused, the professorial pause to allow the class to work out the problem.

"You have a new piece of imbecile mythology, that's what happens. I'm telling you, unless there is an absolutely clear solution to this murder, thousands and thousands of people will firmly believe that a spaceship full of aliens landed in Ann Arbor and murdered Ed Stempel—probably because he found out something about them."

"*Had* he found out anything?" a voice called out.

There were a few mutters, a few giggles. "Oh, for . . . You see what I mean?" DeLeeuw glared in the direction of the voice. "If this is left to the police, that's what a lot of credulous people are actually going to believe."

"Are you suggesting a police cover-up?" someone asked.

"No, of *course* not!" DeLeeuw almost shouted the words. "Nor am I suggesting police incompetence. What I *am* saying is that the police are simply not equipped to expose this particular kind of hoax."

They fired additional questions at him, more out of boredom than anything else, Zoe thought. The crowd around him began to thin out. Zoe too began looking around for something more interesting. She flipped her notebook closed and turned away, accidentally bumping into the guy next to her.

TWENTY

· · · · · ·

"Sorry." She catalogued him automatically: fortyish but trying for younger, bright blue predator eyes, navy blue blazer with a patch that read *WZZE-TV.*

"Stay out of the way, kid." The predator eyes glanced at her, dismissed her, then dropped down to the notebook in her hand, with her name printed in large block letters. The eyes widened slightly. "Hey, you're that reporter, aren't you? The one who wrote up the sightings for the school paper?"

School paper? Zoe wrinkled her nose in disgust. "Yeah, that's me," she said sarcastically. "Zoe Kaplan, girl reporter. Maybe when I'm all grown up I can be Brenda Starr."

"Sure you will, kid, you just hang in there." The guy was about a two on the don't-get-it meter, Zoe concluded, not worth the effort to blow him away. "You actually saw those things with your own eyes, right?"

"Right. So?"

"Great, great." The guy motioned to a young, good-looking black woman with a large camera on her shoulder. "Come on, kid, I'm going to make you a star."

"Huh? You want to interview me?"

"That's right." The guy beamed at her. "You can tell all your friends you were on television. We'll even send you a videotape, so you can show it to them."

"Gee, if I'm good can I have a lollipop?" Out of the corner of her eye, Zoe saw the camerawoman cram her fist against her mouth to keep from laughing. The guy in the blazer looked confused for an instant, then shrugged it off.

"Okay, now you stand right here, next to me. Talk to me, not to the camera. Just pretend you're telling it to your friends, okay?"

"Uh-uh." Zoe figured she'd gotten about as much fun from the guy as she was going to. "No thanks." She took two steps backward and bumped against another camera. "Sorry," she said over her shoulder.

"Oh, come on," the guy in the blazer urged. "Think about it—tens of thousands of people will get to hear what you have to say, not just a few thousand college kids."

"Tens of thousands? Gee whiz." Zoe burbled with laughter. "You mean besides the couple of million reading my stuff every day for the Associated Press? Or the six-hundred thousand a day logging onto the *Daily* Web site?"

The cameraman she'd bumped into, a middle-aged guy whose khaki vest did nothing to hide his large belly, was watching the exchange with interest. So were other media people nearby. Zoe saw faces—and cameras—begin to swivel in her direction.

"So that's who you are." A fiftyish woman with a cap of dark hair—red blazer, *Daily Edition* patch—hurried forward microphone-first. "How did you happen to be there when the first sighting occurred, Ms. Kaplan?"

Zoe opened her mouth to speak, but she was interrupted.

"What did you think when you first saw the unidentified object, Ms. Kaplan?"

"Do you have any conjecture about what the object is, Ms. Kaplan?"

"Have the police asked you to withhold any information, Ms. Kaplan?"

"Have you had any communication from any military or federal officials, Ms. Kaplan?"

Suddenly she was surrounded, the center of a surging, jostling mass, half-human, half-metallic—a seething mass of media people bristling with cameras, videocams, microphones. It was like being in the middle of the Borg contingent at a *Star Trek* convention, Zoe thought.

"Hey! Oi!" She had to shout to be heard over the barrage of questions. "Give it a rest!" The racket subsided slightly. Everywhere she looked, lenses were trained on her. She felt suddenly uneasy, exposed and vulnerable. "Jeez, don't you people have anyone better to hassle?"

"Actually, no." The woman from *Daily Edition* grinned at her amiably. "A reliable eyewitness is worth her weight in gold. Almost literally," she said meaningfully, "if you catch my drift."

Zoe did. For two or three seconds, dollar signs danced in front of her eyes. How much would these guys pay for an exclusive interview? Maybe she could engineer a bidding war between a couple of them. . . .

"Sorry." Zoe shook her head. "Anything I've got goes into my own stories," she announced loudly to the assembled mob. "Back off, okay?"

They continued to shout questions at her for several more minutes, but when she folded her arms and kept shaking her head they finally began to disperse.

"Damn, I almost had you, didn't I?" The *Daily Edition* woman grinned at her cheerfully. Even in the hot sun, her hair was impeccably neat and she didn't seem to sweat; Zoe wondered how she did it. "Here." She handed Zoe a business card. "If you should change your mind . . . "

"I won't." Zoe returned the grin and pocketed the card. "I want control over my own words."

"Yes, I imagine you do." The woman looked at her thoughtfully. "Keep the card. When you get to New York, look me up."

"New York?"

"Right. See you." The woman motioned to the big-bellied cameraman and the two of them moved away. Zoe stood and watched them go, relieved to be ignored once more.

Who the hell were all these people? she wondered, scanning the mob. Some of them she could identify—national and local TV news crews, television tabloid shows, radio reporters hung with tape equipment. Plenty of print media, too, some of them with 35-millimeter cameras draped around their necks.

But there were a lot of other people who didn't seem to fit any of those categories. Like the sad-eyed woman staring almost hungrily at the guarded door; or the two young guys holding stacks of pamphlets and chattering excitedly to each other; or the middle-aged man in jeans and tiny wire-rim eyeglasses cradling a complicated piece of machinery bristling with wires. She set out once again to eavesdrop.

"Vallee says there's a way around the FTL issue. . . . "

"Area Fifty-one is just camouflage—misdirection. The real activity is . . . "

". . . more circumstantial than the Gulf Breeze sightings . . . "

". . . but if Bush really is a member of Majestic Twelve, wouldn't he have . . . "

"Terrifying, isn't it?" She dropped out of eavesdropping mode with a start. Conrad deLeeuw was standing next to her, looking, if anything, even more disturbed than before. His face seemed to have shriveled somehow; his cheeks were hollow, and the skin around his pale blue eyes was puffy and reddened.

"Belief and disbelief. The abhorred vaccuum. Destroy an entire belief system, and another rushes in to fill the empty space. The government lies; therefore rumor and fantasy and mad nightmare becomes truth. That's the game Ed Stempel played; only, madness isn't a game." He mopped his forehead with a handkerchief already sodden with sweat, and Zoe saw that his hand was shaking.

"Are you okay?" She wondered if he was going to pass out.

"Yes, I . . . yes, sorry." DeLeeuw straightened his shoulders, twisted his head back and forth as if to set it more firmly in place. "I'm babbling, aren't I?" He smiled wanly. "Ed's death was a shock, I guess. I knew he was dealing with a lot of deranged people, but even I never imagined they were dangerous. Not this kind of dangerous, I mean. Poor Ed."

"You're going to miss him, aren't you?"

"Miss him? Good Lord, no." DeLeeuw seemed taken aback by the question. "But I never wanted him dead, you know?" He peered down at her earnestly. "And certainly not like this."

You will miss him, though, Zoe thought as she watched deLeeuw depart. Stempel had been a huge part of his life for a long time—his primary antagonist, the person who shaped his ends. The death of an enemy, her mother had once told her, can leave as big a hole in your life as the death of a friend. As she watched deLeeuw shamble across the street, Zoe thought that he was really in mourning.

TWENTY-ONE

. . . . . .

With the media hordes ravening outside, they didn't even consider going out for lunch; Karl was too recognizable a figure. Besides, he was swamped with the endless details of the early stages of an investigation. Anneke left him the pile of printouts and pushed her way anonymously through the sea of reporters, trying to refocus her mind on her own work.

But when she reached her office, after a stop for a quick sandwich, she was instantly barraged with questions.

"Is it true that they found four-toed footprints around the body?" Marcia Rosenthal bounced up from her computer, knocking over a box of paper clips.

"Four-toed footprints?" Anneke repeated, not sure she'd heard correctly.

"Are they really analyzing the ground around the site for traces of lithium?" Calvin asked.

"I have no idea. Why?"

"They're also saying that Karl is actually a staff operative for Majestic Twelve." Ken Scheede teetered his chair onto its back legs and grinned widely at her.

"Good God." Anneke dropped her briefcase on an unoccupied desk and glared at them all impartially. "What the hell is going on? Where is all this—this crap coming from?"

"Need you ask?" Ken jerked his head toward the big monitor on his desk, grinning even more widely. Anneke stalked across the room and looked over his shoulder in growing dismay.

The background of the screen was black shot with gold threads. In each of the upper corners, there was an oval photograph with the caption *Professor T. Edison Stempel, 1956–1998*. The headline, in huge black letters, read: THE COVER-UP BEGINS.

Centered beneath the headline was a picture of Karl.

Someone had dredged up an old photo from his days with the Steelers. He glared out from under the black helmet, the grim game face all the more menacing because it was almost expressionless. On the field, Karl had been famous for being cold and concentrated and utterly remorseless.

She read through the text under the picture quickly. It didn't make a great deal of sense; as near as she could tell, he was accused of working for either the military, or Majestic 12, or the Trilateral Commission, whatever that was. The only thing the writer was sure of was that Karl

Genesko was under orders to make sure Stempel's murder was never solved.

"And this is only the tip of the iceberg," Ken said. "There are already a dozen sites devoted to Stempel's murder."

"One of them even has an interview with the aliens who killed him." Marcia's giggle came muffled from under the desk, where she was crawling around retrieving paper clips. "Ouch."

"This one's actually real impressive." Calvin pointed to his own monitor. "Aerial photographs of North Campus, interview with a forensics expert, bio of Stempel, even a description of crime-scene procedures."

"That sounds rational, at least," Anneke said.

"Well, it would be," Calvin agreed, "except its purpose is to show exactly how the police plan to manage the cover-up."

"Oh, shit." Anneke sank into a chair and reached for a pad and pencil. "I'd better write down some of these URLs."

"Oh, you don't have to do that." Marcia crawled out from under the desk, stood up, and bumped into a chair. "Ouch. Yahoo has a whole special section of links to Stempel sites."

"Oh, *shit*," Anneke repeated with feeling.

She told them distractedly to get on with their work, then went down the hall to her own office and logged on. It was even worse than she'd feared. Yahoo, the best-known of the Internet directories, had Stempel's murder featured on its welcome screen; clicking on it brought up a list of more than thirty sites focusing on the murder, along with dozens of links to "related" sites dealing with

UFOs, conspiracies, and the like. She surfed through about half the Stempel sites before logging off and picking up her briefcase once more.

"I'll be out for the rest of the day," she told Ken, who smiled at her with cheerful sympathy. Clearly, he wasn't taking the Internet explosion seriously. Should I? Anneke asked herself. She wasn't sure; but she thought Karl should at least be aware of what was going on.

The media siege continued. She worked her way through the crush as quickly as possible, the heat from the collected bodies adding to the heat of the sun. She was sweaty and disheveled by the time Linda Postelli buzzed her through, but she went straight down the corridor and opened the door to Karl's office after a perfunctory knock.

And stopped dead in the doorway, staring at the tableau in front of her.

Karl was standing behind his desk. Maddalena Maestra was standing there too, pressed up against him, her arms around his neck. Their faces were inches apart, and Anneke could see a small fleck of dark red lipstick on Karl's lower lip. Both of them had turned toward the door, startled by her entrance, and she saw Maddalena's dreamy smile and Karl's unreadable expression in bright, hard-edged detail.

All of this she noted in the two or three seconds of roaring silence before she dissolved into a fit of uncontrollable giggles.

She gulped desperately, pressing her lips together and gritting her teeth, which only seemed to make it worse. Maddalena, tall and beautiful and sensuous, in an elegant sleeveless dress of pale apple-green linen, stared at her with a puzzled expression on her face. Anneke felt her own silk shirt pasted sweatily to her body, and knew that bits of her short, dark hair were straggling over her forehead. I must look like the local bag lady, she realized, but the thought only increased her laughter.

"I b-beg your pardon, Lieutenant," she choked out finally. "Shall I c-come back later?"

"No, not at all." Karl took a step backward, disengaging himself from Maddalena, who gave him a brilliant, intimate smile before moving from behind the desk. She smiled at Anneke as she passed, adding a small shrug and a wink of sisterhood.

"Please come in . . . Ms. Haagen." Karl's face still wore the same unreadable expression, but as he sat down at his desk he turned away quickly, and Anneke saw the quick twitch of laughter before he turned back. "Ms. Maestra, this is Anneke Haagen. Ms. Haagen is . . . a consultant with the police department."

"How do you do?" Maddalena seemed cheerfully unaffected.

"You were telling me where you first met Professor Stempel," Karl prompted.

"So I was." She looked deeply at him before continuing, a smile playing over her lips. "We met at a conference on alternative healing. No, I'm not a healer, but I've channelled one or two beings who have some healing wisdom to offer."

"And Professor Stempel was there?"

"Yes. He was an interesting man, actually." Maddalena shifted in her chair, as though settling in for a cozy chat. Anneke had quietly taken the chair at the other corner of the desk, and Maddalena turned slightly, making a point of including her in the conversation. "Poor Ed." Her beautiful voice was tinged with sadness. "He tried so hard, but he was so busy counting and analyzing that he didn't have time for feeling. He was so tightly earthbound that he simply couldn't connect to the Higher Reality." She paused. "Poor Ed," she said again. "I hope you find out who did this terrible thing, Lieutenant."

"I take it, then, that you don't believe Professor Stempel was killed by aliens?"

"Good heavens, no." Maddalena's tinkling laughter filled the small office. "What nonsense. Lieutenant, the Greys are utterly incapable of harming the smallest living creature."

"I see." Karl remained impassive. "Perhaps you can tell us something of Professor Stempel's human enemies?"

"Oh, dear." Maddalena shook her head. "I'm afraid there were rather a lot of them, Lieutenant. Ed wasn't the easiest person to get along with. He could be . . . impatient with human frailties. And of course he was rather . . . judgmental." She sighed. "I'm glad at least he's finally at peace."

She answered a string of routine questions with cheerful directness. Her real name—"birth name"—was Sophie Ptak ("Isn't that awful?" she tinkled); she had spent last night alone in her hotel room ("Well, not exactly alone, but I don't imagine you'd accept K'Tel's word for my whereabouts."); she was acquainted with Rudy Giambra, and with Jarvis McCray, and with Conrad deLeeuw.

"Unfortunately, the presence of the Greys has opened a number of atavistic channels to the collective subconscious," Maddalena said ruefully. "They're working to correct that, but it has caused some unfortunate collective mythmaking. The result is the development of a . . . UFO community, for want of a better term. It's not really surprising that many of us are acquainted with each other."

"And dislike each other?"

"Sometimes," Maddalena agreed readily. But she refused to speculate about who might have disliked Ed Stempel enough to kill him. "I'm sorry, Lieutenant. Even thinking about a level of hatred that profound gives me a deep scarlet headache." She rose from her chair in a fluid motion. "I wish I could help, truly I do. If you have any more questions, you do know where I'm staying, don't you?" She purred the last few words, unmistakably suggestive.

"I do have one more question," Karl said. "What exactly brought you to Ann Arbor this week?"

"To be perfectly honest, Lieutenant, I'm not sure." She seemed to ponder the question. "I don't usually chase after UFO sightings, you know. All I can tell you is that I was . . . brought. And I've learned to trust enough not to ask for reasons."

"I see. You are planning to remain here for the next few days?" Karl asked.

"Oh, absolutely." She smiled vividly at him, gave Anneke another wink, and was gone.

Anneke barely managed to hang on until the door closed before collapsing in laughter again. "Oh, my," she gasped. "Oh, God, I wouldn't have m-missed that for . . . "

"I'm glad to be here for your amusement." Karl, too, was laughing. "But it might have been nice if you'd shown a *little* jealousy."

"If you c-could have seen your f-face . . . " And she was off again, whooping with laughter.

When she finally got hold of herself, Karl was looking at her with an odd expression. "Did anyone ever tell you that you're a very unusual woman?"

"Just about everybody. Only I'm not sure *unusual* was exactly the word they used." She found a tissue in her briefcase and wiped her streaming eyes.

"You didn't have even an instant of doubt, did you?"

"No." She shook her head. "I was only surprised that you let yourself get mousetrapped like that. What happened to those linebacker reflexes?"

"Shot to hell, apparently. The damn woman just walked around the desk, and suddenly she was all over me."

"I guess you'd better postpone that comeback." She starting giggling again. "You know, I'm surprised by my own reaction, too." She thought back to the tableau she'd witnessed, her habit of analysis reasserting itself. "After all, she is a very beautiful woman. But there was really only one way it could have been."

"Oh?"

"Well, look. Number one, she's not your type. No, that's not what I mean," she protested when he raised an eyebrow. "Stop that, or I'll only start giggling again. What I mean is, she tries too hard; she's so busy working at it that it feels like an exercise in self-promotion rather than seduction. Number two, even if you were attracted to her, you'd never get involved with a potential suspect in a case. And number three, you'd simply never behave that way in your office, on the job—your work is too important to you."

"And you worked all that out in the two or three seconds you stood there?"

"Oh, no. I trusted you, that's all." She grinned at him.

"But I do think we'd better get a wedding ring on you as soon as possible, Lieutenant—for your own safety."

"It wouldn't do any good with a woman like that," he growled.

"You sound like you're speaking from experience."

"Let's just say that even the best shark repellent can't protect you from a really *determined* shark."

· · · · · · ·

TWENTY-TWO

Zoe hadn't expected much from the official police statement, and she wasn't disappointed. Genesko didn't appear, of course; neither did the police chief. Only Nina Belasco, the department PIO, spoke, and she gave them practically nothing that wasn't in the original bare-bones press release. Zoe thought she'd never heard anyone say "we don't know yet" so many different ways.

Only the "tentative" cause of death created a small stir. "Electrocuted?" The word went muttering through the crowd in an undertone, as though they were tasting it. But Belasco gave them nothing more, and the stir died away.

When Belasco was finished Zoe raced for the lobby, surprised at first that there were no lines at the pay phone until she realized she was probably the only one there who didn't have a cell phone. She called in the basics to the AP for immediate transmission, getting the same minor functionary and telling him she'd call Kaminsky when she got back to her desk. Then she headed toward the bike rack, listening to the snatches of conversation that drifted past her.

". . . big break and this is all . . ."

". . . Brad Pitt, and instead I get stuck in this . . ."

". . . plenty of nut cases, but not one single . . ."

She hadn't actually been told to cover the murder for the wire, of course. But she figured if she simply went ahead and did it they'd probably let her continue. They'd want one simple straight-news piece to start with, but beyond that, what? She worked on it as she pedaled back to the *Daily:* background on Stempel, of course—that part was easy enough. Then, reactions from people in the UFO community. There was probably a real feeding frenzy on the Internet, too; that might make a good sidebar. And she badly wanted to write something about the media hysteria itself, even if she was part of it.

She shook her head as she trotted up the stairs to the city room. You can't do everything, Kaplan. Focus.

"You look like you've heard." Gabriel Marcus looked up from the city desk at her approach, his face registering relief. "I tried to call you, but I guess you were out."

"Just came from City Hall." She waved her notebook at him and sat down at the sports desk, reaching for the phone and the computer simultaneously.

"The police press conference just ended," she told Leon Kaminsky when he came on the line, directing the words to Gabriel as well as the telephone. "I already called in the breaking news, and I'll have a full story for you in five minutes." She cradled the phone between ear and shoulder and opened a file on the old Mac.

"Thanks, Zoe. But this has gotten too big." Kaminsky said. "I think . . . "

"I know, you're going to want more than I can do by myself," she interrupted him, purposely misunderstanding. "Here's what I was thinking. I can do the actual crime coverage, because I'm a close friend of the cop in charge. I've worked on stories with him before—I covered the stadium murder, remember? Gabriel Marcus, who's the *Daily* editor, is also available, and he knows the University better than anyone you could send in from outside. He could cover the whole local angle—background on Stempel, interviews with people in his department, the works." She cocked an eye at Gabriel, relieved to see that he was giving her a thumbs-up. "He's done sports stringing for you guys before, so you know how good he is."

"I don't know, Zoe." Kaminsky sounded uncertain. "I do remember your stadium murder coverage, but . . . " He paused. "Oh, hell, half my people are on vacation anyway. All right, I'll let the two of you carry it for the next twenty-four hours; then we'll see." Zoe broke into a grin and returned Gabriel's thumbs-up. "Have you got any pictures?" Kaminsky asked.

"Pictures?" She said the word aloud, glancing at Gabriel. He shrugged. "Sure," she said confidently into the phone. "We can get you some shots of Stempel out of our morgue files, and I can get a photographer over to the crime scene right away. I'll transmit the initial news story in about five minutes, and a first in-depth piece by—" she checked her watch "—five o'clock? And news updates as they happen, of course." She spoke quickly, in case he was having second thoughts. "And Marcus'll file his backgrounder by four." She grinned as Gabriel made a face at her before jumping to his feet and heading swiftly down the aisle toward the library.

She could hear him sigh. "Okay. I must be losing it, but go ahead."

"You won't be sorry," she promised him. "Is there anything else you want?"

"Yes," he surprised her by saying. "I'd also like something on the whole UFO scene. How they're reacting to Stempel's death, how his death might affect the UFO world, if they think there's a link between his murder and the sightings—anything like that you can get. Hit the high spots, but have fun with it, too." Zoe could almost hear him smile.

"In other words, get out there and cover the nut beat." Zoe laughed. "Sure; I've already met a couple of them. But I may not get that one to you until pretty late—I'll have to locate them."

"That's okay; it'll be a morning feature anyway."

She hung up the phone and pumped her fist in the air triumphantly before giving her full attention to her keyboard. She pounded out the news piece in very nearly the promised five minutes, outlined a more in-depth piece—she'd plug the information in as she got it—then wrote up her notes on Conrad deLeeuw while they were still fresh in her mind. deLeeuw would be the fulcrum of the UFO story, she thought, the nonbeliever surrounded by the faithful. Only, where the hell was she going to find the faithful? Well, before she set out on a search, she'd better see if Barney was available to handle the photography end of things.

"Hey, Kaplan. Got a story on the murder yet?" Barney wheeled around from his terminal as she entered the computer room.

"Yeah, just filed. You can get it out of my directory to put on the Web. Barney, can you take some photos for us?"

"Sure. I wanted some for the Web site anyway."

"Good. Let's get some shots of the crime scene, and then one of the mobs at City Hall. And Gabriel's going to need some pics of Ed Stempel—there have to be some in our photo files somewhere."

"No problem. I think I can find them." He swiveled back to the terminal and reached for the mouse. "Have you seen this?"

"What?" She peered over his shoulder. "Hey, that's the Rock, isn't it?" A large photograph of the Rock, painted white with splashes of orange and brown, was centered at the top of the screen. Beneath it, in hazy pink letters, were the words: *Reclaim the Ancient Power.*

"What the hell is that all about?" she asked.

"Apparently someone's decided that the Rock is a Power Spot."

"A what?"

"A Power Spot." Barney grinned. "A place where—" he turned and read from the screen "—'elemental earth forces come to the surface.' "

"You have got to be joking. The Rock? Why the Rock?"

"Because its pyramidal, for one thing. I bet you don't even know about the transcendent power of pyramids, do you?"

"You mean, like, sitting under a pyramid will cure arthritis, help your sex life, that sort of thing?"

"Gee, you sound so skeptical. Want me to log on to some pyramidology sites so you can learn more about it?"

"Maybe later, when this whole business has softened my brain a little more." She bent toward the screen. "Who's doing this vigil?"

"That girl—Beryl. It seems to be her party."

"Yeah? She's one of the people I thought I'd interview. And we could get some pictures of the action, too. How about we go over to the Rock first, before going out to the crime scene? We might even come up with something the rest of the media overlook."

Some hope, she thought gloomily ten minutes later, standing on the corner of Hill and Washtenaw. Dozens of TV crews surrounded the small triangular plot, spilling out into the streets and ignoring the honks of outraged motorists.

"Shit. Oh well, let's get what we can," she told Barney as they climbed out of the battered Escort. She crossed the street and inserted herself into the crowd, noting something odd about it without immediately knowing what. Then she realized: it was too quiet. There was none of the racket that usually accompanied any press group. She shoved her way forward until she could get a clear view, one of the advantages of being only five-two and change.

About a dozen women in loose-fitting, unbleached cotton pants and short-sleeved shirts were on their knees in a rough circle around the Rock. Each of them was delicately chipping away at the Rock with small metal implements. All of them kept their heads bent to their task, ignoring the crowd around them.

Beryl herself, wearing the same outfit as the others, faced the cameras. She was also on her knees, but her back was straight and her hands rested on her thighs, palms upward.

". . . symptom of the sickness infecting our culture. We cover truth with layer after layer of evil, until the True Power is forgotten. But the time will be soon—sooner than you think—when the True Power will be revealed. You fear everything but the thing you should fear most—the End of Evil."

She spoke in a light, little-girl voice, so innocent-sounding that the meaning of her harsh words hardly penetrated. And her voice was so low that Zoe had to strain to hear; next to her, a TV technician fiddled with dials. Now she understood the unusual quiet—everywhere, people's eyes and ears were fixed on Beryl in the rapt attention necessary to hear.

"Are you planning to do the whole job by hand?" a voice asked—quietly.

"You'd use poisons, wouldn't you?" Beryl said fiercely, but still so low she could barely be heard. "You use evil and call it convenience. But the Power is here, and it rejects evil, as the Power rejected Edison Stempel."

The crowd stirred. "Are you saying Professor Stempel was killed by a supernatural power?" someone asked. A few people tittered. Beryl gazed upward.

"Edison Stempel was evil, and had to be rejected. He stood in the way of the Elemental Power, and it was the Elemental Power that rejected him, that freed us of his evil." Her whispery voice was filled with anger, and with elation. Well, electricity could be called an elemental power, Zoe figured. Beryl directed her gaze toward the crowd, and Zoe shivered suddenly at the look in her light brown eyes. "When the Power of this place is fully released, then all evil will be finally rejected."

"So you don't think he was killed by aliens?" a woman asked.

"The Greys will decide as they will decide," Beryl replied. "The Power is here, but the evil is everywhere."

Zoe had had enough; she backed out of the crowd, feeling her skin crawl. Forget the interview; this chick was stone crazy. She looked around for Barney and spotted his head above the crowd with a gust of relief. She wanted to get out of here. She waved at him and trudged toward the car, wondering as she walked whether Beryl was actually crazy enough to kill.

TWENTY-THREE

· · · · · ·

They drove from the Rock out to North Campus, but there wasn't much to see. The yellow crime-scene tape encircled such a large area that the police activity was barely visible, and the bored-looking cops standing guard refused to say anything but "Don't know, miss." She peered at the blackened mark burned into the grass, but as far as she could tell, it was just burned grass.

Nor was there anyone interesting to talk to. There were half a dozen TV crews lounging against their vans, and maybe a hundred people wandering around at the edge of the yellow tape, but most of them looked like students who were just there for the show. She spotted a couple of guys in camouflage, standing stiffly with binoculars trained on the police in the distance, but Jarvis McCray wasn't among them, and when she tried to question them they just grunted, and waved her off.

Barney clicked off some shots, even standing on the roof of his car to try for a better angle, and when he was done they gave up and headed back into town.

The City Hall parking lot was still where the action was. There were fewer media types, Zoe thought, but more of . . . whatever. Too, the crowd seemed to have co-agulated; instead of a fluid mob, there were clumps of people gathered in numerous groups.

"Oh, jeez." She sighed and turned to Barney. "Look, why don't you get off some photos to show the general scene—maybe from over across the street—and then head on back to the *Daily*. I'm going to see if I can find anyone worth interviewing, and I may be awhile."

"Okay." He looked around for a minute. "I think I'll see if I can get up to the top floor and shoot down. I'll see you later." He headed toward the door, and Zoe stood irresolute for a moment. Finally she eased her way toward one of the groups, this one composed mostly of student types surrounding a short, stocky guy holding a clipboard.

". . . by fomenting this UFO fantasy to cover up their own activities." The students applauded. A single bored-looking cameraman aimed his lens at them.

"Make no mistake," the short guy continued, "the U.S. military wants people to waste their time chasing nonsensical chimera. It's the best cover imaginable for their own illegal activities. We don't know what Professor Stempel stumbled across, but we do know that the CIA will be absolutely delighted if people can be conned into worrying about little green men instead of focusing on the activities in their own secret labs on every major college campus in the country."

Zoe slipped away, attracted by a group composed mostly of women, who were passing out leaflets to everyone willing to take one. Zoe did; it was headed *Abductees-Rights Organizations Demand Reparations*.

"The government allows the Greys to use American citizens like lab animals," it began,

> and then refuses to accept responsibility for our suffering. We demand the following:
>
> 1. That the U.S. government immediately end its vicious and inhumane treaty with the Greys;
>
> 2. That the government demand the immediate removal of all brain implants placed by the Greys;
>
> 3. That the government provide financial reparations to all victims of Grey abductions, including but not limited to payment for lost wages, pain and suffering, medical costs, and loss of consortium.

Zoe read the flyer with growing disbelief, crumpled it up, then uncrumpled it and shoved it into her bookbag. She'd sort all this stuff out later. She worked her way toward the door, passing one group holding chunks of pink crystal aloft while chanting loudly and off-key, and another group carrying picket signs that read: *To a mink, YOU are aliens*.

She saw a few flashes of camouflage, but none of it turned out to be Jarvis McCray. She was searching for anyone who looked newsworthy—and what did a "UFO expert" look like, anyway?—when she caught sight of a compact, muscular figure in a black T-shirt passing through the glass doors into City Hall. She spun around and plowed through the crowd, but by the time she got inside he was already at the window talking to Linda Postelli.

"I need to see Lieutenant Genesko," he was saying. "I'm Rudy Giambra. I have information for him about Ed Stempel's death." Giambra had a large black canvas utility bag slung over one shoulder, and two cameras around his neck. Sweat glistened on the thick black hair of his arms.

"Detective Kramer is handling interviews on that case," Postelli said. "I'll see if he's available."

"No. It's got to be Genesko himself," Giambra insisted. "Look, I knew Ed Stempel, we were working along the same lines, we knew the same people." He swiped at his forehead. "You've got to tell Genesko I need to see him."

"I can give him the message," Postelli said, unmoved by Giambra's persistence. She turned her head and waved to someone behind the door as she buzzed it open.

"Anneke!" Zoe nearly fell on her in delight as she came through the door.

"Well, well." Anneke laughed. "Somehow I don't think that greeting is entirely due to my sparkling personality."

"Look, Genesko is gonna want to talk to me anyway, I'm sure of it," Giambra was saying.

"Did you know your AP story made yesterday's *San Francisco Chronicle?*" Anneke said.

"Did it? Cool."

"Are you a reporter?" Giambra, sharp-eared, swiveled around to face Zoe.

"Yes. Zoe Kaplan, Associated Press." Saying the words gave her such a buzz that it took effort to suppress a grin. "You're the author of *The O(mega) Files*, aren't you?"

"Yes." He drew himself up, casting a you-see? glance at Postelli. "I've known—I knew Ed Stempel for years; I'm pretty sure I know what he was doing out there last night, and I think I know how he died. But this . . . lady . . . refuses to let me speak to the police."

"Number one, Mr. Giambra, you're more than welcome to speak to the police. You just can't speak to Lieutenant Genesko." Postelli looked disgusted. "And number two, I'm no lady. I'm a cop."

"Oh, this is ridiculous." Giambra threw up his hands. Out of the corner of her eye, Zoe saw Anneke motion to Postelli. "You see?" Giambra appealed to Zoe. "I can't get through to her. I have equipment here that Genesko has to know about. Otherwise . . . What?" He turned to Postelli.

"I said you can go in now, Mr. Giambra."

"To see Genesko?" He sounded suspicious.

"That's right." Postelli rolled her eyes.

"Thank God." He pushed through the door as the buzzer sounded. Anneke went through with him. And Zoe, holding her breath, trailed along behind.

"Lieutenant, I've got some things here you've got to see." Giambra started talking almost before he crossed the threshold of Genesko's office. "If I can . . . "

"Please have a seat, Mr. Giambra," Genesko interrupted him. He looked at Zoe quizzically for a moment, and she tried as hard as she could to become invisible. "I imagine you'd prefer to speak to me in private?"

"In private?" Giambra seemed to register the presence of Zoe and Anneke for the first time. "Hell no, let them stay. I *want* the papers to know about this."

"If you prefer." Genesko didn't correct Giambra's assumption that Anneke too was a reporter. "You say you have information for me?"

"Here." Giambra sat down finally, dropped his canvas bag on the floor with a thud and leaned over to unzip it. "Spectroscope," he said, placing a metallic object on Genesko's desk. "Magnetometer. Spectrometer. Geiger counter. Potentiometer." He sat up and pointed to the litter of objects. "I'll bet you found every one of these things in Ed's car, didn't you?"

"Why do you assume that, Mr. Giambra?" Genesko asked.

"Because this is the specialized equipment that all top UFO researchers would have with them if they were investigating a landing site. And Ed Stempel was one of the best."

"He didn't think the same of you, though, did he?"

"That review of my book, you mean?" Giambra laughed without mirth. "Oh, I expected that. Ed was . . . a hard sell. I knew I didn't have the kind of hard evidence that would convince him. If I'd had the time . . . Well, anyway." Giambra shook his head. "But, see, that's what made him such a fine researcher. Ed was out there on the front lines really searching for evidence. And last night, I think he found it." He leaned forward tensely, speaking fast, his New York accent becoming even more pronounced. "I'm no Ed Stempel, but I know my way around a UFO site. You get me to the site, I can run the same tests Ed musta run. I can get you the hard evidence. But the longer it waits, the more the trace elements degrade and the less chance we have of replicating Ed's results."

"So you weren't at the site last night?"

"No, never found it. After the sighting I spent more than an hour driving around over there—that North Campus area." He pronounced it "Nort." "But I don't know my way around, y'know? I kept getting lost on those winding roads, and finally I just gave up and went back to the hotel."

"What hotel is that?"

"I'm at the Sheraton, out by the expressway. I got lost going there, too. I'm a New Yorker. We don't do much driving." He said it proudly, as though the lack of a skill was something to brag about.

"I understand that you know some of the other people who are here in town to view the . . . sightings," Genesko said. "Did you see any of them last night?"

"No. I never got out of my car. I didn't spot the thing until just before it flared, and after that I was just driving around, like I said. Look, Lieutenant, how soon can I get to the landing site?"

"I'm afraid that won't be possible for the present, Mr. Giambra." Genesko shuffled papers on his desk. "We can't release the site until our own technicians are finished analyzing it."

"But your guys don't have a clue what to look for!" Giambra exploded. "You people may know how to scrape up bloodstains, but you don't know shit about searching for trace elements, or measuring radiation levels in plant material, or using black-light photography."

"Nevertheless, we'll soldier on in our own way," Genesko replied.

"So that's the way it is. You don't want to find evidence, do you?" Giambra's face, not pretty to start with, had become ugly. "Y'know, I really didn't think you were part of the cover-up. I guess I was wrong."

"What I would appreciate," Genesko went on as if Giambra hadn't spoken, "is the temporary loan of your equipment." He gestured at the clutter of objects on the desk. "Just for a few hours."

"You gotta be kidding." Giambra scooped up the various devices and replaced them in his utility bag. He stood up. "You heard it yourself," he said to Zoe. "They don't want to get at the truth. You tell your readers that."

"So you think the Greys killed Stempel?" Zoe took the chance of squeezing in a question.

"The proof is out there." Giambra jerked his head. "The cops won't let us find it, that's all. Ask yourself why, then ask them why, and keep asking. Don't let them get away with it." He picked up his bag and stalked out the door.

"Wow." Zoe took a deep breath and slouched back against the wall. "Any of that off the record, Lieutenant?"

"I should say all of it."

"You wouldn't. Would you? Oh, please? You heard him—he asked me to stay."

"*I* didn't." He looked at her so severely that for a moment she thought he really meant to do it. "All right," he said at last. "You can use anything he said, nothing I said. You may not reveal where or under what circumstances you got the information. Understood?"

"Absolutely," she said at once with a gust of relief.

"You may say that he requested permission to visit the crime scene, and permission was refused because police technicians are not finished with their work. You may also say," he added, "that the police will not permit any civilians in the area, in accordance with departmental regulations, to avoid the possible contamination of evidence."

"Have there been other people asking?" she picked up the unspoken inference.

He paused before replying. "You may say that a number of people besides Mr. Giambra have also requested access to the scene, and that all of them have been refused for the reason just stated. You may not attribute that information to any official source."

"Everybody wants to 'help,' don't they?" Zoe said. "Giambra, deLeeuw, God knows who else. They're all so sure the police can't possibly do their job on their own."

"It's also possible," Anneke suggested suddenly, "that one of them wants access to the crime scene for some other reason."

"I never thought of that," Zoe said, thinking about it now. She jumped to her feet. "Thank you. I really appreciate this, a *lot*. If I get on to some of the others who asked to get to the site, can I ask them about it? I'm kind of assuming that one of them is Conrad deLeeuw, but I won't touch it if you say no."

"That's all right. Anything you get from someone else is fair game."

"Thank you," she said again. "I don't suppose there's any information about the autopsy yet?"

"The next press briefing is scheduled for six o'clock." He leaned back in his chair. "I don't suppose it would hurt to give you the autopsy information—there really isn't anything new. As we thought, he was electrocuted, by an object we haven't been able to identify yet."

Zoe scribbled frantically as he described the burn marks on Stempel's body. When he was done, she looked up from her notebook, questions chasing themselves through her mind. She pushed them back firmly; she'd already imposed on friendship enough to make her uncomfortable.

"Y'know," she said, looking from Karl to Anneke, "I'm going to have to figure out a way to pay you guys back."

TWENTY-FOUR

· · · · · ·

"You'd think forensics could come up with some sort of intelligent guess," Anneke said crossly. She poured merlot into Karl's wineglass. "It's Cotswold," she said, pointing to the chunk of dark golden cheese flecked with green onions. She pushed the plate of cheese and French-bread rounds and carrot sticks closer to him. "Did you get any dinner at all?"

"I think there was a pizza somewhere around eight o'clock." He took a sip of wine and reached for the cheese slicer absently, his eyes fixed on the photograph in front of him.

He'd arrived home after ten o'clock, carrying a briefcase full of papers that he spread out on the glass coffee table in the living room. But he devoted most of his attention to a set of photographs showing a nude male torso with two bluish-black marks running down its length. Anneke had looked at the photo, gulped and looked away, but then the fascination of the puzzle drew her back. What on earth could have made those burn marks?

"It's not really a forensic question anyway." Karl returned to her complaint. "The lab's job is to describe the parameters of a possible weapon. It's our job to identify it. Like the dreaded 'blunt instrument'—they tell us the general size and shape of it, but we're the ones who have to figure out whether it's a baseball bat or a fireplace poker." He held up the photograph and turned it sideways. "Usually it's a pretty straightforward issue."

"That's true. The actual weapon isn't normally mysterious, is it?"

"As a matter of fact, there's rarely anything mysterious at all about the average crime. Most of it is just stupid and dreary. If criminals had any brains, they'd be in a different line of work."

"In this case, though, maybe the 'mystery' is the key to the whole thing, exactly because the weapon is unique. It means," she said thoughtfully, "that when you identify the weapon, it should identify the murderer, shouldn't it?"

"Probably." He straightened the photographs into a neat stack, set it aside, and picked up an equally neat stack of papers. "But I have a feeling that we're probably going to have to identify the murderer in order to identify the weapon." He sounded gloomier than she could remember.

"Well then, forget about means," she said, determinedly upbeat. "What about motive and opportunity? I know, I know." She held up a hand. "The police don't usually worry about motive. But you have to start somewhere."

"It isn't that." He fanned out the stack of paper. "It's simply that it's hard to find anyone who knew him who *doesn't* have a motive. After reading these interview reports, I have a feeling that if I'd had to work with him, I might have murdered him myself."

"That bad? Even around the University?"

"I'd almost say especially around the University." He plucked a sheet of paper from the stack and read aloud.

"Professor Ledyard—that's the history department chair—stated that, quote, 'the son-of-a-bitch has been out to get me for years because I wouldn't support his looney-bin think tank.' And, quote, 'do you know what it's like to go to AHA meetings and get razzed about your department nutcase?' And another quote from the good professor—'I told him I'd see him in hell before he ever got another promotion.' "

"That's quite an interview." Anneke laughed. "Who did it?"

"Wes Kramer. You should have heard his oral report." Karl laughed at the memory. "He said Ledyard was practically gibbering by the time he finished. And then suddenly he realized that he was talking about a murder victim, and went all solemn and tried to take it all back. Sometimes," he said, "you can get someone talking and they forget the circumstances. Wes is as good at that as anyone I know."

"I wonder, though—if you were actually a murderer, would you ever really forget yourself in an interview with the police?"

"You'd be surprised. And in any case, everyone in the

department knew about their feud—and was delighted to expand on it in great detail, I might add."

"Charming. So Stempel did have supporters in the department?"

"Well, not exactly supporters. At least, no one who expressed any support for his UFO research. But there were a number of people who had their own problems with Ledyard, and they were perfectly willing to use Stempel against him."

"The enemy of my enemy is my friend," Anneke quoted. "Of course. Still, you know, not many academic squabbles are really life-and-death affairs. If they were, every campus in the country would have bodies stacked up like cordwood."

"True. And these didn't seem to be, either. Issues of course requirements, whether the next new hires would be in American history or historical research, who got stuck teaching freshman intro courses, that sort of thing. And Stempel really didn't have enough power in the academic world to affect anyone's career. For all his pomposity, he was pretty well marginalized in the department."

"What about students? He had power there."

"Oh, the students all adored him. His classes had two-page waiting lists." Karl chuckled. "Wes said that was one of the things that drove Ledyard wildest."

"Did he have any family?" Anneke asked.

"An ex-wife living in Massachusetts, and a brother in Texas. No children."

"All of which brings us back to the UFO world."

"Yes." Karl sounded even gloomier than before. "Where he had enemies he hadn't even met yet."

"You mean the online activity. Yes, but those are just—

well, I suppose you could call them cyberenemies. I mean, they're not here, they're just people scattered all over the country. It's the ones who are actually in Ann Arbor that you can focus on."

"Always assuming that we know who's here and who isn't." He sighed. "At the moment, it's hard to believe there are any UFO believers who *aren't* in Ann Arbor."

"At the moment." Anneke pondered. "You know, one question that has occurred to me is this: Why now? I mean, all the people we're talking about have hated or despised Stempel for a long time. Why did someone kill him at this particular time?"

"An interesting question." Karl nodded. "Ask it this way—are the sightings and the murder linked by more than simply time and space?"

"You mean, the sightings themselves could be the motive. Stempel could have been killed because he discovered who was behind the hoax. That seems to suggest Conrad deLeeuw, doesn't it?"

"Not necessarily more than several of the others. Rudy Giambra, for one, certainly demonstrated sufficient knowledge to pull off this kind of stunt."

"Yes, and probably Maddalena Maestra could, too." Anneke grinned. "I doubt that there's much she couldn't get up to if she wanted to. But both she and Giambra only got to town after the first sighting, didn't they? Whereas deLeeuw is local."

"Well, we know Giambra flew in from New York on Thursday, but we don't know where he was before that. The same thing is true of the others. We're checking, of course, but . . . " He shrugged and took a sip of wine.

"I wish it weren't so hard to figure which of them actually believes the stuff they're all spouting, and which ones are just running a scam," she complained.

"I'm not sure it matters. A true believer might engineer a hoax to get attention for the cause—and might be even more likely to kill to protect his secret."

"I suppose."

"And remember, we're only speculating about the sightings as the motive."

"Well, what about opportunity? Is there anyone you can eliminate?"

"Not really. The only one who even claims to have an alibi is Jarvis McCray, who says his troops can vouch for his presence at his motel all night. But then they would, wouldn't they?"

"Back to motive, then." She sighed. "They say the solution to a murder is in the mind of the victim. I wish I knew more about Stempel."

Instead of answering, he reached for yet another stack of paper and handed her several sheets and a thick wad of photographs. "Stempel's basement," he said.

She looked at the photographs first. They showed a large room lined with shelves and fitted with several long worktables. There were books and journals and notebooks and a huge assortment of equipment of various kinds, all of it aligned neatly on shelves or tabletops.

She examined the individual photographs. There was a powerful-looking computer, along with a shelf holding a variety of circuit boards and soldering equipment, but the photos didn't show enough detail for her to identify the boards. On one of the worktables there was a television, a VCR, a video camera, and what she thought was video editing equipment. On the other worktable there were scatterings of metal and a looseleaf notebook. And everywhere there seemed to be odd pieces of equipment, much of it bristling with dials and gauges, none of it meaning anything to her.

The only thing she was sure of was that it was a remarkably elaborate setup for someone in history rather than one of the hard sciences.

She said as much to Karl, who nodded agreement. "We called in Mark Nolan, from the physics department, to go through it with us. He's still going through some of Stempel's notes, but among the equipment he found was a spectroscope, a Geiger counter, and a magnetometer."

"Exactly what Giambra was showing you," she said. "Wait a minute. You say he found all those things in Stempel's lab?"

"That's right." Karl seemed to be watching her.

"But . . . that's silly. The whole purpose of those things is for UFO research. Are you telling me he went out expecting to see a UFO, and he left behind precisely the equipment he'd need to study them?" She stared at him. "That doesn't make any sense."

"No." He took another sip of wine. "It doesn't."

"What *did* he have with him?"

For an answer he handed her a sheet of paper. In Stempel's pockets: wallet, keys, penlight, gold Mark Cross pen. In the trunk of his car: flashlight, jack, spare tire, half-full bag of road salt. Glove compartment: owner's manual, auto registration, sunglasses, and for a wonder, gloves. And finally, in the back seat: Black leather photographer's case containing:

35mm camera, diffraction lens, two rolls of film
binoculars
tape recorder
100-foot tape measure
ordnance maps of Washtenaw, Lenawee, Liv-
    ingston, and Monroe counties
tweezers
magnifying glass
small notebook (unused)
compass
Victorinox eighteen-piece Swiss army knife
box of large plastic zippable bags

"Where was his car?" she asked.

"Near the woods. He'd apparently driven across the grass to park as close to the burned area as he could."

"It looks like he was carrying a kit of basic equipment, but not the more exotic things." She studied the list again. "But why? I mean, if he didn't haul out the heavy artillery for this sighting, a major event in his own backyard, when on earth would he?"

"Perhaps he was so sure it was a hoax he didn't bother."

"No," Anneke said positively. "In that case, he'd want the best proof he could muster that it *was* a hoax. Besides . . . "

"What?"

"He may have thought it was a hoax, but deep down, I think he was really hoping it was something real. UFOs were the main focus of his life, after all. No." She shook her head again. "I absolutely refuse to believe he'd set out last night with nothing more sophisticated than a . . . a pair of tweezers."

"I can think of one reason he might, you know."

"What?" she challenged.

"If it was his hoax."

"Oh, hell." Anneke picked up her wineglass and set it back down, angry at herself for her lapse in logic.

"Suppose Stempel set up the hoax himself. He could have been putting the finishing touches to the 'landing site' when he was killed."

"Wait a minute. That won't work," she protested. "If someone discovered Stempel himself was behind the hoax, why kill him? Why not simply expose him as a fraud?"

"For one thing, it wouldn't necessarily be that easy. It would just be one person's word against another's."

"But it still wouldn't make sense to kill him. Not if it was his own hoax."

"It might, if someone had staked his reputation on the reality of the sighting."

"Or *her* reputation." Anneke sat up straight. "Maddalena has been milking this for all it's worth, you know. She'll look like an idiot at best if it comes out that she was conned by Ed Stempel." She laughed at his raised eyebrow. "All right, I admit I won't be brokenhearted if it turns out to be her."

"She's not the only one in that category either, of course," he pointed out. "Both Giambra and Jarvis McCray have dug themselves in fairly deeply."

"There's another element to their situation, too," she said slowly. "Both of them desperately *want* people to believe this is some sort of alien activity. They've made it a kind of proof of their theories. Exposing the hoax would be very damaging to their cause." She made a face. "No, that's too crazy. Would anyone actually kill for something like that?"

"Just because it's crazy doesn't mean it's unlikely. I can think of a dozen cases where the motive for murder was even crazier than that. It depends on exactly how obsessed a person is." He checked his watch. "Let's see how bad the news coverage is."

It was pretty much as bad as it could have been, she concluded as they switched among the three Detroit channels. All of them had helicopter shots of the crime scene, making much of the "mysterious" charred marks in the grass. All of them gave a more or less perfunctory thirty seconds to the police investigation. But from there, they all skyed off into the blue yonder.

They saw Conrad deLeeuw, looking pale and sweaty and entirely unconvincing. They saw Jarvis McCray, accusing the police of covering up the truth and hinting darkly of "government collusion" in the death of an "irreplaceable scholar." And they saw "best-selling author" Rudy Giambra everywhere, pleading on-screen for the chance to "help the police in a situation they simply aren't equipped to investigate."

"What did Lieutenant Genesko say when you offered your help?" Liz Epstein asked him.

"He wasn't interested," Giambra said, tight-lipped. "I'm sure he's a good cop, but he's in over his head on this and he refuses to admit it."

Maddalena—"the famous author and spiritualist"—was there, serenely beautiful as she defended the police—and the Greys. And there was a sprinkling of UFO background stories, ranging from Roswell to swamp gas to Area 51.

There was a schizophrenic quality to the newscasts that

would have made Anneke laugh if it weren't so depressing. Should they take the UFO people seriously? they seemed to be asking themselves. After all, their own networks ran UFO "documentaries." But if so, *which* UFO people? Well, Giambra and Maddalena sold a lot of books, so . . . And Beryl had a broad activist following in Ann Arbor, didn't she? They'd covered her activities before. Although this Power Spot business . . . But a lot of viewers really believe this crap, don't they?

You could almost see them puzzling it out as they faced their cameras.

In the end, they seemed to treat everyone and every notion—McCray, a tearful history student, a University spokesman—more or less equally, with a kind of generalized mock-solemnity that made Anneke's teeth ache. When they finally moved on to what she always thought of as the ladies'-magazine segment—"Next, our own Joe Jordan compares dog-grooming salons"—she reached for the remote and savagely clicked the *off* switch.

TWENTY-FIVE

* * * * * *

Breakfast service was just closing up by the time Zoe got down to the cafeteria. She grabbed a couple of doughnuts and a container of milk and carried her tray to the usual corner. At this hour, she expected the table to be empty, but to her surprise the others were still there. They watched her as she shoved a pile of newspapers aside and dropped her tray on the table. More newspapers than usual—besides the *Free Press*, there was *USA Today*, the *New York Times*, and a mass of printouts she assumed were her own stories downloaded from the Internet.

"Is there anything new on the murder?" Ben Holmes asked almost before she sat down.

"Not unless you count six different species of aliens who all called the *Daily* last night to take credit for it." She took a bite of doughnut and swigged milk from the lip of the carton. "I swear to God, I never knew there could be this many freakazoids in the whole world."

She'd stayed at the *Daily* until nearly 2:00 A.M. last night, waiting for a call that the UFO had been sighted again. It never came, but it seemed like every nutcase in the world had zeroed in on the *Daily* telephone number. An oval object "the size of three football fields" had been seen over Whitmore Lake; a three-foot-tall, blue-skinned creature had been spotted disappearing into the drainage ditch along I-94 ("and when we got out to look, *it had disappeared!*"); there were mysterious lights over Toledo, Muskegon, and White Pigeon; there were warnings to Earthlings to 1) shut down the Mars project, 2) prepare for an asteroid collision, 3) save the whales (that one, Zoe thought, had been watching too many *Star Trek* movies.)

They'd dragooned a couple of staffers to answer the phones, and she and Gabriel spent the rest of the evening scrambling to file stories. She made phone call after phone call, disconnecting the latest incoming lunatic without a thought, interviewing Stempel's colleagues and students, interviewing astronomers and physicists, interviewing psychologists and historians, calling in every chip she could think of.

When she'd done everything she could do with the murder and the UFO connection, she turned to the Internet, working with Barney to document the growing on-line hysteria. Newsgroups, Web sites, chat rooms, all exploded with charges and countercharges, conspiracy theories, and flat-out insanity.

That story she filed too, her fifth—sixth?—of the day; by midnight she'd lost count. But she was utterly determined to give Leon Kaminsky everything he could possibly want. She kept checking the wire anxiously, relieved each time she saw one of her pieces transmitted. This was the biggest break of her life, and she was going to make the most of it or die trying.

Which I may just do, she thought, gobbling a doughnut and checking her watch. By nine o'clock there might be another update from the police, and she had to be there when it was released.

". . . was electrocuted?"

"Huh? Sorry, I guess I'm a little distracted."

"I asked," Barry Statler repeated, "whether they were really sure he was electrocuted."

"Yeah, sure. No question about it—there were burn marks on his chest. They just don't know what did it yet."

"I don't understand it," Barry muttered to himself. As usual, he was holding one of his odd bits of electronics, turning it over and over in his hands. Jenna was staring at the thing too, her face tight with . . . anger? fear? What's that about? Zoe wondered; I mean, it's only one of Barry's weird techie things. Isn't it?

Something uncurled in the pit of her stomach and fluttered upward. She felt it in her throat, and she swallowed in sudden dread.

"Barry?" She was afraid to ask the question, terrified of the answer.

"But it's impossible!" he burst out. He looked directly at her, and the fear in his face hit her like a blow. "It *couldn't* have killed him."

"My God." She swallowed again, sick bile filling her throat. "You set me up. It was you, wasn't it?" He nodded miserably, keeping his head down, his face averted; she wanted to lunge across the table, to grab him by the throat and shake denial out of him. "You're the one who ran the whole UFO game, aren't you? *Aren't you?*" she shouted.

"It wasn't just Barry," Jenna said. "It was all four of us."

"It was just a joke." There was a whine in Ben's voice that Zoe had never noticed before. "It wasn't supposed to turn into . . . into this. No one was supposed to *die*, for pete's sake."

"This is where we were gonna laugh and shout 'Gotcha!'" Narique Washington said, looking at his hands.

"But it *couldn't* have killed him," Barry said for the third time. He turned the thing over again, plucking at it with stiff fingers. "It doesn't pull enough power for that, I swear it doesn't."

They really didn't get it, Zoe thought, and then was sickened even more by her own self-absorption. She was only facing the destruction of her career; they were facing the possibility that they had killed a man. She tried as hard as she could to feel as bad for them as she felt for herself. But I'm not the one who did anything wrong, she cried out to herself.

"You've got to tell the police," she said finally. "You should've told them right away." You schmucks, she raged silently.

"We didn't know if . . . We didn't know what to do." For the first time since Zoe had met her, Jenna seemed at a loss.

"All right." She took a deep breath and put both hands on the table to push herself out of her chair, surprised to see that she was still clutching a chunk of doughnut. She dropped it on the *Free Press* and wiped sticky sugar off her hands with one of the printouts. All that her stories were good for, now. "Stay here. I'll call Genesko and set it up."

She stood up, and the sudden motion brought on a wave of vertigo. Unsteadily, she moved toward the stairs.

Morton Oliver was officially off the hook. A decade from now, *Daily* staffers would talk about "pulling a Zoe Kaplan."

Once in her own dorm room, with the door tightly closed, she picked up the phone and started to dial the police department. No; they might refuse to put her through to Genesko. She dialed his home number, hoping that Anneke would be there, but there was no answer. Would she be at work on a Saturday morning? Zoe felt a gust of relief when she heard the familiar voice on the line.

"Anneke? It's Zoe. Can you . . . I need to see the lieutenant."

"Zoe, I . . ."

"It's not about a story. I swear—you know I wouldn't do that. And anyway, I won't be covering this one anymore." She heard the pouring bitterness in her own voice and hurried on. "I know who was responsible for the UFO hoax. Can I . . . can you call and let him know we're coming? And if you could—" Her voice broke, and she stopped.

"Zoe, are you all right?"

"N-not really." The concern in Anneke's voice made it even worse somehow. "Yeah, I'm okay," she managed. "Would you call the lieutenant and tell him we'll be there in—say, about an hour?"

"Of course. And Zoe, if there's anything I can do. . . ."

"Thanks. I don't . . . Thanks." She hung up the phone and lay facedown on the unmade bed, letting the tears flow.

Finally she dried her eyes and reached for the phone once more.

"Mom?"

"Zoe, how nice." Berniece Kaplan's voice sounded pleased. "I didn't expect to hear from you this weekend. I've been following your stories online—you've been doing great work."

"No, I haven't," she said grimly. "Mom, I've got a problem."

"Oh?"

"I just found out that the whole UFO hoax was engineered by four of my friends here in the dorm."

There was a moment of silence. "Oh, shit," Bernie Kaplan said quietly. "And of course, people who don't know you are going to think you were in on it."

"I wouldn't be the first reporter to fake a story just to get something big to write about."

"I know. Shit," Bernie said again.

Thank God her mother didn't go in for soothing platitudes. "Mom . . ." She gulped and tried again. "If you've got any words of wisdom to offer, now's the time."

There was a pause. Zoe sent up a prayer that Bernie Kaplan, Activist Mom, would come up with something out of her 25 years of political experience to get her out of this mess.

"Kennedy Rules," Bernie said finally.

"What?" The words didn't seem to make any sense.

"Kennedy Rules," Bernie repeated. "I mean John Kennedy, of course," she said with a touch of acid in her voice.

"Mom . . ."

"In 1961," Bernie began as though Zoe hadn't spoken,

"John Kennedy presided over a little adventure that's become known as the Bay of Pigs fiasco. You've heard of it
of course, but never mind what it was all about; for your
purposes, the point is that it was very nearly one of the
great political disasters of all time. It could have been
Kennedy's Watergate."

"And?" Zoe, familiar with her mother's dialectic technique, spoke into the pregnant pause.

"He end-played them." Bernie chuckled. "Kennedy not
only took the blame for his own fuckup, he took the blame
for everyone else's fuckup besides. He mea culpa'ed up
one side of Washington and down the other, until people
finally started to say, wait a minute, it couldn't *all* be his
fault, what the hell was wrong with his advisers? Which
was," she added parenthetically, "a very good question.
And then people started to figure: Hey, you know, this
John Kennedy's a pretty good guy, taking the rap for his
subordinates like that, when he could have tried to pass the
buck."

Bernie chuckled once more. "John F. Kennedy was a
very good politician."

Zoe had a feeling there was a point to all of this, but her
head felt too muzzy to grasp it. "And this political fable
means—what, exactly?"

"Zoe, it's all about responsibility," Bernie said soberly.
"Everybody fucks up sometimes, and when they do, most
of them try to wriggle out of it. But the truth is, that just
makes it worse, because then you not only look like a
fuckup, but like a coward besides."

"But what if it really *isn't* your fault?" Zoe protested.

"Oh, honey, as if that matters. Most people won't believe you, and even if they do, they'll consider you a fool

for having been taken in. John Kennedy had been a navy officer, you know," she said. "And one of the primary tenets of the military is that an officer is always responsible. Blaming your men is one of the most contemptible things an officer can do. Zoe, what the Kennedy Rules tell you is that if you stand up and take even more than your fair share of the blame, people will respect and sympathize with you. The fault committed remains, but so does your dignity."

Bernie sighed. "I wish I could offer you advice on how to just make it all go away, but I can't."

"I know." Zoe sighed in turn. "Thanks, Mom."

"Call me?"

"I will."

She put down the phone and straightened her shoulders. Then she headed downstairs.

TWENTY-SIX

• • • • • •

"She's late." Anneke checked her watch, more worried about Zoe than she wanted to admit.

"Only five minutes," Karl pointed out.

"I know, but Zoe's never late." She wasn't sure what it was about Zoe's phone call that had set off alarm bells in her head, but after she called Karl she'd been sufficiently concerned to want to be present. "She said she knew who was behind the UFO hoax, but she sounded . . . wrong, somehow." She tried to explain her unease. "This is Zoe we're talking about. According to her, she's just broken something that will be a huge story for her. But she wasn't bubbling over the way she should have been. She sounded almost as though she were in tears."

There was a knock on the door. Anneke turned around eagerly, but instead of Zoe, Officer Jon Zelisco stepped into Karl's office. He had a sheaf of wide lineprinter output in his hands and a wide grin on his face.

"Got it!" he announced.

"What is it?" Anneke leaned forward curiously as he slapped the printout on Karl's desk. She saw the words *Plant Department*, and as she scanned down the page her eyes widened. She turned to Zelisco with a grin that matched his own.

"Beautiful. Did you ferret this out yourself?"

"I wish." He laughed, teeth flashing white in his dark face. "I don't think I'll ever be that good."

"Sure you will." In the time she'd know him, Jon Zelisco had progressed from adequate computer user to proficient hacker.

He shook his head. "A couple of guys in the computer science department . . . " He stopped as another knock sounded on the door.

This time it was someone Anneke didn't know, a youthful-looking man wearing baggy shorts, a Sorbonne T-shirt, and flip-flops on bare feet. He too carried a sheaf of paper, the top sheet covered with what looked like electronic schematics.

"Come in, Professor Nolan." Karl stood up and waved to a chair.

"I'm just going to drop this and run." Nolan looked more like a student than a professor. He deposited the papers on Karl's desk. "There's a written report with it. I've got to tell you, that's the damnedest Rube Goldberg device I've ever seen. I can describe what it does—I think—but I can't even begin to guess why anyone would want to do it."

"I think I know the answer to that," Karl said. "Thank you very much, Professor Nolan."

"No problem. It's fun to climb off the theoretical merry-go-round and get down and dirty once in a while." He started to leave, then turned back. "I'll say one thing. Whatever that contraption is all about, it could pack one hell of a punch if you wanted it to."

He turned to leave. As he did, Zoe appeared in the doorway. For a minute they did the complicated two-step of people trying to get out of each other's way, and Anneke started to smile until she got a good look at Zoe's face.

The girl looked awful. Her copper-colored eyes were hot and bright in a face gone pale, and her mouth was a tight, grim slash that made her look older than her nineteen years. She nodded briefly to Anneke before addressing Karl.

"Lieutenant." She stopped. "These are the people you've been looking for," she said, jerking her head toward the doorway. "These . . . friends of mine are the ones responsible for the UFO hoax."

There were four of them, all hanging back in the doorway. They looked embarrassed, uncomfortable, even frightened.

"I see." Karl gazed at them for a time. "All right." He stood up and came around the desk, picking up the lineprinter output on the way. "Why don't we move down to an interview room where there's room for all of you."

He left Jon Zelisco watching with bright-eyed curiosity, and led them down the hall to a windowless room nearly filled by a long conference table. They followed him silently and arranged themselves around the table, taking seats as far apart from each other as possible.

"You taping?" The one African American in the group

cocked a thumb at the mirror running the length of one wall.

"Yes," Karl replied briefly. "Now, then. Your names, please?"

They went around the table, announcing their names like children in a kindergarten classroom. Anneke started at Ben Holmes's famous campus name, but Karl only nodded, as if he'd already recognized him. When they were done they waited, silent and self-conscious.

"All right, let's have it," Karl said.

"We're the ones who pulled the UFO hoax." It was Jenna Lenski who spoke first, her head erect, her face under its smooth cap of auburn hair pale but determined. "It was my idea. I was hoping Professor Stempel would f-fall for it, and make a fool of himself."

"It wasn't just your idea, Jen," Narique Washington said. "We all went off on it."

"And anyway, I'm the one who designed and built the thing," Barry Statler said. "If anything . . . went wrong, it's my fault." He looked sick and terrified.

"Believe me, there will be plenty of blame to go around," Karl said. "Ms. Kaplan." Zoe brought her head up and seemed to force herself to meet his gaze. "Did you know about this before it began?"

Zoe looked like she'd been slapped. Her face, if possible, went even whiter. But all she said was: "No, sir, I did not."

"It's true," Narique said. "She didn't, honestly. She was as much of a dupe as . . . " He stopped abruptly; the words *you were* seemed to hang in the air.

"Let it go, Nique," Zoe said to him. "Anyone who

doesn't believe me isn't going to believe you either. If people think I was part of this to get myself a big story to write about, your word isn't going to change their minds."

"Is that . . . ? Oh, Zoe, I never thought about that." Jenna looked even more stricken than before. "We'll tell everyone that you didn't know anything about it, I swear."

"Like I said," Zoe said brutally, "why would they believe *you?*"

So that was it, Anneke realized with a sick feeling in her stomach. No wonder Zoe was devastated. And the fact that she'd been writing for the Associated Press, instead of only for the *Daily*, made it ten times worse—the AP wouldn't view it as a student prank, but as a journalistic crime of the highest order. Professional lives had been destroyed for a good deal less.

"Ms. Kaplan." Karl spoke quietly. "I apologize for the question."

"Why? I deserved it." The pain in Zoe's voice was palpable. Karl didn't pursue it; instead he turned to Barry Statler.

"Describe the mechanism you used, please."

"It was mostly just a simple remote-control device," Barry said eagerly. "Really kind of primitive. The body was black plastic—from garbage bags, you know?—attached to a collapsible aluminum frame painted black. And then the whole thing was hung from three black balloons, one on each corner."

"How big was it?" Karl asked.

"Actually, it was a fair size—almost eight feet on its longest side. It wasn't equilateral," he explained, "it was oblique; made it look bigger, and faster."

"And the motor?"

"Aluminum and titanium. I made it from lab scraps."

"What about the flare-up and disappearance?"

"Oh, that was easy." Barry seemed more at ease talking about technical details. Well, Anneke understood that feeling well enough. "That was just magnesium, like you use in highway flares, with a remote-control fuse. The flare-up popped the balloons and mostly disintegrated the black plastic, and the aluminum framework automatically folded itself up. Then we'd just go pick it up where it landed." His face became anxious again. "Honestly, we were real careful to bring it down where it wasn't over anyone's head. And the total electrical output—remote devices and engine battery combined—just didn't carry enough charge to hurt anyone."

So that's what he was worried about, Anneke thought.

"Besides," Ben blurted, "we retrieved it from behind the music school right after he brought it down."

"Did you now?" Karl leaned back in his chair and gazed at Ben.

The boy turned first red, then white. "There wasn't anyone there, I swear! We didn't see anyone, did we, Nique? And anyway, Stempel's body sure wasn't there. Don't you think if we'd found a dead body we'd have called the cops?"

"No, I don't," Karl rapped out. "You were anxious enough about your own skins that you didn't bother to come forward for a full twenty-four hours after you knew about Professor Stempel's murder. And then you only did so because Ms. Kaplan found you out and brought you here."

"That's not fair," Ben protested.

"Yes, it is," Jenna interrupted. "We didn't think about

anyone but ourselves. No—*I* didn't think about anyone by *my*self—from the first minute I thought up this thing."

"Oh, come on, Jen." Ben smiled nervously at her. "It was just a goof, that's all. We didn't mean—"

" 'We didn't mean'," Jenna repeated scornfully. "We used Zoe, without any thought of how it would affect her; we caused a lot of trouble; and when something really awful happened, we didn't even have the guts to come forward." She tightened her lips and faced Zoe squarely. "Zoe, I know it isn't worth much, but I'm sorry. If there's anything I can do to help, I will." She didn't wait for an answer; instead, she turned to Karl. "Whatever we have coming, we'll suck it up. Do you want us to make a public confession and apology?"

"I can't do that!" Ben yelped. "Do you know what Coach'll do to me?"

"Shut up, Ben." Jenna spoke without turning to look at him, her eyes blazing. "You're busted—deal with it. We fucked up, and we're going to do whatever we can to make things right."

There was hope for the girl, Anneke thought. And after all, it had only been a student prank; they hadn't intended to hurt anyone—well, except for Ed Stempel, but not the way it happened. And they obviously didn't realize what it would do to Zoe. Next to her, she heard Zoe mutter, "Boy, talk about your Kennedy Rules." But when she looked a question at her, Zoe just shook her head.

"I don't know if a public confession will be necessary," Karl said, "but it's all going to come out eventually, so I suggest you be prepared. On the other hand, there may be a way for you to help undo some of the damage you've done, and possibly even come out of it looking less fool-ish."

"Tell us." Jenna glared at the three boys, daring them to object. "Whatever you say, we'll do it."

"Good." Karl laced his fingers together and looked at Barry. "What I want," he said, "is one more sighting of your flying saucer."

"You're kidding," Ben said. "Why?"

"He's setting a trap, you idiot." Barry sat up straight, looking interested. "He figures it'll draw the killer in. Only," he looked at Karl, "won't it just attract everyone, just like the other sightings? How'll you know who the killer is?"

"I think you can safely leave the police work to the po-lice, Mr. Statler."

"Sorry." Barry reddened. "Will you tell me just one thing, though?"

"If I can."

"It wasn't my stuff that killed him, was it?"

"No, it wasn't." Barry slumped in his chair, looking sick with relief. "Now, here's what you're going to do."

He told them what he wanted, laying out details of time and place. The four students nodded eagerly. Then he turned to Zoe.

"Obviously, I don't need to tell you not to reveal any of this beforehand. But I would like you to be there as an in-dependent witness in any case, so you can tell your editor you'll have something for him tonight."

"I can't." Zoe shook her head. "I can't cover this at all, not after this. But there's a worse problem than that." She chewed on her thumbnail. "Lieutenant, I have to tell Leon

Kaminsky at the AP that I'm off the story, so he can assign someone else. And I have to tell him why."

"Zoe, I'm sorry, but that will have to wait until after tonight."

"And I'm sorry too, Lieutenant—I'm sorry as hell. But I've got to." There was pain in her eyes. "Don't you see, he has to know. I won't give him any names or details, but he has to know that his ace girl reporter—" she gave the words a sarcastic twist, her voice breaking slightly "—is going to be accused of inventing her stories. He's got to be ready so he can cover his ass when this all hits the fan. I'm sorry," she said again, "but I owe it to him. He gave me a great opportunity, and I blew it."

"I see." Karl gazed at her for a moment. "How trustworthy would you say Mr. Kaminsky is?" he asked.

Zoe thought about the question. "Very, I think. He's a good newsman with a good reputation, and he's where he wants to be. I mean, he's not some hotshot looking for a big break to ride to the next big job. Like me," she added bitterly.

"Then let me offer a suggestion," Karl said. "You talk to Mr. Kaminsky, and tell him what you feel you need to. Then tell him he may assign another reporter, who may be at the site tonight *if* you are with him."

"Thank you," Zoe said soberly. "Being able to get them the story will help my reputation a little bit, anyway. But you don't have to include me there."

"Oh, I'm not making that provision for your benefit, Ms. Kaplan. I'm making it for my own. You may trust Mr. Kaminsky, but the only one I'm willing to trust in a situation like this is you."

"Th-thanks." Zoe's coppery eyes were bright now with

unshed tears. She gave him a shaky smile. "I think I needed that."

"Now," Karl said briskly to Barry, "about that charred area in the grass."

"You want that, too?" he asked.

"Yes, I do. I assume that won't be a problem?"

"That depends. I can make them *look* the same, but I can't replicate them exactly."

"Why not?"

"Well, see, remember that the whole point of the thing was to suck in Professor Stempel. And he's no fool—I mean, he wasn't a fool." Barry corrected himself uncomfortably. "We had to give him something he'd be likely to get excited about. So we seeded the area with some special chemicals."

"Boron and lithium," Karl said.

"How did you—oh." Barry looked sheepish. "Of course. Your own lab analysis."

"Out of curiosity, why those particular chemicals?"

"Because, after the 1966 sightings, someone did a soil analysis of one of the areas where something was seen, and discovered that there were elevated levels of boron." Barry laughed. "It didn't seem to bother them that boron is a normal element to find in soil. Anyway, I figured that'd be one of the things Stempel would definitely test for, so I gave it to him. The lithium was just because I could get my hands on it and I thought it sounded good. The thing is, though, I don't think I can get my hands on any more of the stuff."

"That won't be necessary. Just as long as you can get enough magnesium to reproduce the charred area."

"Yeah." Sheepish was becoming Barry's permanent mode. "That part was easy."

"Good. Now, I have one more question, Mr. Statler. How did you arrange for the lights to go out each time it came down?"

"That was—" Barry stopped. "I don't think I better say anything about that."

Karl tapped the lineprinter output. "Unfortunately for you, you don't need to. When Ms. Kaplan informed me after the first sighting that the lights went out over the athletic campus, but stayed on over city streets, I was fairly sure where to look for the answer. You left traces in the plant department computer when you hacked into it."

"I never did," Barry said, stung. "I can get in and out without—shit." He shook his head at his own stupidity. "Sorry, but I don't know what you're talking about."

"Obviously, I don't have to tell you that computer invasion is not only a felony, but a federal crime. Even if you avoided a jail term, conviction would at the very least cost you your fellowship."

"There is nothing in that printout that has anything to do with me," Barry said stubbornly. "It may show that someone broke into the plant department's control computer and jiggered some lights, but there's nothing to show who it was."

Karl sighed and tossed the output aside. "You're all very bright and very silly children," he said. "If I didn't know Ann Arbor as well as I do, I'd find it unbelievable that four intelligent people could put this much time and effort into a practical joke this elaborate."

"You've got to understand, Lieutenant," Barry said with a grin. "Summer in Ann Arbor is always the silly season."

TWENTY-SEVEN

• • • • • •

"What's this Genesko like?" Pete Cantilio asked. He was maybe in his late twenties, short and wiry, filled with a nervy tension that made Zoe twitch in response.

"The best," she replied firmly. "If he says it, you can take it to the bank."

"If you say so." He looked unconvinced. "How soon do we get this show on the road?"

"Not till about ten-thirty. They want it full dark."

"Shit." He checked his watch. "I'm gonna go grab a sandwich."

She watched him speed-walk down the aisle of the city room, slapping the oak cabinets along the way as if discharging energy. Well, Kaminsky could have sent someone a lot worse, she admitted to herself; at least this guy didn't patronize her. Or sympathize either, which she appreciated. In fact, he barely paid any attention to her; she wasn't a person, just a means to an end.

She'd called Leon Kaminsky from a phone in the *Daily* library, with the door firmly closed and Gabriel present. He also had to know, after all. She spoke quickly, getting it over with as fast as possible, seeing the growing consternation on Gabriel's face.

"I'm sorry as hell, Mr. Kaminsky," she said at last. "You gave me a real break, and you got a real mess in exchange."

"I'm sorry too, Zoe," he said. "Your stuff has been excellent. And for the record, I believe you when you say you didn't know anything about it. You wouldn't have voluntarily taken yourself off the story if you'd been running a game."

"Thanks. I appreciate hearing that."

"And I appreciate the fact that you arranged to get us the story even after you're off it."

"That wasn't my doing, actually," she admitted. "Lieutenant Genesko was the one who set it up."

"But he wouldn't have if he didn't trust you." There was amusement in Kaminsky's voice. "Zoe, don't make the hair shirt any rougher than it has to be. Now, I'm going to send a guy named Pete Cantilio down there to cover this. He'll meet you at the *Daily*. I'm counting on you to make sure he gets everything he needs, okay?"

"He'll have it all, I promise." She hung up. "We'll have to run with just the AP story," she said to Gabriel, trying to ignore the pity in his eyes.

"God, Zoe, I'm sorry." He came around the library table and laid a hand on her shoulder.

"Whatever *did* happen to Morton Oliver?" she asked, trying for a light tone. She wished he'd take his hand off her shoulder; she didn't think she could stand much more sympathy.

"Oh, come on, you're no Morton Oliver," he said. "You didn't do anything wrong."

"Then how come my life just turned into a pile of shit? Because," she quoted, answering her own question, " 'Stupidity is the only capital crime. There is no appeal.' " She stood up and managed a small grin. "Robert Heinlein's *Notebooks of Lazarus Long,*" she said. "Come on. We've got work to do."

"I don't understand about this trap," Pete Cantilio complained, shifting gears (badly) and squealing his Toyota around the corner. He drove pretty much the way Zoe'd expected, in bursts of speed punctuated by jerky stops. She gritted her teeth and tightened her grip on the windowsill.

"If you mean you don't know how it's going to uncover the murderer, neither do I," she said. "But if Genesko says it will, then it will."

"Maybe." Cantilio took two more corners and headed northeast out Fuller. "And why the hell out here?"

"He needed a place to fake a landing site," she explained patiently. "It had to be secluded enough for them to set up the operation without being seen, and it had to have a flat area big enough for a UFO to land there. And it had to be reasonably easy to get to. Huron High has a lot of open field around it, but it's also got woods to block the view and the whole place is pretty much out in the middle of nowhere. Besides, this time of year it's empty, so there isn't anyone around to see anything anyway."

Cantilio grunted but said nothing more as they passed the VA hospital. "Over there," she directed when the bulk of Huron High School came into view. "Pull around behind." She found herself talking in low tones even though there was no one around to hear. "We're supposed to put the car back into the woods so no one can spot us."

"No way. It'll scratch the hell out of my car."

"Tough. It's either that or we quit. You want to tell Kaminsky you didn't get the story because you didn't want to scratch your car?" She was getting increasingly edgy, here in the dark with this yuppie jerk. She'd promised Kaminsky and Genesko both that she'd be totally responsible for him; the trouble was, Kaminsky and Genesko had very different agendas.

"All right, all right." He pulled the car in behind a stand of trees, grumbling all the way. "Now what?"

"Now we wait." She tried to compose herself, preternaturally aware of Cantilio's twitching impatience. She looked around for any sign of Genesko, but if his Land Rover was anywhere around she couldn't see it.

"Is that it?" Cantilio asked suddenly.

"Where?" She followed his pointing finger; in the night sky to the south she saw the familiar triangle of lights. She opened the car door and scrambled out, her feet sinking into a thick mass of moss and dead leaves and who knew what else. "Let's go, Cantilio. It's showtime." She led him along the edge of the woods, trying not to wonder if there were snakes in Ann Arbor.

"Jesus, Kaplan, you could've warned me that we were going to be hacking our way through a jungle."

"Shush. Keep your voice down. Who the hell told you to wear Cole-Hahns on an assignment? Stop here."

"Is this where it's coming down?"

"Yeah. See that?" She pointed at the dark landscape, where an even darker circle was faintly visible.

"Got it." He peered forward, then up. "Here it comes."

The lights were doing their thing, a herky-jerky dance that made it hard to maintain focus. Clever, Zoe thought; you could never quite keep it in view. She watched as the thing wheeled out over Huron Parkway, to the east of the school grounds. It began to drift back over the school.

"Shit!" Cantilio swore. The lights suddenly blazed, impossibly bright. Zoe's eyes squeezed themselves shut, as they had done during the other sightings; when she opened them, the sky was dark once more. She blinked, trying to clear her vision, and out of the corner of her eye she saw the movement of a dark figure, barely visible. Nique had just retrieved the remains of the UFO.

They could hear the sounds of honking horns, and the ironic cheers of drivers, drifting through the night air from the parkway.

"Now what?" Cantilio muttered in her ear.

"Now we wait some more," Zoe told him.

"How can the cops be sure the guy they're after will even find the place?"

"They gave this one a good long ride," she explained. "It was over the city for nearly an hour before it headed out this way. Anyone who wanted it badly enough wouldn't have had any trouble following it."

"But that means a lot of other people'll follow it out here, too, especially other media people." Cantilio sounded angry. "I thought your guy promised us an exclusive."

"Relax. The other guys may be here, but they won't

have a clue what they're really seeing. We're the only ones who know it's a police trap, and we're the only ones who'll know the truth about the UFO hoax."

"I guess," Cantilio grumbled. "But I still don't understand how this Genesko'll know who the perp is if a whole mob shows up."

"I don't know." It was a point that had bothered Zoe, too. "Give it a rest, Cantilio, okay? Genesko knows what he's doing." She wished she were as confident as she tried to sound.

The first wave arrived almost immediately—a gaggle of students who trudged across the field on foot, coming in over the berm from Huron Parkway, laughing and shouting to each other.

"Hey, let's go over this way!" one of them called.

"You spot any little grey men yet?" another yelled. They all laughed uproariously, waving beer cans aloft, guys and girls with their arms wrapped around each other.

"Maybe they're hiding in the woods," one of the girls suggested. "Why'dn' we go flush 'em out?"

"Nah, that's dumb. You couldn't land a flying saucer in the woods. Let's go look around the other side of the building." The pack bumbled noisily past, and Zoe breathed a sigh of relief.

"Hey, look at this!" Someone had found the charred circle at last. A few cars bumped over the grass, coming in off Fuller. People were beginning to gather; some of them raced headlong across the lawn; some sauntered, curious but not excited; a few, Zoe noted, approached slowly, with nervous upward glances.

"Over there." Zoe touched Cantilio's sleeve. "That

woman—that's Maddalena Maestra." She kept her voice low, but didn't bother to whisper; there was now plenty of noise out in the field.

"Right; the one who wrote that book about channeling." Zoe had filled him in on the various players earlier in the evening. "Think she's gonna be the one?"

"Beats me." They watched as Maddalena circled the charred area slowly, then looked up and smiled. Her lips moved, speaking to the sky. Then she suddenly turned.

"That's Conrad deLeeuw," Zoe said. "The Rationalist." DeLeeuw was carrying a large bag covered with flaps and pockets. He spoke to Maddalena, who continued to smile. DeLeeuw set the bag on the ground, rummaged inside, and began to pull things out of it and fiddle with them.

Suddenly there was light, a harsh glare focused on the charred spot, the edges of illumination picking out the growing crowd. DeLeeuw moved the light around on its tripod until he was satisfied, then bent down to the bag again.

"Come on," Zoe said. "There are enough people here that we can go blend into the crowd now. But remember, stay with me."

"Yeah, yeah." He looked itchy, and Zoe wondered if he was thinking about ditching her. She felt perfectly prepared to peel the hide off him in strips if he even tried it.

They moved away from the woods. There were more lights now, being held aloft by TV camera people. Zoe spotted a couple of media vans, their round white antennas gleaming faintly as they bounced across the grass. She hoped Genesko would get this over with before the entire horde descended.

By some unspoken agreement, people had gathered in

a ragged circle around the charred spot on the ground. Every now and then someone bent down and touched a piece of the blackened vegetation, or broke off a brittle blade of grass and raised it for a closer look. But no one walked across the spot, or stood on it. Zoe and Cantilio ambled toward the circle and stood a little away, watching.

"Uh-oh. Here come McCray's Mounties." Jarvis McCray approached the area at the head of half a dozen camouflage-clad guys in a stumbling semblance of close-order drill.

"Halt." McCray led his troops past the circle and stopped them a few feet from the woods. "Fan out," he ordered. "Nick, you and Jimmy take the woods and work your way south. Frankie and Bill, go with them but work your way north. Lenny and Mac, the far side of the building. You know what you're looking for. Move out." McCray's eyes glittered. Nick and Jimmy were going to wonder about Cantilio's Toyota, Zoe thought. And Frankie and Bill were probably going to be real surprised when they came across the police.

"Stay out of my way, Jarvis." DeLeeuw was doing something with a high-powered camera.

"Yeah, as if," McCray said dismissively. The teen jargon made Zoe wonder how young McCray actually was. She hung back, outside the area of deLeeuw's light, not wanting to be recognized.

"Now, now, Jarvis." Maddalena's silvery laugh sounded sweetly. "Let poor Conrad get on with his work, drearily earthbound though it may be. Just as we allow you your less-than-charming toy-soldier games."

"Up yours, bitch." There was nothing youthful about McCray's snarl.

"Oh, my." Maddalena laughed again. "*Such* a clever comeback. How *do* you think of these things, Jarvis?" Around them, the crowd tittered. McCray took a step toward her, then stopped as she stood her ground, the cheerful smile unchanged.

"Y'know, there are an awful lot of innocent bystanders here," Cantilio muttered in Zoe's ear. "Isn't it risky for the cops to set up a trap with all these people around? What if someone starts shooting?"

"I don't know." Zoe turned toward him, frowning uneasily. She'd been wondering the same thing. "I guess Genesko just—" She stopped at the sound of a car engine, and jumped back as a small white Buick bounced across the grass and stopped with its nose at the edge of the circle, its lights adding illumination to the area.

"What do you think you're doing?" Rudy Giambra leaped from the car without turning off the engine, his voice loud and angry. "You idiot, you're contaminating the site!" He glared out across the charred circle; at its center, Beryl sat in what Zoe assumed was the lotus position, although she wasn't exactly sure what the lotus position was. Beryl was gazing straight ahead, ignoring Giambra completely.

"God, some people have absolutely no sense," Giambra stormed. He opened the back door of the car and withdrew a large photographer's case, and then a second. He set them both down on the ground, carefully outside the charred area, then opened the hood of the Toyota. He knelt down, opened the larger of the two cases, and lifted something heavy out of it; Zoe could see his muscles tighten with the effort. When he stood up, she had the sudden notion that some creature had wrapped itself around him.

There was a large, squarish object strapped to his chest, something metallic that gleamed dully in the Toyota's headlights. He leaned over the car's engine and did something inside; when he withdrew, Zoe saw that there were wires running from the object to the engine. From the other end of the object, more wires connected it to a long wand that ended in a wide, flat rectangle—like a vacuum cleaner, Zoe thought suddenly. Or one of those metal detectors. Giambra held the wand stiffly, hovering the rectangle over the charred ground.

"What the hell is that?" DeLeeuw looked up at him from the ground, a pair of tweezers in one hand and a plastic bag in the other.

"Something he has no business having." Genesko stepped forward into the pool of light. "Please remove that and give it to me, Mr. Giambra."

"No!" Giambra took two steps backward, until he was standing in the charred circle, hugging the thing to him. Behind him, Beryl began to chant, a thin, keening sound that brought grimaces to the faces of some of the spectators. "What do you know about any of this?" Giambra demanded of Genesko.

"I know that that device doesn't belong to you." Genesko took a step forward. The crowd had quieted, aware of some sort of drama without knowing exactly what it was. In the near-silence, Beryl's tuneless chant rose painfully to the ear. Behind her and to both sides, Zoe could hear the faint whirr of TV cameras.

"Oh, belong." Giambra shrugged, still hugging the thing to his chest. His face was shiny with sweat. "This is the key to everything, don't you realize that? This is *proof*. When I turn it on and get the readings, you'll know I'm right." He fumbled at the box on his chest with one hand, pressing the rectangular end of the wand against the burned grass.

"Mr. Giambra." Genesko's voice was a whipcrack. *"Don't flip that switch."*

He leaped forward. From behind her, Zoe heard someone cry out "No!" Genesko grabbed Giambra's arm, pulling it away from the box, wrestling him to the ground as Giambra kept screaming, "No, no please, just let me show you, please, let me show you!"

And it was over. Half a dozen cops galloped from the woods; behind them Zoe saw Anneke, white-faced, a fist pressed against her mouth and an expression of terror not quite gone from her face.

She turned back. The crowd had broken into a high-pitched babble, pressing forward to see what was going on. TV reporters were shouting questions in high-pitched voices. But all of them remained outside the circle, she noted with an inward grin; and the cops were already beginning to move them along.

"Come on." Once more she plucked at Cantilio's sleeve and darted toward the woods. Giambra was on his feet, hands cuffed behind him, Genesko's huge hand on his shoulder; the thing, whatever it was, was being carried away by that cop, Wes Kramer, who was looking at it like it was a poisonous snake; and Anneke stood at the edge of the circle, her eyes enormous, gazing at Genesko as if she were afraid to take her eyes off him.

"Is that him?" Cantilio had followed Zoe reluctantly.

"Yes. Wait here. He'll be along." As if on cue, Genesko steered Giambra toward the woods, leaving the rest of the media cut off by the police. Anneke was a pace behind, still white-faced.

"Why'd he kill Stempel, Lieutenant?" Cantilio had his notebook out, pen poised, almost before Genesko reached them. "Is that the thing he electrocuted him with? How'd you get on to him?"

"Cantilio, will you knock it off? Sorry, Lieutenant." She rolled her eyes in Cantilio's direction and let a beat of silence elapse. "Okay, what can you give us? *Is* Rudy Giambra the one who killed Stempel?"

"A good question, Ms. Kaplan. And the answer is—no, he isn't." Genesko had a funny expression on his face, but Zoe couldn't figure out what it was.

"But . . ." She stared at him.

"In fact," Genesko said, "he just came within an inch of killing himself." In the harsh light, she thought suddenly that the expression on his face was amusement.

"So it was Rudy," deLeeuw said.

"Poor Rudy," Maddalena said sadly. "Fear takes its toll, you know. If only he'd been more open to the positive reality."

"Oh, knock it off, Maddalena," deLeeuw said in a tired voice. In the background, Beryl's keening continued.

TWENTY-EIGHT

* * * * * *

"It's the Associated Press, not an afternoon daily," Cantilio said urgently. "I've got to file a report of the arrest right away, before these other people get it out. I can worry about details later."

"He's right," Zoe admitted. "Can you give him the basics now so he can get it on the wire?"

They were standing next to the Land Rover tucked behind a stand of trees. Rudy Giambra, weeping and mumbling, had been led away by Wes Kramer. The mob of reporters were being held back by the police, but Anneke knew it was only a matter of time before they caught up with Karl. She tightened her grip on his arm, reassuring herself that he was all right.

"The basic facts are these," Karl said. "Professor Edison Stempel died as the result of an accident caused by a malfunctioning electrical device of his own manufacture."

"Are you kidding?" Zoe blurted.

"Then what's Giambra been arrested for?" Cantilio asked.

"For the theft of that device, as well as for withholding evidence from the police, and possibly for obstruction of justice."

"You mean that thing he had was actually Stempel's? That's what killed him?" Zoe asked.

"That's right. Stempel made the device himself, but when he tried to use it last night, it overloaded and he was electrocuted. Mr. Giambra came upon the body and took the device, intending to pass it off as his own." Karl was speaking for the record, sounding formal and stilted.

"How do you know that's what killed Stempel?" Cantilio was scribbling rapidly in a small notebook. It seemed odd to Anneke that Zoe wasn't.

"For the moment, that is a conjecture based on evidence found in Professor Stempel's home. We believe that an examination of the device will show that it matches the burn marks on the body."

"How do you know the thing didn't belong to Giambra in the first place? Couldn't he have made it himself and used it to kill Stempel?"

"We found plans for the device in Professor Stempel's home."

"Still," Cantilio pressed, "couldn't Giambra have found Stempel with it and used the guy's own machine to kill him? How come you're so sure it was an accident?"

"Because he tried to use it himself!" Zoe exclaimed.

"Exactly." Karl smiled slightly. "We weren't positive of

that until tonight, when Mr. Giambra came very close to electrocuting himself."

"If you hadn't stopped him." In the darkness, Anneke could see the whites of Zoe's eyes as they widened in realization. "If you'd been a second later, you'd've been fried right along with him, wouldn't you? Jeez." She glanced toward Anneke. "So that's why you were so freaked."

Anneke shuddered and pressed her body closer to Karl's, replaying the moment in her mind. It hadn't occurred to her, knowing the reason for the trap, that there would be any danger; she'd been unprepared for the red terror she'd felt when Karl reached for Giambra. She found herself thinking suddenly: Maybe we could move the wedding up to August after all. As if, she laughed at herself shakily, the act of marriage would keep him safe.

"So that's what the trap was about?" Cantilio said. "To see who showed up with the thing?" Karl nodded. "And the whole UFO business was really done by a batch of college kids. What's going to happen to them?"

"The UFO question is no longer a police matter," Karl replied, and Anneke was sure there was relief in his voice.

"Okay, that should do for a first lead." Cantilio snapped his notebook shut. "I'll call it in from the car. When can I get the details?"

"There isn't likely to be any further information until tomorrow morning," Karl said. "Why don't you and Zoe meet me at my office at nine o'clock?"

"Fine. See you then."

"Hey, wait up," Zoe called as he trotted away. "You've got to drive me back. See you in the morning," she flung over her shoulder to Karl as she ran after Cantilio. She grinned and rolled her eyes. She's back, Anneke thought with relief.

Sunday morning it was Cantilio who was late. A different kind of reporter mentality than Zoe's, Anneke thought when he strolled in without apology at nine-fifteen. He's only interested in getting the story; he's not really interested in the story itself. She was fairly sure that Zoe's approach would pay greater dividends in the end.

"All right, Zoe." When they were more or less settled in the cramped office, it was Zoe that Karl spoke to. "Fire away."

Anneke was surprised at the girl's first question. "What's going to happen to Jenna and the others, Lieutenant?"

"Through the legal process, probably nothing," Karl said. "But they'll have to be publicly identified, if only to convince the more extreme UFO believers that this really was a hoax."

"Some of them are still not going to believe it, you know," Anneke warned him.

"Oh, I know. Some people don't believe the earth is round."

"Okay." Zoe bounced impatiently in her chair. "You say Stempel invented this machine, and that he managed to kill himself with it. So what the hell *was* it, exactly? And what was he doing with it Friday night?"

"I can answer the second part of that more easily than the first. We believe he was using it to analyze the supposed UFO landing site."

"So it was a kind of alien detector?" Cantilio asked the question without humor, a straightforward collecting of facts.

"As near as anyone can tell," Karl said, "it was a combination boron-detector, spectrometer, and Kirlian camera."

"What kind of camera?" Zoe tilted her head. "I think you lost me on that one."

"A Kirlian camera—K-I-R-L-I-A-N," Karl spelled out the word for Cantilio, "is used to photograph auras."

"Auras." Zoe threw up her hands. "Why not? We've already had everything but leprechauns."

"What went wrong with the thing?" Cantilio asked. "How come it killed him?"

"Well, according to his own schematics, it carried a hefty charge to begin with—it ran off car batteries. And Professor Stempel wasn't as practiced at electronics as he thought he was; we found a loose wire in the casing. But the most important point is that Kirlian photography is a contact process. The camera has to be touching its object in order for the aura to appear on the plate."

"It rained Friday night, didn't it?" Zoe exclaimed.

"Exactly. According to Barry Statler, they prepared that charred area late in the afternoon. And there was a thunderstorm around seven o'clock."

"So when Stempel pressed his machine against the wet ground and flipped the switch—*psssst.*" Zoe made a noise like bacon sizzling, and Anneke laughed in spite of herself. She should have felt sorry about the death of Edison Stempel, but what she actually felt, she admitted, was relief that Zoe was back to her usual obstreperous self.

"So you found plans for this thing at Stempel's house," Cantilio said. "But how did you know he'd actually built it?"

"We didn't know for sure. But he had a workshop full of sophisticated equipment, and he didn't have any of it with him, even though he was setting out on a live UFO hunt. Why would he leave all of his equipment at home, unless he had something even more elaborate to use?"

"Okay." Cantilio scribbled in his notebook. "So Stempel takes this machine out into the field, and he zaps himself with it. Then why did Giambra take it?"

"Because he wanted it," Karl said simply. "For one thing, he had no idea that's what killed Stempel. Remember, it was dark. When the device malfunctioned, it drained the batteries of Stempel's car, but Giambra couldn't know that, either. All he saw was his old antagonist Edison Stempel, dead on the ground at an 'alien landing site,' carrying the wonderful device that Stempel had apparently been hinting about for months. He says he disconnected the machine from Stempel's station wagon, took it back to his hotel room, and more or less figured out how it worked. But luckily for him, he didn't get a chance to try it out until last night.

"He still insists that's not what killed Stempel, by the way." Karl made a face. "He claims the Greys did it because Stempel was about to provide evidence of their presence. He seems to think Stempel was a true genius."

Zoe's eyes widened. "Wait a minute. Are you telling me he actually *believes* all the stuff he's been spouting?"

"Apparently so." Karl spread his hands.

"But that crazy book he wrote—did he get that stuff in a brainstorm, or what?"

"It's hard to say. He says he wrote it 'to make people understand.' If I had to guess—and it's not a guess for publication," he said to Cantilio, "I'd say he wrote what he believed to be true, hoping to convince others by claiming that he'd been told about it directly by aliens."

"Sheesh." Zoe shook her head. "I just figured him for a con artist. Instead, he's a real nutcase."

"It's not as easy as you might think to tell the difference," Anneke said. "The same thing is true of cult leaders. We tend to assume they're all frauds—that they don't really believe in alien visitations, and Power Spots, and comets coming to take them away, and all the rest of it. That's why it's hard to imagine that a famous author would do what he did just to steal what we know is a bogus machine."

"Sidebar," Zoe said, laughing. "How to tell the frauds from the nuts."

"I've got everything I need." Cantilio jumped to his feet. "See you, Kaplan." He sketched a wave and left without a thank-you. Zoe shrugged and sighed, watching him go.

Cantilio's story was perfectly adequate, but Zoe thought it was boring and predictable, not at all what she herself would have written. It ran lead on the *Daily* Web site, with the AP ligature but no byline, just as it had come over the wire. She sighed and clicked the mouse, and read her own piece once more, running as the op-ed lead.

> Every now and then a reporter gets scammed. It would be easy to claim that it's not our fault, that people will always try to use the media, that mistakes happen.
> All of that is true, and none of it is relevant.
> I have just spent four days reporting on the UFO sightings over Ann Arbor. Yesterday, I discovered that those sightings were a student

prank, perpetrated by four of my friends, four people I knew well.

The fact that I had no idea those friends were the source of the hoax doesn't make my reportage any less suspect. Nor do I expect it to.

I should have been more cautious. I should have been more suspicious. If I hadn't been so anxious to get a great story under my byline, I might have wondered why I was lucky enough to be the only reporter who was personally escorted to that very first sighting. I might have investigated the prank aspect more thoroughly.

Instead, I accepted the coincidence without a thought.

There were some more mea culpas; Zoe read to the end.

"Tough break," Barney McCormack said sympathetically, reading over her shoulder.

"Yeah, well . . . " She shrugged.

"There you are." Gabriel stepped into the computer room holding a sheet of paper. "Thought you'd like to see this."

"What is it?" Zoe took it from him. It was a printout of an AP story, headed *Update: Formal Charges Against Rudy Giambra in UFO Death Case.*

"Great." She made a face and handed it back to Gabriel. "More stories I don't get to cover."

"No. That graf there." He pointed to a paragraph at the bottom of the page.

" 'Note: Associated Press stringer Zoe Kaplan,' " she read, " 'took herself off coverage of this story when she discovered that the perpetrators of the UFO hoax were four friends of hers living in the same dormitory. Kaplan had no prior knowledge of their involvement.' "

"Oh, wow." She forced the words out past the lump in her throat. "He didn't have to do that, did he?"

"No, he didn't. And notice something else?" Gabriel said. "It doesn't say 'former' stringer."

"Can I come in?" Jenna Lenski stook in the doorway of Zoe's dorm room.

"Yeah, sure." Zoe stuffed towels into the bottom of a cardboard carton and dumped a pile of notebooks on top of them. "My mom's due any minute to pick me up, and I'm not even packed yet."

She was inordinately glad the summer session was over. She hadn't seen much of Jenna and the others since Stempel's death, and she hadn't seen much of anyone else either. Aside from her weekly chores at the *Daily*, she'd hunkered down and actually gotten some studying done.

"What are you going to do for the rest of the summer?" Jenna took a few steps into the room, placing her feet carefully to avoid the clutter of papers and clothes and bedding waiting to be packed.

"Veg out," Zoe said, shrugging. "How about you?"

"Probably the same thing. I lost my summer internship in the history department."

"Bummer." The word was perfunctory; Zoe wasn't sure she could work up any sympathy for Jenna yet.

"I'm damn lucky that's all that happened. They could've yanked my scholarship."

"Well, you and Ben can just hang out until school starts in the fall."

"Ben's gone back to Indiana for the rest of the summer. We haven't been seeing each other since . . . you know."

"Sorry."

"Don't be. I guess we were never really compatible. The coach ordered him to move into an apartment next fall. Assigned him his roommates, too. Two offensive linemen, both over three hundred pounds. One of them's a chemistry major, the other's a philosophy major planning to go on to divinity school." Jenna grinned. "It's gonna be a l-o-o-ng year for Ben Holmes."

Zoe chuckled. "And Nique finally got a nibble, you know." When she'd run into him a few days ago he was still so apologetic that he didn't tell her his good news until she asked. The Chicago Bears had called and offered him a tryout after one of their defensive backs blew out a knee in a pickup basketball game. She hoped Nique would make it.

"What about Barry?" she asked, suddenly curious. He'd moved out of East Quad immediately after Rudy Giambra's arrest, and she hadn't seen him since.

"Same old same old." There was a note of bitterness in Jenna's voice. "He's been offered a fellowship at MIT. Apparently they really get off on a good high-tech prank up there."

"It figures." Zoe giggled, struck finally by the absurdity of it all. "He can help them reprogram the Harvard campanile to play 'Hail to the Victors.' "

"Or reset all the toilets to flush backwards." Jenna too began to giggle.

"Or turn on all the campus lights at three A.M."

They both broke up laughing. Well, why not? Zoe thought. It was the silly season, after all.

AUTHOR'S NOTE

• • • • • •

Mention the 1966 "UFO sightings" to anyone who was in Ann Arbor at the time, and they're probably going to start giggling. What it was, was pure comic relief, at a time of intense involvement with great national events, at the height of the Vietnam War and the political and social upheaval of the sixties.

When the first "sighting" hit the news, we grinned. When sheriff's deputies insisted they'd seen a UFO, we snickered. When J. Allen Hynek declared the phenomena "swamp gas," we howled with laughter.

Why aren't people laughing anymore?

Well, a lot of people still are. It's just that you can't hear them over the endless UFO "documentaries" on television that seem to proliferate like rabbits. And on the Internet, no one can hear you laugh.

In *Bleeding Maize and Blue*, I extrapolated the notion of "flash rumors" from science fiction writer Larry Niven's "flash crowds." But until I began work on this particular book, I didn't realize how right I'd been.

I spend a fair amount of time on the Internet. I believe—if we can save it from corporate greed, political hypocrisy, and social-control freaks—it can be as revolutionary as the invention of the automobile. But folks, I've got to admit, the Internet has a lot to answer for.

This is where lunacy goes to procreate, the Koffee Klatch at the End of the Universe. This is where any idea, however bizarre, can become a topic of endless discussion and speculation. The Internet is where, when you have to go there, they have to take you in.

On the other hand, sometimes the Internet is where you go for a nice, cool splash of honesty.

The Heaven's Gate affair happened to occur while I was writing this book. I read and watched and listened to every report I could find about it—not so much because I was fascinated by the event, but because I was fascinated by the *coverage* of the event.

Within hours of the first reports, the Internet exploded with Web sites devoted to Heaven's Gate, anything and everything to do with it. Yahoo (http://www.yahoo.com) immediately set up a special page of links; newsgroups and chat rooms exploded with rumors and opinions and horrible, hilarious jokes.

While the mainstream media were forced into serious coverage, complete with solemn, portentous analyses, the Internet wallowed happily in Hale-Bopp hysteria and black humor—exactly what most people were thinking in private. (Come on, now—you mean you didn't swap even one or two Heaven's Gate jokes around the water cooler?) Not for the first time, the Internet was a better mirror of society than the media.

What does it all mean? I have absolutely no idea. That's why this book was written as a comedy.

If you happen to be one of the True Believers in the Greys/Majestic-12/Hangar 18 mythology—if you think *The X-Files* is a documentary—you probably didn't read this far anyway. As for me, I'm an unregenerate, Western-linear-thinking, scientific-method type, unalterably wedded to the precepts of the Snorg Hypothesis.

And finally, let me give full credit to the Skeptics Society for that last. You can find invisible Snorgs, as well as a whole lot of other cheerful debunking, in their online FAQ—Frequently Asked Questions—file, at http://www.skeptics.com. I recommend it highly for all you reality-based folks.

CONTINUE READING FOR AN
EXCERPT FROM
SUSAN HOLTZER'S
LATEST BOOK

THE WEDDING GAME

AVAILABLE IN HARDCOVER FROM
ST. MARTIN'S MINOTAUR

You are standing at the southern end of a long valley illuminated by flickering red light from the volcanic gorge behind you. Carved into the walls of the valley is an incredible series of stone faces. Some of them look down into the valley with expressions of benevolence that would credit a saint; others glare with a malice that makes the heart grow faint. All of them are imbued with a fantastic seeming of life by the shifting and flickering light of the volcano.

—ADVENTURE: THE COLOSSAL CAVE

This was where she downloaded mail from GameSpinners, a private mailing list for computer game designers. Today there were twenty-seven messages from the list, and a quick glance told her that at least half of them were from the same half dozen or so people.

Which meant that the dreaded games-for-girls flame war had broken out again. And unfortunately, she herself was the reluctant center of the storm.

It had begun a couple of months ago, when she'd made a passing reference to her wedding preparations, and Kell Albright's antic imagination had caught fire.

Kell was their resident party girl, the one who insisted that "games should be fun, or why bother?" They'd never met face-to-face, but Anneke's imagination clothed Kell in short, tight skirts, multicolored hair, and several tattoos, dancing the night away at underground clubs before hitting the keyboard in the morning. It was hard not to envy her cheerful energy or enjoy her persistent humor.

Kell was also a true idea-hamster, notions spinning from her mind like sparks from a flywheel. She always seemed to be working on half a dozen game ideas at once, and never seemed to be seriously engaged in any of them.

Until now. Kell, it seemed, had decided to write a "Wedding Game."

<Kell>Wow, what a great idea for a game! It'd be for, say, young teenagers--maybe twelve to sixteen? You could have lots and lots of possible wedding scenarios, lots of different choices-- players could even design their own wedding gowns. And then you could give them all sorts of problems to solve--nasty in-laws, fights about bridesmaids, drunken bachelor parties, stuff like that. It'd be great! Anneke, can I ask you questions about it while you're planning it?

Well, what could she say?

<Anneke>Sure, Kell, if you want to. But I think I'm probably not what you want. I mean, no traditional wedding gown, no mother of the bride, no in-laws at all, for that matter. And it's going to be just a small, private wedding. Wouldn't you be better off talking to a friend your own age who's having a traditional wedding?

<Kell>Au contraire. It's easy to get stuff about regular weddings from magazines and Web sites and stuff. It's the less traditional weddings that'll make the game really interesting, you know? Besides, you'll be making a lot of the same decisions every bride does--things like location, guest list, maid of honor, all that sort of stuff.

And anyway, none of my friends are even close to getting married. We're all still in girls-just-wanna-have-fun mode. ;-)

The smiley was typical of Kell. Most women computer professionals scrupulously avoided using them, but Kell happily, or perhaps purposely, sprinkled her postings with graphical smiles, winks, and nudges. Kell had a way of provoking flame wars even as she seemed merrily oblivious to them.

Today the battle had erupted under the topic heading "Finding decent beta testers." Not unusual for GameSpinners, where no one worried overmuch about staying ontopic. Generally, people just kept hitting Reply and posting away, even when the subject had drifted, as one had recently, from "Game Reviewers" to whether an AK-47 was better than an Uzi for taking out a Ninja attack squad.

<Kell>Why should girls get stuck with all those boring, repetitive shoot-'em-ups just because that's what boys like? Does every game in the world have.to be written for 15-year-old boys?

A good question, Anneke thought, but in the context of the computer gaming world, not an easy one to answer. It was Seth Conroy (of course) who made the obvious comment. Seth spent his days slumming (his word) in the Information Systems department of a Los Angeles bank, instead of rapping with a hot game company. He wore suits instead of jeans and T-shirts; he punched a time clock instead of happily programming when and where he wanted to; he earned just enough money to be furiously envious of the Armani-clad hotshots above him in the rigid hierarchy. He felt overworked and underappreciated; he probably was; and it showed.

<Seth>::Does every game in the world have to be written for 15-year-old boys?::

Nope; only the ones that make money. If you want to be some kind of pro bono programmer, that's fine with me. But I want to do this for a living. And face it, it's boys who drop the big bucks in this marketplace.

Well, yes, but . . . Anneke selected the last sentence to copy it into her posting, and hit Reply.

<Anneke> Well, yes, but which is cause and which is effect? Maybe girls don't spend money on games because the only games out there to spend money ON are designed for boys.

She hit Send and clicked on the next posting. She was pretty sure Dani Noguchi would be in full attack mode.

Dani was young and bright and angry. She'd been on the fast track with a hot new startup, in Houston, a company that was going to "revolutionize the Internet." Well, weren't they all? Except, Dani had bought into the promise of a big payoff and had taken the fat stock options instead of a decent salary. When the company went belly-up, the "bold entrepreneurs" who'd run the scam walked away with a couple of million in their pockets and venture capital for the Next Great Thing. Dani had walked away with a pocket full of worthless paper.

<Dani>And what SHOULD girls like--some Martha Stewart game where the winner is the one who makes the best Christmas wreath out of used toilet paper? Come on, girls have as much anger and hostility to get out of their system as boys do. Maybe more--God knows we have more to be angry ABOUT. The problem isn't the game TYPE, it's the game PLOTS. Give girls a strong female protagonist who isn't just boobs and ass, give them a real grrrl game, and they'll put their money down.

Not entirely true, though, Anneke thought. There were a few action games on the market that did just that, and while they did attract a certain number of girls, they still appealed more to teenage boys. Girls just didn't get into gaming young enough; by the time they're old enough for action and adventure games, we've lost them.

<Dani>Besides, girls NEED action and adventure games, for the same reason boys do--it's empowering, and it helps them learn about conflict. Shit, there's a lot more of the real world in Forsaken than there is in Barney's Great Adventure. The last thing we need is another generation of sweet little girls who never grow up and smell the shit.

<Kell>Sorry, but the last thing the world needs is another generation of women trying to act like men. The world already has a lot more testosterone than it can handle.

Anneke hit Reply, stared at the screen for a minute, then aborted. In essence, the argument was the central conundrum of the contemporary women's movement, and she wasn't sure herself which side she came down on. She moved on to the next message with the mixture of trepidation and anticipation that Vince Mattus's postings always engendered. Vince was *always* in attack mode.

<Vince>Why doesn't it surprise me that you're both wrong? Actually, there IS a market out there for girl games. And the great thing is they don't even have to be any good. All you have to do is package it in pink, and some dumb mother's gonna buy it for her little Susie. I mean, it's not like she's gonna be able to tell if it's any good or not.

In fact, the chick market is a great opportunity for a third-rate programmer, because they wouldn't know a good game from a tic-tac-toe clone anyway. Girls don't really play games. All they want to do is jerk around and look at the pretty pictures.

As usual, Dani rose to the bait.

<Dani>Vince, you are such an indispensable icon of the women's movement. Every time we begin to get complacent, you remind us what men are really like. How far did *you* get on Tomb Warrior without a cheat sheet?

And as usual, Kell didn't.

<Kell>Poor Vince, you're so good at yanking people's chains, and so bad at everything else. When was the last time you actually had FUN? (I mean, without a centerfold and a towel. :-)

Anneke snorted with laughter as she read the rest of Kell's posting.

<Kell>Besides, the real problem is that teenage boys are so PATHETIC. I mean, the poor things are so hormone-sodden that they can barely speak in coherent sentences. Where's the fun in writing Yet Another game for an audience that feeble? >:->

<Seth>In a way, much as I hate to say it, Vince is right. But before you flame me, here's the thing--that's true of boy's games too. Most of the stuff we argue about here, like playability, is just a series of bullshit factors, at least for the action-adventure genre. If you give it enough flashpower, the kids'll buy it for the graphics and the scenario. Even if it's not the greatest game in the world to play, so what? By then, they've already paid out their forty bucks.

Oh Lord, not the old playability-vs.-plot argument. She was about to pass on the rest of the thread when she saw Jesse Franklin's name at the top of the next response.

<Jesse>But where's the creative challenge? What's the point of being a gamer if you're going to think like that? You might as well be an investment banker.

Jesse was an icon in the computer gaming world, one of the great hackers back in the days when the word was an accolade, not an accusation. "Mordona," his brilliant adventure game written for the old Apple][, had been a triumph of programming, almost a tour de force. For a machine with only 32K of RAM, no hard drive, and a floppy disk that held a bare 128K, Jesse had created a game that grabbed you by the throat and dragged you into its world, all of it written in the tightest, most elegant code Anneke had ever seen. She felt privileged to have him on the list, but in this group, of course, not everyone felt the same. Maybe it was an age thing.

<Vince>Seth may be a money-grubbing whore, but in this case he's got a point. Jesse the Purist used up his One Great Idea twenty years ago, and he hasn't done anything since but sit around and pontificate, like he's the Second Coming of Steve Wozniak. If you want people to actually buy your games, you've got to give them something that grabs them by the balls in that first look. If they don't buy it, it doesn't matter how great it plays. And once they do buy it, who cares what they think of it?

<Dani>It figures that Vince would blow off playability, considering what he churns out. Anyone ever actually try to PLAY Tombs and Tokens?

<Vince>Anyone ever try to play any of YOUR games, Dani? No? Oh yeah, that's right--you've never actually written and marketed anything, have you? Now why doesn't that surprise me? Oh, right--you're a grrrrrl.

<Elliott>Yeah, but if the playability sucks, how you going to get anyon to by it, at gunpoint? Hey Vince, here's a news flash--15 year olds TALK TO EACH OTHER!! How the shit do you think we decid what games to buy, with a ouija board? Besides, only a 36K brain would lay out 40 or 50 bucks for a game with out downloading the demo and tryng it out first. So KIDS KNOW if its any good BEFORE we by it.

Anneke chuckled. Elliott held the high ground when it came to talking about fifteen-year-old boys. Elliott Washburn wrote like what he was—a fifteen-year-old hacker/computer wonk/semi-genius who understood everything about games and nothing much about reality. Anneke wasn't sure if his parents deserved jail time for screwing him up, or canonization for not killing him in his sleep. Either way, she didn't envy them.

Elliott was self-taught, one of those intuitive programmers who could look at a blank monitor and effortlessly visualize the correct lines of code crawling down the screen. Unfortunately, he couldn't seem to visualize anything else; his high school grades hovered dangerously just above the magic 2.0, and people, it seemed, were a complete mystery to him. His postings were usually stream-of-consciousness affairs that might or might not have anything to do with the subject under discussion, beyond topic drift to the realm of total non sequitur. His spelling and grammar were so atrocious that Anneke would have considered the possibility of dyslexia if his code weren't so perfectly written.

He wrote about high school only rarely, and about local friends never, and Anneke had wondered occasionally if she should feel sorry for him. But his postings revealed a rich network of online friends, and a cheerful disposition that never seemed forced. Once he got beyond high school hell, she reasoned, he'd find face-to-face relationships that would work for him.

Elliott had never actually finished a game; he seemed more interested in creating endless modules featuring hand-to-hand battles, slavering monsters, and violent assassinations, all of them filtered through liberal gobs of splattered blood.

The flame war ended there for the moment, although Anneke had no doubt it would continue for a while. She wished both it and the next one would go away—the one headed "Wedding Bell Blues," in which Kell peppered her with daily questions.

<Kell>Anneke, how about some last-minute crises? I figure that the closer you get to the event, the more likely it is that something will go wrong, right? AND the more likely it is that whatever goes wrong will produce the greatest amount of trouble. Sort of a Murphy's Law of Weddings. :-)

I thought I'd program each crisis as a separate module, so that theoretically it's possible for the player to be hit by all of them either simultaneously or sequentially, and at almost any point in the game. But the later the crisis occurs, the more difficult it'll be to solve.

<Jesse>Just don't backload all the excitement, Kell. Remember, gamers deserve small payoffs as they go along, not just one big one at the end. Not many players are going to stick with it to the very end, after all, and they shouldn't have to in order to enjoy playing it. "Life's the journey, not the destination."

<Elliott>Hey, Kell, how about having the bride kidnaped by a ninja attack squad? They culd be disgised as gests, see, and theyd snatch the brid and then the groom would get his own squad to- gethr and chase after them. It wuldnt have to be sexist either you could have the bride be an Amazon warrior and she culd be res- cud by her own troops who are really an Amazon legion.

Anneke laughed out loud as she clicked Reply.

<Anneke>Hey, works for me, Kell. Sounds a lot more fun than dressing up like a Christmas tree and listening to people snicker. I might even have my Amazons kidnap Karl and force him to elope. As for last-minute crises, sorry to disappoint you but so far the only thing that's gone wrong is that Karl's best man had to cancel at the last minute, to go on a scouting trip to Seattle. I admit I'm really pissed about it, too, and I hope the Baltimore Ravens rot in last place. (Jay's a scout for them, and they're insisting he go on a scouting trip that he could easily put off a week.) But other than that, everything seems to be falling into place very nicely.

>BONNNNNGGGGGGGGG<
A hollow voice says, "The Galloping Ghost Tortoise Express is now at your service!" With a swoosh and a swirl of water, a large tortoise rises to the surface of the reservoir and paddles over to the shore near you. The message, "I'm Darwin—ride me!" is inscribed on his back in or- nate letters.

—ADVENTURE: THE COLOSSAL CAVE

The final subject heading, "See you at GameDev," was from Larry Markowitz, the nominal list owner. Larry was a senior programmer with Gallery3 Software, which produced, among other things, a graphics programming package loathed and loved almost equally by most game developers. They used it, they relied on it, and they railed against it, in almost equal proportions. Nothing else could do what Gallery3 did; why, developers screamed, couldn't it do it better?

<Larry>Wanted to remind everyone that we'll be a major player at GameDev this year. We've got a triple booth right at the front, and I HOPE we're going to be demoing the Gallery3 upgrade (if the Marketing mavens get their shit together in time). Anyway, I'll be at the booth nearly the whole weekend, so if any of you folks are planning to attend, I'd love to have you drop by and chat for a while. In fact, I'm going alone, so if enough list members are around, maybe we could plan a pub crawl after hours Saturday night.

<Dani>You mean you're not bringing your wife, Larry? Ooh, count me in.

<Elliott> Shit, Id give anything to go to that, but my mother trets me like Im about six years old, you know? Larry, will the upgrade speed up the collision detection routines? because when I get my gladiators moving I really want to see those tridents whiping around, you know?

<Vince>I hope the upgrade is better than the piece of crap you've got now. Did anyone bother to fix the bug in the texture mapping module? Or did your marketing trolls tell you no one would notice?

<Anneke>What a shame. Larry finally on the loose and I don't get a shot at him. Sorry, gang, but I've got something ALMOST as important this weekend--my honeymoon.

As she typed the words she felt a pang of real regret. GameDev was a major event in the gaming world, a place to check out new developers' software, to learn about the latest in hardware advances, to meet and chat with other game programmers. She'd never gone before—until now, "Whitehart Station" had been too ephemeral for her to commit herself to it. This would have been the perfect year for her to attend.

With a sigh she quickly ran through the rest of the posts, pausing briefly at one headed "Lighting Call Question."

<Elliot> I wrote a function to calculate ligting intensity but I cant get it to work riht. Anyone know anything about how to do this?

<Vince>Shit, where did you learn programming, anyway, off the back of a cereal box? Besides, last time I looked this was a list about game DESIGN, not a tutorial for retards who've never even heard of the TestIntersectionS test. There's a whole set of formulas at http://www.csu.org/~lola/light.html where you can find what you need without bothering the rest of us.

<Elliott>Up yours, Vince. Big fat hairy deal-- just because you can find some freaking website, you think your some kind of genius.

Vince was presumably right about the Web site, though. It was why he was tolerated—because, wrapped inside the anger and vitriol, he nearly always had the answer to any question. Still, lately he seemed to be getting even nastier than usual, his act getting less amusing and more annoying. She wondered if even Larry Markowitz, the most laissez-faire of list mavens, would pull his plug one of these days.

With the thought in her mind, she saw the next thread with a start of surprise. It was also from Larry, and it was headed: "Vince Is Dead." So he'd finally kicked Vince off the list. She discovered that, in a weird way, she was going to miss him; he may have been a vicious jerk, but he brought a certain edge and energy to the conversation.

<Larry>I'm posting this to report that Vince Mattus was found dead in his apartment this morning. He was killed by a letter bomb that exploded when he opened it. Sorry, gang, I don't have any other details. I'll post more information as I get it.

It took her a second to shift mental gears, from list exile to actual death, and another moment to make the connection. Letter bomb . . . Vince lived in Ann Arbor . . . then *that* must have been the explosion Karl had been called out on. Quickly she clicked on the next posting.

<Dani>A letter bomb? Awesome. So someone finally found a useful function for snail mail.
<Jesse>Jesus, are you sure, Larry? Where'd you hear it?
<Seth>Are you kidding? You sure it was a letter bomb? Maybe he just got in the way when his personality exploded.

The responses came quickly, out of order, tripping over themselves as they shot through electronic relays.

<Larry>It's right off the AP. It showed up in my newswire mailbox just a couple of minutes ago.
<Kell>I'll be damned. Boy, some gamers are REALLY sore losers.
<Dani>Watch your backs, everyone. If there's a mad bomber out there targeting bad game programmers, get ready for a bloodbath.

Anneke laughed without guilt, accepting the culture of the Internet. You didn't find a whole lot of *nil nisi* hypocrisy in cyberspace, where black humor was more the norm than the exception. The Internet was where people said what they really thought, and what they really thought of Vince Mattus was that he'd been a vicious, nasty, self-absorbed prick.

More postings were pouring in even as she read the current ones. She scanned them all quickly, but there was no further information, only questions, expressions of amazement, and more one-liners.

And one last topic thread, arriving late to her mailbox through who-knew-what stutter in the great system of relays that was the Internet. This one was headed: "Where Should I Start?" from a teenage newbie named Toby Weintraub.

<Toby>My problem is I've got all sorts of games in my head, and I can't decide what to do first. What's the best kind of game for a beginner to start with?

<Jesse>It's always a tough question, Toby. There are so many choices, aren't there? Card or board or RPG? Action or adventure or puzzle? Turn-based or real-time? 2D or isometric? Every decision changes the design parameters of every other decision--just like real life. You just have to do what feels right to you. Start with the kind of game YOU like to play, and go on from there.

<Vince>Oh shit, another one. Hey kid, if you send me a dime, I'll send you a clue, okay? This is a list for professional game developers, which you are not, because if you were you'd already know what you wanted to do. And no, we don't know how to get you a job with Electronic Arts--I assume that was going to be your next question, right?

<Toby>Up yours, Mattus. Thanks, Jesse. The trouble is, the

kinds of games I like to play are the real complicated kind, you know? I suppose I could start with something simple, but that sounds so boring.

And that was the last of it. So that would be Vince Mattus's last word, on this or any other subject. Anneke reread the posting, thinking about Vince. What did she know about him? Hardly anything, she realized, and she'd been happy to keep it that way. She searched her memory for personal information he'd dropped into his postings, and came up empty. He lived in Ann Arbor; he had two games on the market; nothing else. She'd always assumed he was young, but only because most gamers were. She didn't even know if he was a Michigan student or not.

Well, was that so unusual, for someone she'd never met in person? Actually, yes. After being on the GameSpinners list for a little over a year, she considered most of the regular posters to be her friends, and she was pretty sure the others felt the same. True, their connection was only along a thin slice of each other's lives, but personal elements had a way of leaking through. Just as she'd chatted about her wedding plans, the others had chatted about their own daily lives. She'd heard about Elliott's sister's chicken pox; about Kell's apartment-hunting travails; about Dani's despised former employers. She knew that Larry's wife was an intellectual-property lawyer who was on the road far too much; she knew that Seth had just broken up with an aspiring actress; she knew that Jesse was suing a local rancher for diverting water from his New Mexico homestead.

About Vince, she knew nothing.

She returned to the "Vince Is Dead" thread and hit Reply.

<Anneke>Did anyone here ever meet Vince f2f? Larry, what do you know about him? How'd he come to join this list?

She clicked to send this and the other items in her outgoing mailbox, then clicked on the Netscape file menu. What was Vince's game company called? Gooseberry Software, that was it. She did a search, then clicked on "gooseberrygames.com."